LOVE AND FURY

By Samantha Silva

Mr Dickens and His Carol

Love and Fury

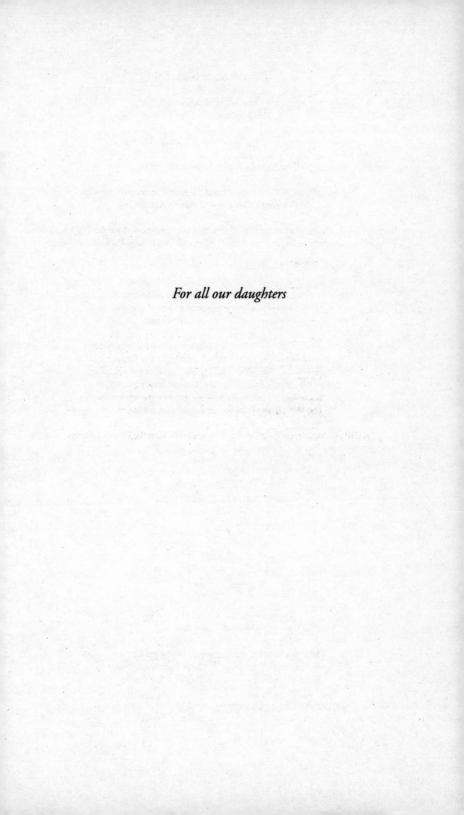

For all our daughters

You who were darkness warmed my flesh
where out of darkness rose the seed.
Then all a world I made in me;
all the world you hear and see
hung upon my dreaming blood.

'Woman to Child', Judith Wright

Mrs B

30th August 1797

Mrs Blenkinsop arrived at a neat circle of three-story houses at the edge of North London, surprised to find her charge at the open door, holding her ripe belly with both hands and ushering her inside with an easy smile and no apparent terror of the event to come. The home and its mistress, in a muslin gown and indigo shawl, smelt of apple dumplings. Though they hadn't met, the woman took the midwife's hand and led her past half-furnished rooms, introducing them as she went, waving away stacks of books on a Turkish carpet, anticipating shelves, and the occasional wood box and leather trunk, as 'the old life still finding its place in the new.' Mrs Blenkinsop had seen far more disarray in her time, and liked the simple touches, cut flowers in every room and a single oval portrait, just a face (that looked very much like the missus herself) gazing out from over a mantel. In the garden out back, which was enjoying its first late-summer bloom, the midwife caught sight of a little girl, three years old, she guessed, playing with a young woman who seemed to be telling her the names of plants.

It was a fine house, with fresh white walls and open windows, tall as Heaven, inviting a cordial breeze that followed them down a hall, up two steep staircases, and into the airy bedroom where the missus led her, answering each of Mrs Blenkinsop's questions with an uncanny calm: her waters had started as a trickle but ended as a gush as she'd stood in the kitchen that morning. She'd felt a dull ache and scattered pains, with no sensible pattern, but she wasn't unwell, and remembered eating, only two hours before, a small breakfast, which she hoped was enough nourishment to sustain her for the labour to come.

'I don't imagine there'll be much for you to do, Mrs Blenkinsop, but sit by and wait for Nature to do what your art cannot.'

'No objection by me.' The midwife put her old bag and bottle of gin on the floor.

'I can't abide the lying-in. I was up next day with Fanny.'

'Sweet girl in the garden just now?'

'Yes, with our dear Marguerite. Both too sweet for the world, I'm afraid. But Fanny wasn't shy coming into it.'

The midwife took off her brown cape and folded it over a chair. 'Well, I've never seen two births the same. Not in all my time. But we'll hope for the best.'

'I told Mr Godwin I'd be down for dinner tomorrow afternoon.'

'Let's have a look, then,' said the midwife, eager to attend to the business at hand. 'D'you mind if I take off my cap?'

'Of course, Mrs Blenkinsop. We don't stand on ceremony here.'

'"Mrs B" ought to do fine,' she said, taking some almond oil from her bag and rubbing her hands clean with it. 'Shortens things up.'

'Mrs B, then.'

A servant appeared with a pressed apron for the midwife, which she wrapped around her own dumpling of a stomach and tied at the back. She removed the woman's slippers, squeezing the arch of each foot before lifting her legs onto the bed, then laid her palms on the great taut womb, and closed her eyes as a way of gathering all her senses to feel the child inside. Satisfied that the baby had fallen down proper and headfirst, she sat on the edge of the bed to raise the missus's knees to a slight bend, rolled her gown to the crest of them, pulled off her underthings, and lightly pressed her legs apart. They had the give of a woman who'd done this before.

As the midwife inquired into her case – dilated only one finger's worth across – the pregnant woman exhaled a slow breath and talked to the ceiling.

'I told Mr Godwin over breakfast I had no doubt of seeing the animal today, but that I must wait for you to guess the hour. I think he was somewhat alarmed at the prospect of it all, but relieved when I sent him away. Though I promised I'd send word throughout the day.'

'Then it'll just be the two of us, for now.' The midwife wiped her hands on her apron. The custom of gathering a gaggle of female relatives and friends, as far as she was concerned, did nothing to serve the cause, or the patient. None of them, in her experience, could agree on a best course going forward or backward: was it oystershell powder for weak digestion, or crushed chamomile flowers? Cayenne pepper or laudanum for morning sickness? A 'cooling' or a 'heating' diet throughout? (Mrs B had seen too many women living like a horse on grassy food and water.) If a woman's pains weren't strong enough, her attendants promoted large quantities of strong liquors, and if very strong, even more. The only thing worse, in her mind, was the calling of a doctor, who was always quick with the forceps and short on patience with a woman in pain.

'We ought to have a good long time together, looks as if,' said Mrs B, rolling the woman's gown back over her calves.

'Are you sure?'

'We must have a little patience.'

'Those were my mother's words to me as she was dying.'

''Tis true, comin' or goin'.' The midwife gave her a quick pat on the bodice of her dress. 'Let's get you out of this into something easier.'

The woman signalled toward a wardrobe, where Mrs B found a clean, pressed chemise, not a single heavy bedgown in sight, typical for lying-in but much too warm. She was of the view that nothing should be added to dress or bedclothes that the patient wasn't accustomed to in perfect health. When she turned back, the woman was on her feet, arms surrendered to the ceiling, at ease in her body. Her hair was all soft chestnut curls, brown eyes to match, her figure like a bulging flower vase.

'Not to worry,' said the midwife, undoing the gown at the back and coiling it up over her belly, head, and arms. 'Everything's in a fair way. You'll meet her soon enough.'

In seconds the new garment replaced the old. '*Her?*'

'Mmm.'

'But we were expecting "Master William." We've been expecting him from the first.'

All the bending and up-and-down had Mrs B blotchy in the face. She stopped to blow a few strands of hair away, and saw the surprise on her patient's face.

'Everyone does. Expect a boy. But you're fleshy all over, not just out front. Feet nice and warm. Skin smooth as a plum.' The midwife put her hands on her hips to squint at the woman's eyes. 'Pupils closed up and small.' She put her nose in the air and took a satisfied sniff. 'But it's that smell of apple dumplings gives her away. You've a yen for sweets. That means a girl. Who'll take her time with you, upon my word.'

Mrs B bent over for her bag. She set the gin and satchel on a near table, and began unpacking.

'Another girl,' said the woman almost under her breath, 'in this world.'

Something in the cadence of her voice made Mrs B turn to take her in. The missus had stepped back into her slippers and redraped her shawl. She was very still, hands circling her swollen belly, staring down through the thin white linen with a wistful smile on her lips, as if saying hello and goodbye all at once. She'd looked so unafraid of everything until then: an older woman, late thirties maybe, experienced, with the way of the world about her. The midwife thought most women made far too much of the difficulties and inconveniences of childbearing, that it was a natural condition – not a disease at all – and ought to be treated as such. The woman in front of her now seemed not like them at all. No, she seemed the sort to look the task in the face, let Nature take charge, but help it along where she could, a short country walk, she guessed, gentle ride in a carriage, walk up and down the stairs, or busy herself in the early going with the distraction of dumplings, the spiced scent of a groaning cake. But standing there, some softness bled through the woman's strength.

'Shall I call you "Mrs G", then?' asked the midwife. 'Just to shorten things up, same for both of us?'

'Mrs G?'

'Or Mrs Godwin, if you like.'

'Mrs Godwin? Who the devil is that?' the woman said with a bright laugh.

Mrs B looked at her, confused.

'I'm sorry. It's only that I don't think of myself that way. "Mrs Godwin." Though it's been four months already.'

Mrs B made the count of months in her head. She was a Christian woman but didn't judge. 'Well, then, new married. Congratulations, I guess, are in order.'

'Except that it goes against everything I believe.'

'What's that?'

'Marrying at all.'

Mrs B was accustomed to women in her state saying things they might otherwise not, especially as the pains came closer together – sometimes things they would later regret, causing them to swear her to silence. She had heard secrets and gossip, pleas and gibberish, screaming, moaning, crying and curses, but never a declaration so clearheaded as this. Mrs Godwin seemed to be staring at her, almost daring her to disapprove. But Mrs B only smiled, in a way that didn't show her teeth.

'Well, we've a bit of a wait on our hands,' she said, setting out the last of her tincture jars. 'What shall we do with it?'

'I asked Mr Godwin to send me a newspaper, a novel, any book. Some amusement to while the hours away.'

'Maybe tell her your story, why don't you?' said the midwife, nodding toward the missus's womb. 'Just for her.'

'Why do you think she's taking her time?'

'Ooh, the darkness can be a comfort, I s'pose,' said Mrs B.

14

'It's the darkness binds you to her, and her to you. S'where we all begin, don't we?'

When the missus didn't answer, Mrs B turned to see a shadow sweep across her face as she gazed outside, pulling her shawl close around. Mrs B took her as chilled, and stepped toward the open window.

'Let me close that for you.'

'No!'

Startled by the sharp edge in her voice, Mrs B let go of the tall panes, and felt her own fleshy shoulders drop. She was tired, there was no way around it, eleven days straight, the thrumming chaos of the Westminster Lying-In Hospital, and now this, before a day of rest. Rhythm, routine, as long as was possible, she thought. She could bear up one more time, she told herself, letting the soft breeze dry the water pooling heavy at the back of her eyes. She wouldn't say a word, never would. It wasn't her place. She was tired, that's all.

'I like the feel of it on my face,' the missus said, by way of apology, Mrs B supposed. 'I cannot abide still air. I can't breathe.'

'Open's fine, till you tell me different.' Mrs B set her shoulders and returned to the table. She poured a dram of gin from the bottle.

'You think she can hear me?' asked the woman.

'Oh yes. Same as the *whoosh-whoosh* of your heart. Has done, all along. Why, you and her've known each other a good long while already.' She held out the small glass, an offering. 'And with God's blessing, you'll have a good long time to come.'

The pregnant woman took the glass, held it high, and swirled it, watching the gin catch the light.

'And you think I can talk her into the world?'

'Well, there's no talking her out of it.'

The woman's eyes smiled. She tipped her head back to drink down the gin in one swallow, closing her eyes for the burn of it down the throat, which seemed to fortify her. She put the glass in Mrs B's hand, cupping her own slender fingers around the midwife's.

'Call me Mary,' she said, as if restored.

'I am Mary Wollstonecraft.'

MARY W

Another girl. In this world. Like so many passages, it begins
with water. Not the wide grey water of chopping seas, not
pulling tides or rocky shores, not harbours. This water pools
on the floorboards beneath me, clear liquid, splashing like an
ephemeral fall from my own body, sputtering news of your
imminent arrival. Mrs Blenkinsop trundles across the circle
in my direction, it must be her: good round face and ruddy
cheeks, summer cloak flapping behind, clutching a leather bag
and glass bottle to her ample chest. Her white ruffle cap's fallen
down, showing her woolly hair (holding more to red than grey)
swirling in a great bun, illuminated by the tender sun of the late
summer morning. When she opens her mouth to speak, I see
that her teeth are crooked and yellow, and that she resists smiling
because of it. But her eyes are insensibly kind; a primordial
mud-green, like a flashing creek after a storm, with twigs and
leaves, sediment and rain all mixed together, flecks of light dancing
on its rippling surface. Detritus, and all that is necessary for life.

Which is enough to set us on our long, strange journey together.

At the start she warns me that I won't be relieved of my load anytime soon, though she assures me I'll be safely delivered, head foremost, and all is as it ought to be. Some part of me believes in this seasoned midwife so thoroughly that when she announces your sex (with no fanfare at all) I am won to it like a trumpet call – *réveillez-vous!* 'Awake!' she says to me, to the daughter who stirs within. In an instant you spring from my imagination, entire. Never mind those who espouse the art of getting pretty girl babies, who would've had me gaze on cherry lips and lily-whites throughout my pregnancy, sitting quietly doing needlepoint, taking care not to think thoughts at all. Indeed, many in my state take up the cause of a nursery in the months before their confinement, if not the refurbishment of an entire house, always with an urgency that resides in our most primitive animal natures. Burrow deep, spin a steel-silk orb, feather the nest. For my part I cannot unpack a trunk without a thought bounding in, a rush to nearby fields and forests, a cold lake-bath, or the desk, the paper, the pen. There is no confinement that can hold me, no drawing of the curtains, but wide-open windows throwing fresh country light across the page, illuminating the blackest ink.

Now, daughter, I'm to tell you a story to coax you into the world. When Mrs B says it's the darkness that binds us, I know she means nothing by it; they are words to ease my time. But the River Fleet, in the far distance out my window, demands that I look. More water, flowing across time, beyond pastoral fields and nursery gardens that remind me of the villages of my girlhood and the best part of my youth, out past the occasional brickworks that remind me of the worst. Here, at the edge of

Somers Town, and the farthest reach of my vision, the river runs clear under an ancient elm with great gnarled arms. It bows its graceful canopy as if to mark the water's progress to St. Pancras Church, where, this spring, that same old elm burst with frothy yellow buds that swayed with the wind, and bowed to us, your father and me. The day that I *married*, defying my own nature and betraying all I held dear.

My womb quickening with you.

It was the thirty-eighth anniversary of my birth, the day I chose, and Mr Godwin consented, to begin this life together, this new world we've made for you. I didn't tell him, but am keenly aware that every year, without knowing it, we also mark the anniversary of our death. For however untroubled the Fleet is here, in this midlife paradise, I know that by the time it joins the Thames, it will be sullied by the bloody scraps of butchers' stalls, the bloated corpses of cats and dogs, dead flowers, and human excrement.

My own story is no prettier, far from it. There are triumphs in it, a scattering of joys, but the beautiful sits side by side with the grotesque; I cannot separate them. All the brutality is there, the hurt I've suffered at the hands of others, but so, too, my own mistakes, missteps, and missed understandings. I have held it close, afraid to unleash it into the world. So how could I tell you, my almost-born daughter, the story of that vivid darkness as if it would persuade you of this place? Would you survive the deepest bone-secrets of our brief shared being? You inside me. Me inside you.

No, I think not.

But then true labour comes, quick and hard.

'Perhaps it's time to call for Mr Godwin, when he finishes

his supper,' I tell Mrs B.

She gives a note to the housemaid to deliver to him, and asks that some fresh butter be sent up. She helps me to the bed, where I'm to kneel, sit, crouch, lie down, as the pains permit. When the butter comes, she stretches my loins to ease the way for your head. I can hear Godwin's footfalls up and down the hall outside, imagine him wringing his hands. He knocks on the door, but I can't hear his exchange with Mrs B. I want to call his name, to reassure him, but can't find my voice.

The closer the pains, the more I grow quiet and withdraw into myself. Mrs B mops my brow and whispers into my ear that a child cannot be far behind.

And then at last you slip from my body.

Mrs B tips you upside down and slaps your feet to wake you into the world. But the moment lasts longer than it should, and I begin to doubt. Then you gasp for air, at last, and live, not with a wail so much as a chirp and squeak I think only I can hear.

Oh little bird!

Your father bursts into the room at the sound of my giddy relief – was I laughing? He startles at the sight of you naked and trembling in Mrs B's hands.

'Is it—'

'Breathing, sir, she is.'

'Oh, darling,' he says, coming to my side. 'A little girl.' He half sits on the bed and presses his forehead to mine. His joyful tears, my ragged hair matted against my forehead, as Mrs B cuts the umbilical cord and washes you with all the ceremony of scrubbing a turnip just plucked from the ground.

'Made us wait for you a good long time, yes you did,' she

says, sponging your tiny face and chest.

But I know I have waited for you, for this, all my life.

'Let's give your limbs some liberty, shall we?' Mrs B wraps you loosely in cotton cloth and delivers you into my arms. I free the blanket even more, to survey the whole of you, count your fingers, your toes. I can see in your father's eyes that you aren't what he expected, or what our gentle confederacy of perfections rarely admits: a child at birth is a shocking thing. Your skin is coated, as if with wax the colour of jaundice, so thin it bares the atlas of dark veins beneath. Instead of feathers you have fine white down, barely visible, all over your body; instead of wings, arms like spindles, held tight to your heaving rib cage, not much bigger than your father's palm, which he holds against your quick-beating heart.

The love, instantaneous!

Mrs B tells me to hold you to my breast, but with your eyelids too swollen to open, your lips unaccustomed to the ways of sucking, your little beak searches but cannot find me. I see the worry in her eyes; she needn't say so. You're too small, your lungs work too hard, each breath a jagged try. But I would tell her I will not let you die, my own life force now inextricably tied to yours, a thousand times knotted together. And though we cannot choose which day we are born, into what time or place, a day chooses us. Never forget, little bird, that the day that chose you comes at the end of a month when a comet blazed across London's skies, heralding your arrival.

Another girl, in this world!

And so I *will* tell you the story to fill you up and bind you to this wondrous vale, if you stay with us, little bird. Please stay. I will tell you the moments that begin and end me – because

21

we are made of them all – strung like pearls in time, searching always for where the new circle begins its turn, the place of our next becoming. Where the line becomes an arc, and curves.

Mrs B

31ˢᵗ August 1797

'Mary W safe delivered at 11 hours 20 minutes last Evenin of a daughter after a long travail. Placenta not yet delivered,' Mrs Blenkinsop wrote in her pocket diary when the patient finally slept for a few moments. Mr Godwin refused to set down the child, but sat in a chair pulled up close to the bed with their 'little bird' tight in his arms. Mrs B thought she ought to rethink him, after her first impression last night when he'd knocked on the door to inquire whether they ought not call a doctor, given the unexpected length of the labour. He'd been told by friends at dinner, and could confirm, having once read in a book, that it is the fashion to call a doctor or at least a male accoucheur to assist, to have the benefit of those with real medical training.

'Not at all necessary, sir. I prefer to trust in Nature,' said Mrs B. 'Great and marvellous is the goodness of Providence.'

'I am an atheist, Mrs Blenkinsop. That is of no use to me.'

Mrs B had never met an atheist, but she had encountered

nervous men. In her experience, the bigger the brain, the greater the worry. She judged, by the way Mr Godwin wrung his hands as he spoke, that this was his first birth. He seemed an awkward man, like a stiff chair that hadn't been sat on enough – the opposite of her own husband, whose life force had always pulsed in his large, rugged hands. Mr Blenkinsop, whom she'd tried to put out of her mind these last days.

Still, Mr Godwin was right that it was the custom nowadays, this sending for men, even when it might be no more than a common labour. It would be one thing if they were as old as she, with as much practical experience. Instead Mrs B saw mostly boyish pretenders who, having attended an anatomy course and seen one or two dissections of female bodies, believed themselves experts in the field, as if they'd invented it themselves. Nothing filled her with more dread than the sight of a chamois leather bag opened to reveal its forceps, perforators, blunt hook, and a pair of bone cutters. She had yet to meet a doctor who believed that doing nothing was the best approach.

'I'm sorry, Mrs Blenkinsop,' said Mr Godwin, patting his glistening forehead with a cambric handkerchief. 'I meant nothing by it.'

'Nothing taken, sir. The waiting's hard, I know, but there's no cause for worry. None at all.'

She'd seen the way he burst into the room immediately after the birth and sat at the edge of his wife's bed, right up against her hip, how they pressed their foreheads together, knit their fingers. While she'd attended to the just-born child, scrubbed away the scurf with warm water and wine and put a flannel cap on her head, she couldn't help hearing Mr Godwin speak to his wife of a joy he'd never known; how sheltered he'd been

24

before knowing her, and how wrong to let a Miss Pinkerton pursue him of late; how sorry he was for any pain he'd caused her because she must never doubt his love for her, and here was proof of their love, this little girl. As if a child had never been born on this good earth.

Mrs B was reluctant to ask him to leave his post by his wife's bed, but Mary looked to be in the afterthroes, which she took to mean that the placenta was soon to follow.

'It's not finished, then? She's not out of danger?' Mr Godwin asked in a furtive whisper.

'There's no danger, sir, just Nature, taking its time.'

He suggested, more gingerly than before, and with more respect, that they might call a doctor at any point she thought it necessary. She squinched her eyes in agreement, which seemed to satisfy him, but he only consented to leave the room when Mrs B allowed him to take the child with him. Just for a little while.

'Watch over her, darling,' Mary said with a weak turn of her head.

'I promise,' he said, and forced himself from the room, their eyes not leaving each other's until the last possible moment.

Despite two hours of effort, the afterbirth refused to budge. Mrs B tried her old recipe of hyssop, wild mint, pennyroyal, and balm, good for easing gripes in the belly and cleansing impurities from the womb. Hyssop could even bring away a dead child, but mostly it helped beckon the soft, warm placenta, whole and unto itself, to slide into the midwife's waiting hands. The less she intervened, the less blood would be lost, she knew, but there was a boundary of time, and they were near it.

When the herbs failed to move things along, Mrs B gave

the cord a gentle tug, then rubbed and pressed on Mary's belly.

The patient, at the start, was uncomplaining, even cheerful. Never mind her long and arduous labour, Mary now radiated elation at being delivered of her daughter. She was enthralled with her 'little bird,' and couldn't wait for Fanny to meet her new sister. The matter of the placenta seemed an inconvenience she was anxious to have behind her, so she might hold her new babe in her arms, and urge her to suck. This, she'd told Mrs B, she believed in above all things – that the best sustenance for a newborn child was its mother's own milk, and the love that flowered between them. But Mary began to tire, and the boundary of time drew closer.

'Will it come on its own?' she asked Mrs B. 'Why isn't it coming?'

'I think your placenta's a bit shy.'

'That would be the only thing shy about me.'

'It's not just yours, it's hers too. Belonged to both of you.' Mrs B thought that talking was the best way to ease Mary's mind. 'It's like a tree, I think,' she said. 'How the placenta makes the roots, and the cord is the trunk that grows from the roots, and your little girl is the fruits and flowers of all that.'

'I'd like her to be a tree of her own,' said Mary.

'Why shouldn't she be, then?'

'You have a poetic soul, Mrs B.' Mary squeezed out a smile and laid her head on the pillow with a sigh.

Mrs Blenkinsop told her to have a little rest, said they'd take it up again when she woke. She knew she must alert Mr Godwin to the risk of infection, however unlikely, given that he'd not stopped pacing the hall, and every twenty minutes asked for news through the door. She still believed, by faith *and* experience, that Nature would take its course, given time.

'It's hard to think clearly,' Mr Godwin said, rubbing his temple.

'We could wait till morning, sir.' She was careful not to mention God again.

'But waiting has its own dangers, yes?'

The swaddled child chirped low in her cradle. She seemed to grow weaker by the hour. Mrs B could tell that her little cries nearly broke Mr Godwin.

'We've a French Dr Poignand, from the hospital. Maybe it's for the best.'

Mr Godwin looked from the cradle to his sleeping wife, his tall forehead collapsing into folds. Mrs B had seen it before, a husband wrestling with his helplessness. Men believed in action above all.

'What would the missus want? Maybe think of that.'

'Yes,' he said, pressing his kerchief three times across his brow. 'What would Mary do?' Mrs B could see him thinking it through, never taking his eyes off his wife. 'To think that not much more than a year ago I believed in my solitariness with the greatest vehemence. There was not a woman in the world worth giving up the life I kept very much for myself, to do and think and write and dine and sleep exactly as I wanted. Marriage, I believed an intolerable oppression, a prison, a compromise I would never make. I was . . . delineated, and I liked it that way. And now? I can hardly find the line between us. Her thoughts are mine. Her feelings, mine. Our difficulties, ours. I am a different man because of her, Mrs Blenkinsop.' He looked squarely at the midwife in a way men rarely did. 'My love for Mary has freed me from the prison that was my life. And I cannot comprehend going on without her. What man I would then be.'

Mrs B nodded. There were words he'd said that she didn't know, but she had the sense of the thing, and was touched by him telling her. In the hundreds of births she'd attended, she could not remember a single man baring his whole soul. Pray, yes. Weep, yes. Punch a wall, she'd seen that too. But never this. She tried to imagine her own husband, what he might say, in far fewer words.

No, she told herself, don't think of that. She must keep in the room.

Mr Godwin held the handkerchief to his lips and regarded his wife with a look of despair.

'She would want to live, Mrs Blenkinsop. For her daughters. But I need her to live . . . for me.'

Mrs B kept both hands bearing down on the missus's belly, at Dr Poignand's instruction. Mary moaned and writhed, her hair stringy with sweat. In moments she fainted altogether, which the midwife counted as a blessing. When conscious, she tried to lift her head to look between her legs. Mrs B was determined that Mary not see the horror down below, the bloody mess, the doctor up to his elbow inside her, peeling the placenta, piece by piece, from her womb. The pain, she knew, was worse than childbirth itself.

Mrs B knew a good deal about pain. She was childless herself, not for lack of trying, but that was long ago, so long she hardly remembered what trying was like, though she never forgot the wanting. In the early years, as apprentice to a country midwife, she found herself jealous of the pain that childbirth brought, though she never told a soul. How willing she would have been to suffer it, had she a child to show for it in the end, just one, that's all she'd asked of Him. Instead, over time she convinced herself that God had spared her from her own travail that she might serve other women in theirs, and with that, her desire gave way to duty, her jealousy, to joy observed. But to pain, she became obedient mistress. To her way of thinking, it wasn't enough to call a birth 'lying-in,' or 'groaning,' or 'crying-out,' as if a woman could be measured by the amount of noise she made. No, pain had a thousand likenesses, each as different as rough weather, every variation and never two days the same. She had seen women claw at their bedclothes, beat their own thighs, and try to climb the walls in hopes of escape.

But this was pain of another reach.

'Look at me,' said Mrs B, pointing to her chin. The midwife disapproved of Poignand's method, of doctors who believed if there was room enough for a child in the womb, surely there was room for a hand. But she had sympathised with Mr Godwin wanting to do something, anything, that might turn the tide in his wife's favour. She'd watched him from the window, frantic at being unable to find a carriage in the middle of the night, set off almost at a run for Parliament Street where the doctor lived. She wondered if she'd been too tired to press her point, but it was out of her hands now. Mr Godwin'd returned shortly before dawn with Poignand, who sprung to action, refusing even almond oil to cleanse his hands.

Mrs B found it hard to look herself. 'Keep your eyes right here,' she said to Mary, tapping the round button of her chin.

Mary, in a delirium, tried again to lift her head, to form her parched lips into words, but couldn't. It was as if she'd lost her voice altogether, Mrs B thought, with everyone else talking for her. She squeezed some drops of water from a cloth into Mary's mouth.

'What is it, dear? Tell me.'

'I want to die, truly,' Mary whispered, 'but I cannot leave her . . . I am determined.'

Mrs B pressed the cool cloth to Mary's brow and clutched her hand. 'Then don't leave her,' she said.

'Both hands on the belly, Blenkinsop,' said Poignand. 'And can we not give the poor woman some laudanum?' By now he was sweating too.

'I promised her, Doctor. No laudanum.'

Mrs B thought she felt Mary squeeze her hand back. She leaned down to her ear. 'It'll soon be over, Mary, God willing. Think of your new little girl.'

But Mary had faded away again, and couldn't hear. Mrs B had seen it before. The pain with no name, no sound, neither screams nor breath. A prayer no more use than the tip of a chin.

Mary W

Little bird. My true life begins not with my birth, but with a death, the shock of which will draw a line in my life that separates everything that's gone before from all that lies ahead. I was thirteen years old, fiery but unformed, feared the wrath of my parents, hated my brother and my life, loved the countryside and my sweet spaniel, Betsy, who feared nothing, knew only joy.

We'd moved to the little village of Walkington, which, compared with the stink of Spitalfields, I was sure must be Paradise, or as close to it as I'd ever come. Best of all, I'd met a girl, in nearby Beverley, who I was quite sure had all one should ever want in life, and *was* all anyone should want to be. This day was Jane Arden's birthday, and the hope that'd sustained me was that I'd be invited to her party. I'd had my one good dress, such as it was, washed and pressed for a week, hanging on a nail at the back of my door, with my pinchbeck quizzing glass, dangling from its velvet ribbon, looped around its collar, my single accoutrement. I'd waited every day for a letter to come, been on my best behaviour, not argued, and done my chores in hopes Mama would let me go should the longed-for invitation come. But it hadn't.

Then my brother crossed me again, and I couldn't help myself. He was the oldest, best-loved, do-no-wrong Ned, but I knew his secret. My fingers clenched the gathered corners of the kerchief I took from his room and now I stole past the village gates, Betsy cantering beside me. When the bare kiss of spring grazed my cheek, I set down the tied kerchief, pried off my boots, and peeled away my worsted stockings. I knotted them twice around my waist, wondering why all clothing was cumbersome to me, my chemise like a winding sheet, never mind my practice corset, my skirts. My spaniel crouched, then lunged at my feet, beckoning me to keep walking. Papa had tried for a year to make her his hunting dog, but she'd yelp at the blast of gunshots, bury her nose in the hedgerow, and run away when he raised his boot. Betsy was mine now, as loyal a friend as I had (perhaps my only friend, if Jane didn't prove true), and freed from the necessity of recovering dead birds, she'd become an enthusiast in all things, even tromping on the year's first columbine, worried about nothing at all.

I started off again, my rage at Ned propelling me, and counted my steps, which is how I measured whether my legs had grown, because there was talk in town of a desirable height for a woman, and I was sure I'd end up too short or too tall, but never just right. My body changed like a brewing storm, every day something new and unwelcome. Not so Jane Arden, whose skin had not a mark on it, where I was a map of imperfections: knobby knees, great white knuckles, freckles all over. She was the open, rolling countryside of those Yorkshire Wolds; I, the bulbous rocks and uneven ground beneath my feet. I imagined her parlour the best in all of Beverley. Even her French was impeccable, her grammar irreproachable, and I, a pretender, with dull pens my brother Ned refused to fix for me.

I confess I even wished her father were *my* father, for I couldn't separate Jane from John Arden, with their noble noses and keen grey eyes. For weeks I'd secreted myself in the back row at his scientific lectures, pretending to be a Beverley girl. He spoke of things beyond all my knowing, of electricity and gravity, of 'animalcules,' invisible to the eye, that are borne by the air and reach all the way inside of us. I could see she was his daughter by the way she looked at him with pride from the front row, only occasionally staring out the window, when I could see her long neck and regal profile. Finally, with jangling nerves, I introduced myself to her, Jane of the fine manners. Wanting to impress, I pretended to know things I'd only just learnt. But she smiled as she took my cold hand in her gloved one. Here was a buzzing electrical current; here, gravitational pull. This, then, was the science of my heart. I had a sudden determination to overcome any obstacle to possess her friendship. I wrote her my first letter that night, and one every day after, with a third as many replies from her, polite enough. She didn't know that it burned like a bonfire – a bone fire – inside me, the desperate wishing for her life to be mine, or for some sign of returned and equal affection, some inkling that she found me worthwhile.

When she asked me to sit beside her at a demonstration of her father's portable scientific instruments, I couldn't contain my joy. I thought Mama only assented because she, too, longed for us to be part of the Beverley crowd somehow. Jane sat in her chair, her hands folded as neat as a napkin in her lap. I tried to do the same, but kept inching toward the edge of my seat as John Arden revealed one instrument after another: an equinoctial sundial in a fish-skin case, a folding botanical microscope you could slip into your pocket, a compass with a steel needle 'blued' at North.

When Jane led me by the hand and introduced me to him after his lecture, I saw up close how sympathetic his eyes were, but sad too. I'd heard whispers that his wife had succumbed to tuberculosis when Jane was small, and that he'd raised her to young womanhood by himself. He looked at Jane with the same pride that she did him, didn't talk down to her, but straight across, as if she were capable of any understanding. He cocked his head when he asked her a question, waiting to hear her opinion. Had he covered the material too quickly? Too much history? Enough explanation of each instrument's capabilities? I felt, by the way he shook my hand firmly, that Jane's endorsement of me was good enough for him. We lingered over his cabinet of curiosities, laid out on green velvet, which I was careful not to touch. When Jane excused herself to say goodbye to a group of girls near the door, I didn't know whether to follow.

'Here,' said John Arden, offering a small magnifying glass from his collection, beautiful in its simplicity. 'Look through this, and tell me what you see.' He held out the walnut he'd used in his demonstration.

I pulled the glass close to my eye, but it made the world all wrong.

'Move it near and far until things come into focus. It's different for everyone, since our own eyes are a convex lens, infinite shapes, no pair alike.'

I soon found the walnut shell in full relief.

'It's said we have the Romans to thank, Emperor Nero, I think, who looked through a chip of some gemstone or other to better see actors on the stage. Don't remember who figured out how to concentrate the sun's rays to coax a flame. Useful, that. But our own Sir Francis Bacon was the first to turn it to a pure scientific use. Imagine, simply because the glass is thicker in the centre, it changes everything. Marvellous, really.'

'It is,' I said, studying the intricate grooves of the shell.

'Also called a quizzer,' he said. 'I suppose you know that. Jane reminds me I need not always explain everything.'

'Oh, not at all. I've heard of them. Just never held one in my hand.'

'Not the finest example. But I like the pinchbeck. Not as good as gold or brass, but that's the point, really; it won't tarnish either. Look, you can give it a ribbon and wear it, so it's always with you.' He took it from my hand, pulled a velvet ribbon through, and tied it around my neck. I blushed at the feeling of his fingers near the collar of my dress, not for any impropriety; it simply felt what it must be like to have a father who cared for you, who might have once tied your laces, or patched a scraped knee. I raised the pinchbeck glass again to study the walnut, its grooves like dry riverbeds crusted with mud.

'How much the small world resembles the large,' I said.

'Untold worlds, big and small, right in front of us, everywhere.'

I lowered the glass and looked at him. His high forehead was shiny and smooth as a peeled potato. He was dressed plainly, like a clergyman, but his sparse hair misbehaved, as if ideas sprouted from the top of his head. A thought flew into me that maybe he'd turned all his grief over his wife's death to curiosity, looked away from the pain inside to the wonders without, whether for himself or his daughter, I couldn't guess.

'I can almost see the wheels turning,' he said.

'I can't stop it, no matter how hard I try.'

'Why would you?' he asked, tilting his head as he did with Jane.

'Because it hurts sometimes,' I said, without thinking first.

He looked at me and smiled, the creases at the corners of his eyes deepening. 'It's a gift to be a thinker, to like ideas. But it's a burden too. One can never turn away.'

'I don't know many ideas, not really.'

'But you must be a great reader. All the girls at Jane's school—'

I wanted to lie. I was embarrassed to tell him what counted as an education for me. I stammered instead. 'I'm afraid I don't go to school with—'

'Oh,' he said. 'Apologies. I just assumed—'

'Though I do love to read. But books are . . . hard to come by.'

'Well, I've enough of my own for a small circulating library. When you come to Jane's birthday, I'll be glad to lend you whatever you like.'

My heart sank. I looked at the gaggle of girls by the door, all perfect curls, fine lace, and frippery. I would never be one of them, no matter how much I wanted it, or how hard I tried. Jane had not seen fit to invite me, or seen me fit to invite. 'That's kind of you,' I sputtered, trying to hide my hurt. But he saw it.

'I'm sorry. I'm sure Jane means to ask you. Still plenty of time. Hard to keep up with her social swirl.'

'Of course,' I said, embarrassed and grateful, a melange of feelings unknown to me. I started to untie the ribbon from my neck. 'Thank you for allowing me—'

'No, please. Consider it yours. I've more quizzing glasses than any one man should, and I'm afraid Jane's had her fill of them. I've got her every colour of ribbon known to man, and still she refuses to wear them. I cannot keep up with what's au courant.'

I wrapped my hand around it, clutched it to my chest. 'I shall treasure it.'

'Don't treasure it, Miss Wollstonecraft, just look through it every chance you get.' He took the glass in his hand, and wiped it with his kerchief. 'But best keep the fingers away from the glass itself.'

I was mortified that I didn't have gloves on. But he skipped right past it, breathing his fog on the glass and wiping it clear. 'You want clarity above all. You'll be startled by what you see.'

I had never been so near a man who was not my father or brother, neither of whom had ever treated me with the regard I felt from John Arden in that moment. I realised I had never felt regard before at all. I mumbled a thank you, bade a clumsy goodbye, and started for the door.

'Miss Wollstonecraft!' he called from behind. I turned back.

'Never worry. Ideas will find *you,* wherever you are.'

If only you could see me, little bird, clutching my brother's kerchief so tight I almost forgot what was inside, my anger at Ned mingling with my envy of Jane, and my longing for her father's regard. I wished I didn't have feelings at all. But when I broke free of rough ground, the soft loam bulged between my toes and filled the arches of my feet. The sky threw a glimpse of morning the colour of seawater. Even if I couldn't see it, had never seen the sea, I smelt and tasted it on my lips. It stirred everything in me. I was thirteen, yes, but I *was* a soul, could feel it rising inside me like high tide, feel the pull of it in my belly.

Nature was my only home on earth, a place to rest, unbound.

Betsy sprinted ahead of me. She knew the way, the only path to it, the one we'd made ourselves. I tucked the hem of my skirt into its waist to climb the final 'stairs': flat rock, grass, flat rock again, and at its peak, the large, buff limestone where I sat sometimes on its carpet of moss and lichen, master of my own world, that small circumference with a view, I pretended, all the way to Calais. I pulled my knees up, wrapped my arms around them, and laid my cheek there, bone to bone, breathing it all in. Betsy panted in the grass, head resting on her speckled paws, feeling the wind in her fur. No one but Betsy wanted it, or would walk that far, so we kept it our secret. But I would have let Jane Arden come. Because then she would know me, then see me. On my hillock that spoke everything of who I was.

That, little bird, the only true happiness I knew.

The barbed edge of my anger fell away. I knelt to the ground and set the kerchief on the level surface, untied the top, and peeled its corners away until one, two, three, and then thirty spiders at least, with what seemed like a thousand legs, skittered across the rock, under it, away, and into the wild. My realm had been theirs all along.

Could Jane Arden ever understand? She was refinement and elegance, knowledge and hope. How could I explain my letting loose a kerchief full of spiders on a nothing hillock that meant everything to me? How could I make her see that those spiders needed refuge, wanted to live as all beings want to live? Free.

* * *

I stood on the threshold of the cottage when Ned confronted me with his empty jar.

'Where are they?'

Eliza and Everina turned to him because Ned's mood of the moment, whatever it was, preoccupied all the household, except when Father was home. I brushed past him, defiant. I was second-born, a girl, but I never knew which was the greater crime. I paid for it every day, but that day I was tired of paying.

'Take them off,' my mother said, before she even turned to face me. She could point to my stockings with the back of her head, from that spot the size of a pin cushion where her hair was always uncombed and ratted. Though she wore a cap most of the time, there were eyes underneath, I swear it.

'Don't you want to hear my side?'

'And not a single word.'

I pinched my lips to hold in not a single word but a thousand. I untied my brogans and rolled the stockings down, one by one, seams inside out, my toes poking through. I held them out to her, an offering: yes, I did it again, Mama, ruined everything. What shall we do now? She wanted me to fear her, but it wasn't fear. It was boredom with our ritual, sadness that here it was again instead of anything else.

Ned stood between us, snorting like a bull. 'Make her tell what she's done with them, Mama!'

Eliza and Everina looked up sideways from their cross-stitches awaiting my next move, pretending not to. Their blank faces took no sides, as usual. Poor Henry, twelve years old, sat on the stone floor in the corner playing with dust balls and drooling into the rag tied around his neck. 'I kn-kn-know where your spiders are, Ned.'

'Where, then?'

'Outside, l-l-lots of them. I'll get some for you.'

'You imbecile,' said Ned.

'Don't call him that!' I said.

'Not a single word, Mary, unless you're prepared to tell Ned why his jar is empty,' said Mama, shooing little James away from her skirts. Not yet three, he came to clutch at my skirts instead.

'He stole my quizzer!' I pulled the magnifying glass, freed of its ribbon, from my pocket and held it up as evidence of his crime. 'It was hanging on the back of my door, but I found it in his room. And a pile of spider bodies, without legs!'

'No one cares,' he said. 'They're spiders!'

'He pulls their legs off, Mama. And then burns them with the magnifying glass. In the most cruel way.'

'It's science,' said Ned. 'But you wouldn't know that, would you? You go to a school for *girls*.'

'I'm the one who told you!' I shouted, but I couldn't disagree. Of all my grievances against him, that Ned was seen worthy of a real education while I was not cut the deepest. 'You're not a scientist. You're a torturer! Who pulls helpless spiders' legs off to watch them suffer and squirm!'

'Mary!' Mama raised her voice to silence me.

But I was beyond her wrath, unafraid. 'They're not *his* spiders. They don't belong to anyone! Why do you always take his side?'

This drew a slap across my face so weak I almost wanted to laugh. I knew she couldn't stand me looking at her with pity. Betsy whined and scratched outside the door.

'Stop that dog's scratching. Now.'

'She just wants to be inside, with us.' But Henry had already let her in. Mama narrowed her eyes, resenting even that small defeat. But she preferred to admonish me and ignore Henry. Sometimes she seemed bothered by the presence of so many daughters, when she'd only wanted sons. Henry she didn't count, but doted on Ned as if he were her husband, a husband she might like to have, or wished hers was. I saw her once giving him dancing lessons in the drawing room. Ned was clumsy and four-footed, but she didn't care. The way she looked at him, her face shining like a smitten young girl – maybe one she once was – who knew how to hold herself, and where a young man's hand might rest on the small of her back.

Reliving this now, little bird, I feel some splinter of sympathy for my brother. I'm sure I saw him blush, not at the thought of touching his mother, but touching any girl at all. I see that despite his bravura, he didn't know anything, and that my mother, who loved him best, was trying to prepare him for the world she thought he deserved, which was one she'd never had. Sometimes I'd pretend she loved me like that too. Pretend she did *not* send me to a wet nurse for the first two years of my life (unlike Ned, whom she let suckle at her breast) – that she delighted in my first smile, first word, first step, first anything. Even then, I visited five-month-old baby Charles in secret. His wet nurse, in the poorest part of town, had lost her one child, an infant, and had only my youngest brother's care to shape her days. She was glassy eyed, and said nothing to him as he sucked, just stared at the wall. But she didn't mind when I sat beside her and said nonsense words to him, wiggled his tiny feet, watched him laugh. I wondered if my wet nurse did the same for me, whether I took her as my mother, and then, when I was taken from her, the only home I'd known, found my own mother a stranger, as she found me.

If only Mama had looked at me that way, once, the way she looked at Ned. The way I'm looking at you now, little bird. I would've retreated to my hillock and been happy for all my days.

Mama took Ned's jar from his hand. I was to wash my stockings and stitch each hole, then sit by the hearth for three hours, looking at a spot on the wall and saying not a word, an exquisite torture. Everina was careful not to make eye contact, but Eliza stole glances when she could, and I saw some mixture of awe and pity in her eyes, but wasn't sure which of us she held in awe, and whom she pitied.

When Mama turned to her needlework, I looked out the window that perfectly framed my mighty oak in the near distance, half as big around as I am tall, with an elephant's foot for a trunk and strong, knurled arms. I took shelter in its leafy world when Ned banished me from playing the boys' hardy games, and so declared it 'my tree,' where I'd go to read, or make my own school. Eliza and Everina, when they weren't playing with dolls, consented sometimes to being my students, and Henry as a last resort, who let me pretend to teach him things. I wished I were up there, cradled in my favourite bough, as strong as a hammock, reading whatever book I could find, or even my father's *Town and Country*, filled with the latest London scandals.

An old housekeeper had taught me to read with the help of some alphabet cards, left over from Ned, no doubt, and her own Bible, tied with a ratty ribbon. I don't remember the woman's face so much as her thick, wrinkled finger moving across the page, word by word, as I sounded out each one. I think now that she meant to tame me – I was all scabbed knees and dirty elbows – but it was she who made books my companion, when I could get them, sating a hunger of the mind more compelling than the twitching of my eager legs.

Mama caught me staring at my tree, and gave me the eye. But when she turned to attend to James and give instructions to the cook, I reached down to stroke Betsy's head, feel her brindle fur through my fingers. It was then that Eliza swept past to press a letter into my lap. I thrilled at seeing my own name in Jane Arden's fine curling hand, and half turned my body to gently break its seal. Just as I did, the door opened and slammed shut, signalling that Father's workday was done, such as it was. He fancied himself a 'gentleman farmer,' though his true penchant was for failing at it. (He spent what money we had to hire others to do the work, then barked orders at them.) My life to that point had been an ever-shrinking circumference *he* drew for us, dragging us from Spitalfields to Epping Forest to Barking to Walkington – whatever his diminishing inheritance would allow – to get far away from his own father and the silk weavers of London's Primrose Street. He was ever in search of a living off the land, or at least a place we might pretend to be a small, genteel family (we were neither small nor genteel). Someplace near a pub and a racecourse suited him best. He sought erasure of his past in each new place, but who he was went with him everywhere. And we went with him, a household ever in thrall to his whims and deficits. Suffering for his mistakes.

Betsy lifted her head, alert to his presence. We were all alert to him, but it was better not to look, not to draw his attention. There was no pretending he wasn't drunk already. Henry hummed in the corner, tracing raindrops on the window with his finger.

'What're you singing about, Henry?' But he just kept on humming.

A worn-out Betsy, ever the optimist, lumbered to standing and went to greet Papa. When he slapped his chest, inviting her paws, and rubbed her head and ears, our cottage sighed and let down its guard.

'Ah, pup, how was your day? What a good dog, a good dog, yup.'

Mama appeared from the kitchen to gauge Papa's mood. 'Give us a hug, why don't you, then?' he said, walking toward her. She shook her head with a wilted smile and let him pull her to his unbuttoned waistcoat.

When he trained his eyes on me, I looked into the fire, my letter tucked safely between my dress and the seat of the chair. 'What's Mary done now?' he asked, still in a good-enough mood.

'She stole my spiders!' said Ned, standing from his seat with that pouty face.

'I know where the spiders are,' said Henry, half singing it.

'What's this about spiders?' Papa looked to me for an answer.

'She's not to say a word, not one word, for one hour more,' said Mama.

'Oh, let her go, Elizabeth. What's the point of keeping Mary from talking? Mary will talk-talk-talk all day long. But it's harmless. Nothing that matters.'

Papa's greatest gift with words was that he could sting two people at once. I looked between them, but I could see Mama had acquiesced already. When I stood, at last free of my penance, I forgot Jane's letter, which drifted to the floor. Papa pinched it between his dirty fingers. Out of instinct I grabbed for it, but he pulled it away, looked at the envelope, and laughed.

'Ah, our Mary has a little friend in Beverley, does she?'

I pulled my shawl close as he finished breaking the seal, unfolded and read it.

'"Dear Miss Wollstonecraft, I am pleased to send this letter in return for your staying from church yesterday to write me. There is no need to excuse the badness of your writing, as you call it, nor should you beg pardon for not writing sooner."' He read it with contempt, in a high-pitched voice, with nothing of Jane Arden's assurance and delicacy. '"I delight in your having enjoyed my father's demonstration Friday last, and his rather discursive lecture on magnetism." Magnetism? What use is that in the world? Rubbish, is what that is.'

Ned smiled, enjoying my humiliation.

'"And presume we will have the pleasure of your company on Thursday evening in Beverley at six o'clock, when we will enjoy supper and light a cake (as the Germans do) to celebrate my fourteenth birthday—"'

My heart lifted. Jane Arden wants me there! Me! Tonight!

Papa must have seen the look on my face. 'Think you're too good for Walkington, do you?'

This from a man who pretended to cultivate an air of leisure without reading a single book, as far as I could tell. I fought not to shrug my shoulders. If I didn't make a fuss, he'd move on to something else. I could wash up and dress, I still had the gown pressed and ready for just this, and be in Beverley by six.

'No, Papa,' I said.

'Think you belong in Beverley, do you? Fancy friends. Assembly-room dances. Think a young man wants to dance with *you*?' I glanced at my sisters, who looked at the floor. 'No man'll want you, Mary. You're not pretty. You're not good at things men care about.'

'I don't mean to be good at things men care about.'

His neck jerked back into his collar. I could almost feel his stinging hand across my face.

'I'm sorry, Papa.' It griped me to say it.

He cackled, leaning to the side of my face, practically spitting in my ear. 'You think you're better than all of us, don't you, Mary? Better than me, that's what you think, isn't it? You think you're somebody.'

'Please, Papa. May I go? This once?'

'What about my spiders?' Ned cut in.

'He stole my quizzing glass!' I protested.

'What use do *you* have for it, Mary?'

'Spiders, spiders, spiders,' Henry sang, crawling his fingers up the window.

'He can have my stupid quizzer!' In an angry instant I pulled it from my pocket and threw it at Ned's chest. He tried to catch it, but it landed on the hard stone floor. He picked it up and held it to the light, cracked in two places, the length of it.

'Look at that,' said Papa. 'It's no good to anyone now.'

Ned smiled again, victorious. It sank me to see what I'd done. Was I no better than he was?

'Please, Papa!' I heard myself begging, which is what he wanted from me. I looked into his eyes, trying to find some shred of kindness in him – some remembering what it was to be young, to want to belong to the world.

'You're nobody, Mary. Less than nobody. That's who you are.' He crumpled the letter, but he might as well have crushed my heart in his fist. 'You're not to set foot out of this house. Do you understand?'

My eyes burned, but I looked at him, saying nothing. My fury a mirror of his.

Eliza and Everina looked at their laps. Betsy stood, ready to defend me. Smug Ned waited for my inevitable answer. For Papa must be answered.

'Yes, Papa,' I said, wishing I were dead. 'I understand.'

'Spiders, spiders, spiders,' Henry sang.

'Shush, Henry. Dinner's nearly on,' said Mama, who appeared at the door.

'I'll take mine at the pub,' said Papa, who would use Jane Arden's invitation to justify drinking another meal. He let the door slam, the thin windows shuddering behind him. Betsy whimpered, and then silence. I leaned down to snatch up the letter and held it dear in my trembling hands.

I refused dinner and retreated to my room where, by tears and candlelight, I wrote a thousand letters to Jane, raging against my fate, my brother, my father, the tyranny of men. I wanted to ruin him, tell all his secrets, say that my father was everything *hers* was not: a failure, a gambler, a drunkard. He beats his children, I wanted to say, even if sometimes he wrestles them onto his lap and kisses their heads, he withdraws his affection as easily, a double cruelty. Ned is the only one he won't touch, protected as he is by my mother's skirts. Henry, who is his shame, he boxes about the ears until my sapling brother cowers in the corner. We girls he always hits with a wide-open hand, careful to leave no lasting marks that might be seen by curious townsfolk. I wanted to tell her that he stopped hitting me a year ago when Betsy bit the arm he raised to strike me, piercing cloth and skin. I had never seen him afraid before, and now I see it in everything, even his refusal to let me go to Beverley.

Polite society would find him out to be the pretender he is.

I knew I wouldn't send any of it. Because they were my secrets too. I was railing against the night, but it only agitated poor Betsy, who laid her head in my lap, then on my feet, circled around her own tail, and finally settled in a sighing heap. When my hand hurt from writing, I paced the room, telling myself what I ought to have said to him: look at you. You're less than nothing. That's why you hurt everyone else. Because it's the only thing you can do. The only thing you're good at. I looked out the window and saw my tree, its quaking leaves dipped in moonlight. I sat on the floor with Betsy and laid my head on hers, to feel her velvet warmth against my skin.

But I knew I was waiting for him. I was done ignoring my mother's bruises, done covering my ears trying to drown out his nightly pawing, her refusals and pleading, then surrender, followed by grunts and moans, and a bedstead that banged like a hammer against the wall. Even worse, his drunken snoring while Mama whimpered until she finally slept. I didn't know what I would do, but I could stand it no more.

Betsy heard him first. I followed her to the top of the short flight of steps, and waited under the low ceiling, alert to the sound of his shoulder pushing open the front door, the creak of it closing, heavy footfalls. He stumbled, then cursed the furniture. There was something like a song on his breath, but he didn't know the words. I watched his dark figure careen into the wall at the bottom of the stairs.

When he climbed to the top, it took him a moment to realise that I was lying across the threshold of my mother's room, blocking his way.

'Mary? What're you doing? Go to bed, stupid girl.'

48

'Not tonight, Papa.'

'Outta my way.' He nudged my side with his boot. Betsy gave a low growl. 'And tell that feckin' dog to shut up.'

'Not any more nights,' I said.

He teetered on the landing. I thought he might fall backward. Hit his head and die and be gone for ever. And then hated myself for thinking it. Betsy stood close by, ready to defend me.

'I could just walk over you.'

'Then walk over me,' I said. 'But you'll have to do it, Papa. Every night from now on.'

I woke in my bed that morning, with no memory of how I got there. Heard Betsy downstairs, pawing at the door to get out, and was surprised to hear Papa's voice: 'C'mon, girl. Out this way.' As if all was forgotten. Soon little James was crying – I can still hear it now – the clatter in the kitchen, the cook's voice, Everina singing a nursery rhyme. I heard Eliza tell Mama that I was sick and ought to stay in bed, as if they knew what I'd done.

When I got up and dressed, pulling my shawl tight around me, and ventured downstairs, everyone but Mama looked at me. I stood on the threshold.

'Good morning, Mama.'

'Morning, Mary.' Her shoulders sank with shame; I could feel it, but she didn't turn to greet me. 'Too sick to fetch some eggs from the chicken house?'

The cook offered to do it in my stead.

'No. I need the fresh air.' I took the basket from a shelf and left by the front door, stopping to take in the bright morning. I looked around for Betsy, who ought to be waiting for me at the front step. I called her name, then headed down the path, still calling, thinking she would rush from the hedgerow any moment to frolic by my side. Maybe we'd breach the gates of Walkington this fine day.

And then I saw her. Dear Betsy.

Hanging in a noose from my tree.

Mrs B

1st September 1797

As the sun rose in the new September sky, Mrs Blenkinsop lay awake in the adjoining study where Godwin had insisted she rest for the first time in so many hours, or was it days? It all seemed to pour from one vessel and slip through her fingers. The settee was too small for her, but she adjusted, as she had all her life, to whatever circumstances allowed. She'd slept in fits and starts, but with the door cracked open, as agreed, that she could be alert to any stirring in the bedroom. Mr Godwin now took his turn at watch, sitting on a chair pulled up close to his wife's bed, with his 'little bird' tucked into his arms. Mrs B thought she heard him softly humming. It sounded like a hymn, one from childhood, maybe, that he didn't know still lived inside him.

Mrs B rearranged her aching body, put her arms behind her head, and tried to recreate the last day in her mind, something to keep her tethered to the waking world. If the sun was up, so must she have been, as was her daily habit. She could remember Poignand closing Mary's loins with dry cloths, that was yesterday morning, when Mary shut her eyes and slept at last. Then she'd offered him a clean towel, his shirtsleeves rolled to the elbow, to wipe his bloody hands. It was coming back to her now, clear and in the right order. The sight of his wife's blood, mixed with ecstatic relief, had required Mr Godwin to steady himself on the back of a chair.

'You're sure, then?' he asked the doctor.

'She's out of danger,' said Poignand. 'Get some rest, or you're no good to her at all.'

Mr Godwin asked him to inspect the newborn before he left, but assured Mrs B, taking her aside, that it was not a slight, and she took none.

'Do you mean for me to go, sir?' Mrs B whispered.

Mr Godwin rubbed his forehead in that way that was now familiar to her. 'I don't think so. Honestly, I think Mary will want you here when she wakes. Unless of course you're needed elsewhere.'

Mrs B was used to carriages and messages coming and going from the Westminster Lying-In, all the time, but none had come, and she was glad of it. She wanted to be here, only here. Some part of her never wanted to leave, though she didn't know why. She was old enough to stop delivering women altogether. Her husband had wanted her to. She could go home now and rest for good. But even if Mary no longer needed her, the languid infant did.

She laid the babe at the foot of the bed, near her sleeping mother, and loosed her swaddling cloth. There was no visible trauma to the baby, except some bruises not uncommon after a long labour, the swollen eye and lip.

'I've treated the black-and-blue with an ointment of chamomile and hog's grease,' she said, anticipating Poignand's questions.

'Any evidence it swallowed meconium?'

'Not that I could tell. But I'll give her honey and castor oil when she's strong enough.' Mrs B didn't like him calling the infant an 'it.' She was a girl, even if she didn't yet have a name.

'You cleaned out its nose?'

'I did.' Of course she'd done this thing and that thing, and more, as she had for years and years, probably before Poignand was born.

Poignand looked around the room, searching for something else, no doubt, to judge. 'Why is the window open? And no fire lit?'

'Because it's August.'

'It's September, Blenkinsop.'

'The missus likes the open air. She can't breathe.'

'It's not *her* breathing that worries me.'

He pressed his ear to the baby's chest. Mrs B hadn't told the anxious parents that when she was washing their newborn with warm wine, it seemed the child had stopped breathing altogether. She'd scrubbed her little feet with a rough cloth, sprinkled wine in her face, eyes, nostrils, ears, and, feeling her own heart pounding, blown puffs of breath into the baby's mouth and lungs until she let out a squeak and seemed to breathe again on her own.

After assuring Mr Godwin that mother and child would no doubt gain strength with each passing hour, Poignand asked that Mrs B see him to the door. He was all put back together, leather bag under his arm, but something in him seemed unsettled.

'For god's sake, the woman needs some rest. Remove the child to another room, and no visitors at all. She must not be disturbed, except to suckle, only if she insists.'

'She did mention it, sir. No spoons or papboats for the little one. Mary made me promise. Like the laudanum.'

'You call her Mary?'

Mrs B tightened her jaw. 'She told me to.'

'Well, formalities fall away, I suppose. But so do promises, when necessary.' Poignand wiped his sleeve across his forehead and looked up at the ceiling. 'I feel certain I got it all,' he said, as if reassuring himself.

'I'll keep watch, sir.'

'And don't forget yourself, Blenkinsop. They need your strength.'

'I take care of myself, sir, and drink porter like any fishwoman.'

The rest of the day and night swirled in the midwife's head, but she remembered a sort of peace settling on the house while Mary slept. Mr Godwin had showed her his wife's study, a sliver of a room with one tall window, a writing desk, a chair, the settee. A housemaid brought up a blanket. The cradle was moved in. Whenever Mary stirred, Mrs B propped her up with some pillows, gave her something to drink, and laid the baby at her breast, with no success. Even when Mary pleaded with pretty words, the child's cries grew fainter every hour, her little breaths shallower.

When Mr Godwin took his turn to rest, Mrs B gave Mary clean linen pinned lightly around her waist, and then set to work, as quietly as she could, making the chamber sweet and fresh. She opened the door and window, asked that the room be brushed, the carpets cleaned and aired. She'd seen enough births in small houses, crowded hospitals, and jails, where the whole air was foul and unfit for breathing. She'd seen women, new-delivered, covered up close in bed with extra clothes piled on, curtains drawn and pinned together, every crevice stopped up, even the keyhole. She wanted Mary to feel September on her skin, to breathe free and grow strong after her ordeal. It was her child's best hope.

When it was Mrs B's time again to rest, her mind wouldn't stop turning circles. She smelt bread baking, heard little footfalls on the stairs, Fanny crying, begging to see her mother, then laughing outside just minutes later. She could see a slice of Mr Godwin through the crack of the door, clutching his fragile newborn with ink-stained fingers, opening to a page from his journal, it looked like, reading to Mary, soft and low.

"'I am overcome with love . . .'"

Mrs B closed her eyes and let his voice, and the faint morning breeze, wash over her.

"'Never shall I forget in the moments after her birth, the effusion of soul, the kindness which animated us, increased as it was by peril and suffering, the sacred sensation, the way we read in each other's eyes a shared and melting tenderness and inviolable attachment . . .'"

Mrs B could hear his voice catch in his throat, feel a lump in her own. This was why she meant to stay with them. She had delivered, over some forty years, the wives of traders, shopkeepers, innkeepers, sailors, clothworkers, artisans, but never this. Two people who seemed to think and write for a living. Who pressed their foreheads together, who said things, in all her years, she'd never heard anyone say. These married people made her own home seem wanting. Her whole life, wanting.

'"Let other lovers testify with presents and tokens, we record and stamp our attachment in this precious creature – the result of our common affection, the shrine in which our sympathies and our life have poured together, never to be separated."'

'What shall we call her?' Mrs B heard Mary say in a rusted voice. 'Our little bird.'

She crept to the door to see Mary's eyes wide open and shining, gazing on her husband and child. She turned onto her side and reached to feel the tuft of hair peeking out from the blanket wrapped around the newborn still tight in her father's arms. She saw Mr Godwin take her outstretched hand and kiss it.

'We have time and time some more to choose,' he said.

Mrs B had not the heart to tell them she thought the child might not live.

Mary W

Picture me, little bird, near Whitsuntide. A different springtime, full of hope. At a ball, in gleaming new assembly rooms.

Of course, my father hadn't wished me a happy fifteenth; we'd barely spoken for two years. But when he gathered us around to say we were to leave Walkington for Beverley, my young body buzzed with joy. He'd taken a place in Wednesday Market, where the new terraced houses were 'elegant at an easy rent.' I took it that he'd determined being a farmer was beneath him, never mind that the sick sheep and failed crops made it so, and that he'd now be a gentleman, without the farmer part. When he broke out a bottle of gin to toast his new endeavour (speculation of some sort that was sure to make him a fortune), he cursed the uncongenial land, the middlemen, the labourers. Anything but himself. And then celebrated with a shot.

'What about school?' I blurted, my mouth always a furlong ahead of my mind. But I held my breath for the answer.

Mama didn't look at me. She walked to where Ned was

standing and considered a wayward curl on his forehead, gently moving it to one side. 'The grammar school for Ned, of course, for "gentlemen of the best quality."'

'But for us girls?' I shifted my stance. My fear was that we'd be consigned to the charity school, whose students wore white straw bonnets, brown wool frocks, and blue cloth cloaks with orange trim. How dreary they looked, like prune-faced old women.

'The local day school will suit you girls fine.'

I had to quell my excitement. No more sneaking to town to attend John Arden's public lectures, trying to pass myself off as a Beverley girl. Now it would be truly mine: the handsome town with its chipper clatter of hooves on broad, clean streets, neat gardens, the assembly rooms in North Bar Within, rumours of better ones being built at Norwood, a playhouse in Lairgate, even talk of a circulating library! But best of all, I would be at school with Jane.

Eliza, reading my face, squinched her eyes and smiled. Everina clapped silently. Henry, subject to contagion of all kinds, followed suit. Imperial Ned looked to be calculating already the social ladder he would climb. But Mama looked worried when Father mentioned Whitsuntide come next May, not because it was known to be the acme of the social season, but because it revolved around horse racing – my father's preferred occupation above all others. Beverley's racetrack boasted a brand-new grandstand at Hurn, and had added a Gold Cup race, already the talk of the town.

'They have concerts, too, Mama, plays and fine dances every night during racing week. My friend Jane told me so.'

Father downed his second shot and took Mama's waist, twirling her around. 'Fine dances every night, do you hear,

Elizabeth?' He was in a grandiose mood.

Mama pulled away from him and ran a finger along one brow.

'I don't have a proper dress, not that fits me.'

'But there are shops with everything one might wish for. Brocaded silks, ribbons, and hats, corsets, and shoes!' I said.

'I still have my French silk shoes somewhere. I'm sure I have.'

'Imagine, Mama, the finest dress to go with them, made just for you.' Me, always trying to ingratiate myself with her.

'For me too?' asked Eliza.

'Dresses for everyone!' Father toasted with a third shot.

'That will do, then,' Mama said. But I saw her look out the window, out past everything, where her own girlhood must have lived. 'How many years it is since I've been to a ball.'

Mama had become isolated in our small cottage, and while she'd once imagined herself part of polite, cultivated society, it seemed she didn't know her place in it anymore, or what one did, exactly, to belong. I fancied that I could be indispensable to her – show her a Beverley that might bring her out again – and, for a moment, guessed she might even be grateful for it. It would be a coming-out for both of us. But for now I was glad to be the unintentional beneficiary of our father's latest reinvention of himself.

Why shouldn't I feel lightsome?

I had an inner certainty that things would change, my life expand. Even our two-story brick house in Wednesday Market was the opposite of the cottage in every way, with handsome doors, sash windows, and classical mouldings. The ceilings were high, the paint new and bright. Mother allowed that we girls should have two new gowns for school, and Eliza and I, one each for the assembly-room dances.

School at last! Assembly-room dances! I thought Heaven could not be far behind.

When the day came for Ned to move away for school, I was surprised to see that Henry was also to go, standing with his small bag, hair parted in the middle and slicked down with beef suet.

'I don't think he can manage, Mama. Latin? Algebra? Rhetoric?'

'They do some account of animals, I think. He likes animals. And they study the globes, that might be a good thing. They'll look after him, know what to do.'

'It's above Henry. Even *I'm* better prepared than he—'

'*You* would be wise to yammer less and embroider more. Be glad we're sending you to school at all.'

I determined not to let her ruin my high feeling. When we girls left for day school in our new muslin dresses, my eagerness spiked at the sight of Jane Arden presiding over a circle of girls, all chattering at each other, except when Jane spoke, and everyone stopped to listen. I caught her eye and waved. She beckoned me over and introduced me. Imitating her as best I could, I introduced my sisters, who only smiled demurely. The other girls peppered me with questions, but I kept my answers clipped, for now. It seemed they were all bred of Beverley society, knew its customs and requirements, their place in it. Their fathers wouldn't be like mine. There'd be no Walkington in them, no holes in their stockings. It was best to tell them little, and let the mystery of the Wollstonecrafts disguise us. Then I'd win them over one by one.

We were shooed into a room like clucking chickens, and took our desks. I tried to mimic the way the girls gathered their skirts into their seats, hands folded on their laps. Eliza and Everina copied my every move, which was a poor copy already, all three of us pretending not to be the awkward rustics we were. We then had a small lecture 'for the benefit of the new girls' on the merits of needlework – learning precision and patience – and the domestic value of simple addition.

'Which languages will we study?' I asked, causing a rustle among the skirts. I thought I heard one girl gasp. Even Eliza blushed at my brazenness.

'A smattering of French,' said the teacher, 'is all that is required in the sphere of Beverley women.'

Jane caught my eye and shook her head subtly to indicate that the asking of questions was frowned upon. The rest of the day I sat at my desk and fumed. I knew how to read, how to write. I had taught myself addition, taught my sisters, even Henry. There would be no learning in this place to add to my own. Every day, if like this one, would be agony.

'Father lets me come so that I might be in the company of girls,' said Jane, when she took my arm gently after school as we walked. 'But my education happens elsewhere.'

'What sort of education?'

'The world of knowledge according to John Arden, I suppose. Philosophy, history, belles lettres, every sort of science—'

'French?'

'And German he thinks important.'

'The globes?'

'The celestial world entire.'

'Then how can you tolerate this; this nothing of an education at all?'

'For the sake of friendship, Mary. Frankly, the tedium is a

welcome relief. To be the singular focus of my father's intellectual fervour is, at times, exhausting.' She stopped just then and put a firm hand on my forearm. 'Why don't you come one day?' Jane said, more polite command than question. 'Father would welcome a hungry mind.'

I kissed her cheek, impetuous. And so began my education by other means.

The Arden household welcomed me wholeheartedly, down to the servant who greeted me with a brisk *bonjour* and took my coat. The parlour was better than I'd imagined, without affectation, only sincerity and taste: portraits of people who looked worth knowing, or being related to; one above the hearth that I took to be Jane's mother, the same regal neck as her daughter. There were Turkish carpets mellowed by years of afternoon sun; cut blooms of all colours spilled from a cloisonné vase. And the wood-panelled library, where our lessons would be held, sported tiers, like towers of endless books with rich leather spines the colours of autumn, softened by human hands, and smelling, the whole room, of wood smoke. I had a yearning to belong there as I'd never felt for any place, save Nature.

John Arden's tutorials, twice a week after school, were a lesson in everything, but enthusiasm most of all. Jane seemed relieved to share her father's attention, and he seemed glad to have a second pupil. He treated us as he would young men, without limits on what we were capable of understanding. And while Jane was first with answers, eager to be released to her 'social swirl,' I was first with questions. He stacked my arms with books, gave me a swan feather quill, 'for its excellent toughness,' and showed me how to sharpen it myself. He told me to write, write anything, because it was capturing from the ether ideas and thoughts and putting them to paper that willed them into the world. This above all.

I don't know why Father let me go, except that it seemed he wanted the town's acceptance as much as I did. He washed and dressed every day, took his London papers, joined the conversations at coffeehouses, drank at the more respectable inns. A strange peace descended on our house. Father had long ago stopped raising his hand to me, and without Henry to pummel, found Eliza and Everina too docile to bother with. He showed affection, at times, to young James and Charles, was solicitous of our one new housemaid, Lucy, who was a pleasant presence, and even stopped his nightly punishments on Mama. (I believed it was a credit to me: that he knew he would have to step over me to get to her.)

But the lessons became the centrepiece of my life. That, and Jane's friendship. We took walks, arm in arm, on my darling Westwood Common, our lungs breathing the same bracing air. It was hard to keep my shoes and stockings on, but I might lose her if I didn't. I slowed my gait instead, content to share with her my ease among the woods and windmills, the names of trees that tumbled off my tongue: grey alder, beech, wild privet, yew. I pointed out the shapes in clouds, hoping she saw the world as I did.

Jane lifted her skirts and stepped over things I wouldn't consider puddles, wanted to talk about anything aside from the day's lesson, but mostly her circle of friends. I asked about them each: which was the one with the sweet upturned nose? The striped bonnet? That one with hair the colour of pennies? She had command of their details, their fine points and foibles, the sort of man each imagined for her future, as if Jane were a registry of all the young Beverley women who mattered, and all the men who might marry them. She asked in turn about my family, my father and mother. I spun a tale about the silk weavers of Spitalfields, mostly true, how we had come from money, what my father aspired to. I heard myself repeating his lies, amplifying his prospects. I didn't mention Henry. But Jane seemed satisfied to know a girl so different from herself, as if *I* were the exotic creature, and that was enough.

She demanded to know when she could expect us at the assembly rooms, now that it was October and the season was upon us, with a dress ball on Monday nights, a Wednesday concert, a fancy ball on Thursday, and a card assembly on Friday. I hadn't the nerve to tell her she might wait for some time, as neither I nor my sisters knew well enough how to dance, and so made excuses. But she'd abide no excuse when it came to Whitsuntide in spring, because the Norwood Rooms would be done by then, and there was talk of the officers of the East Riding militia planning a dance.

How desperate I was to please Jane, to win her to my cause, which was simply the cause of me. I wrote to her again and again, keeping up the semblance of my pretend gentility. At night I'd labour over my letters to make them seem I hadn't, spewing quotations wherever I could, copying out whole poems or passages, exhausting myself. I begged her pardon for the freedom of my style, such as it was, equal parts mimicry and faux philosophy, weak in grammar and spelling, at which Jane excelled. I felt singularly toward her, and wanted her to feel the same. I knew the other girls talked mostly of hunting husbands; all I wanted to will into the world was a perfect friend.

So, if the East Riding ball was Jane Arden's magnificent

obsession, it would be mine as well. If Eliza and I could get through it, show that we were worth knowing, worth dancing with, worth anything at all – the trajectory of our lives would be for ever altered. At school we had dancing lessons, paired off girl with girl. I managed to be with Jane some of the time, volunteered to play the man, and occasionally held the soft curve of her waist, felt her palm in mine. But she was the best dancer, graceful and sure of herself. Everyone wanted her.

We sisters danced in our room till late at night, practising our steps. Eliza counted down the days in her diary, with a list of dances we must know, and by when. No, I said, we don't have time to learn them all, but must concentrate on one or two, and dance them well enough that people assume we know the rest. Everina was too young to go to the ball, but I let her try on my gown and walk about in my shoes. She read the rule book aloud to us, committed parts of it to memory: 'Young ladies are cautioned not to cluster together . . . No improper company should be permitted . . . Brides and strangers are permitted to call the first country dance of the evening . . . If there are more Ladies than Gentlemen, two ladies may dance,' and so on.

Eliza pressed me at least once a week, 'Please secure a promise from Mama to be our chaperone.'

I was an unlikely emissary to our mother. She missed her darling Ned, often taking to the settee like a scorned lover; if not napping, reading sentimental novels with preposterous plots full of flushed cheeks wet with tears and an excess of exclamation marks. I wanted her to revel, as I did, in our new life, and felt sure, given time, that I could replace Ned in her affections, have some piece of her for myself. The ball might be the very thing to unite us. Our luck turned when spring showed its first tender buds. She had a letter from Ned saying he meant to be home for Whit week, which lifted her spirits considerably.

'Did he write anything of Henry?' I asked.

'Why should you worry about Henry? *I'm* his mother.'

And so I let my younger brother slip from my mind. It seemed enough that dresses had been made and fitted just right. Mama had her one good necklace repaired, let Everina practise curling her hair, even giggled when her old silk shoes, recruited from a trunk, still fit her.

But there was no escaping Whitsuntide and the truth of our life.

Two weeks before, Henry appeared on our doorstep with his sorry bag of clothes and a letter from the schoolmaster explaining that he'd been deemed 'unteachable.' Mama refused to look at him, except to ask after Ned, who'd stopped writing home altogether. I took Henry under my wing, buttered his toast on both sides, the way he liked it, and tried to shield him from Father, who took his ejection from school as an affront to our family's 'good name.' He turned back to hard drinking, a tonic for his own self-loathing, and came home in the wee hours so drunk he couldn't even climb the stairs. During the day he raged at whoever was in his path, Henry most of all.

Often sick to my stomach, I excused myself from John Arden's lectures to rush home and steal Henry away to the haven of my favourite oak on the Common, where we were both soothed by my reading to him, even if he hummed while I did. One day I shut the book hard and glared at him while he let a woolly caterpillar inch toward his wrist. He was trying to feed it a leaf.

'Why aren't you listening, Henry? You never *listen*.'

'*Polygonia c-album*, that's its real name. Just a baby, this one, and he likes the undersides of leaves, but when he grows up, he'll like the top side.'

'How do you know that?' I asked, my irritation waning.

'I learnt it. At school. And their favourite food is hops, but they like stinging nettles too. And some day it will be a butterfly, and fly away.'

Despite my impatience, I was struck by his gentleness, his awe of the natural world.

'I'm sorry, Henry, that Father hurts you.'

'Don't be sorry, Mary. He's just sad. Sad-sad-sad.' He was humming again, even misery a song.

Henry was carted off the next day to the charity school, since neither parent could bear the sight of him. I confess I was relieved. He was out of harm's way for now; maybe he'd learn something, maybe thrive, fly away. The whole household felt the respite from Father's ire. Even Mama turned back toward planning for the ball: what Ned would wear, which sort of carriage would be called to take us, what time, fashionably, to arrive. It seemed a promising moment to share some intimacy to unite us. I found her on her favourite settee, gazing dreamily out the window.

'Would you teach me to dance, Mama?' I saw she gripped a letter in her hand. 'Then I could teach Eliza too.'

'I am hardly the one to teach you girls to dance.'

'But I saw you, with Ned. Showing him. You knew just what to do.'

'You spied on us?'

'No! Not spying,' I said. 'Admiring. How gracefully you

moved.'

'Darling Ned,' she sighed. 'How I miss him.'

'Yet here am *I*, Mama,' I said. 'Asking you to dance.' She spun around. Her eyes, I now saw, were red ringed.

'Your brother's not coming for Whitsuntide.' She tugged on a loose thread where the piping was pulling away from the settee's edge. 'So there will be no ball for the Wollstonecraft women.' She looked right at me. 'Not for me, not for you.'

I sat beside her, gingerly taking her hand. 'I'm sorry for you, Mama, about Ned. But we can still make our own joy from it.' I felt her hand go limp.

'If only I could learn to step and twirl half as well as you,' I said. 'All the girls at school know how—'

'Then let them teach you.' She shook my hand away from hers, as if my touch were a sullying thing. 'Or maybe your friend Jane.'

The way she said it, Jane's name dripping off her tongue in disgust, made my chest cave. She put her fist under her chin and looked outside again.

'Do you know that I met your father at a ball?'

I shook my head and looked into my lap.

'He cut a fine figure once, trim, robust . . . could dance like any fine young gentleman, at least I thought he was. Not what he is now. A drunk and a failure.'

'What about his . . . speculations?'

She let loose an exasperated huff. 'Gambling by another name, is what it is. Wealth without work, that's what your father believes in. And like all his other schemes, doomed from the start.' She looked at me with a flat stare. 'We are always clinging to the edge of ruin, Mary. Surely you feel it.'

I shrugged my shoulders. I'd only wanted to dance with her, just that.

'Does your dear Jane Arden know how wretched and low we truly are?'

I shook my head.

'That you lie across my threshold at night?'

Now I was swallowing tears.

'And when all of Beverley discovers who your family is, do you think you'll be welcome at the assembly-room balls?'

I stood, towering over her, not because I'd grown, but because she had diminished. I wiped my nose with the back of my hand.

'Don't you want me to be better than we are?' I asked. 'To try? For all of us.'

She looked up at me. 'Your father's right about you, Mary. You think you're better than your own family. That you deserve better than what *I've* had.'

'I see your unhappiness! Why should I want that?' The cords in her neck tightened.

'You think you can hide the truth of us, our failures, of you? Hide behind fancy John Arden and his cloying daughter?'

'You don't know her!'

'No, Mary. She doesn't know *you*. But she will, soon enough. Everyone finds us out in the end.'

She stood and swept past me out of the room.

I hadn't the heart to tell Eliza the ball was in jeopardy. I was sure I'd think of something to salvage it, to keep up appearances, and secure for us a place our past couldn't touch. But I lay awake every night with a roiling pit in my stomach, the fear of Father being found out, and the rest of us dragged down with him. I felt a rising panic to belong. The person who could save me was Jane. But the less I felt worthy of her, the more demanding I became.

Like a horse sensing its rider's fear, her friends resolved to form a close knot around her and keep me away. They were cruel to me and my sisters. The one with the sweet upturned nose tied a kite to Eliza's hair, another sent Everina to fetch striped paint and pigeon's milk from a store, where the clerk laughed in her face. Jane asked me to the theatre, but the girl with the penny-coloured hair told me the play would be above my understanding, and I shouldn't bother. Jane didn't seem to be part of it, but she didn't step in to defend me.

'I am singular in my thoughts of love and friendship,' I told her on our last walk together on the Common. 'I must have the first place with you or none.'

'Silly you,' she said, threading her arm through mine. 'You'll meet a man at the Norwood ball, an East Riding man, and then the world will change its colours, and you'll change yours.'

'I don't want to meet a man.'

'I don't believe you,' she said.

'But why don't you trust my colours now? These that I am, without a man?'

She tugged my arm to stop. Her cheeks were hot pink. 'Do you not believe in your future happiness as a wife?'

'Is there no happiness without being a wife?'

'What other life is there?'

'A governess. A schoolteacher.'

'So, living without security of any sort.'

'Living free.'

'Of what?'

'The tyranny of marriage. Of men.'

She laughed in a nervous way. '*My* father, a tyrant?'

'No! Not your father. Who worships your mind, and holds you in the highest regard. Yet you betray him by playing girl games and pretending your own intelligence doesn't exist.'

'Mary, what are you saying?'

'That I don't think this ball should be the apex of our lives, the all and everything, and a single dance the promise of happiness, and the end of this, who we really are, without men. Just us.'

'I am sixteen years old,' she said, enunciating each word, her lips taut. 'This ought to be my coming-out year. And while we don't have the means for a ball in my honour, and I may not have the pomp and circumstance I've dreamed of, I tell you now, Mary, that I intend to pin up my hair, hold my neck long, dance my steps, and hope for a husband.'

She didn't say goodbye, just picked up her skirts and hurried in the direction of home.

'Tell me where I've erred?' I wrote to her that night. 'I hope my owning myself partly at fault, to a girl of your good nature, will cancel the offence. I have a heart that scorns disguise, and a countenance which will not dissemble.'

I couldn't bear to go to school the next day, but decided to deliver the letter myself at our usual lesson time. Their servant led me to the study, where John Arden was bidding goodbye to an older man with small round spectacles and cheeks like wrinkled apples.

'Oh, Miss Wollstonecraft,' he said, surprised to see me. 'I'm afraid our Jane isn't feeling well today. I assumed she'd have written to tell you so. I hope you don't mind.'

'Of course,' I said, embarrassed. I stuttered, he stuttered, both searching for something to say, when the old man offered his white-haired hand to me, to save us both.

'Marmaduke Hewitt, at your service.'

'I do apologise!' said John Arden. 'Miss Wollstonecraft, meet Mr Marmaduke Hewitt.'

'Always a pleasure to meet another fresh-faced friend of Miss Jane's. What a collection she has!'

'Oh no,' said John Arden. 'There are none quite like Miss Wollstonecraft. Just as there are none quite like you, old friend!' He gave Hewitt a warm pat on the back. 'Mr Hewitt is apothecary by trade, but scientist, bird-watcher, bug-collector by nature.'

I managed a small smile. 'I have a brother who knows quite a bit about bugs – anyway, he seems to.'

'My next apprentice!' Hewitt said with a jollity so unmatched to my mood that I was nearly disarmed.

'You see, *I* was his apprentice when I was quite young,' said John Arden. 'He allowed that I might serve him, doing nearly nothing of value, in exchange for hours at liberty with his microscope. We still meet once a week merely to trade observations of the natural world.'

The old man's face brightened, looking at his friend. 'I do think my young apprentice keeps the world alive for me. It was a bargain well worth making.'

He allowed that he must be on his way, shook my hand again, and offered to show himself out. When he was gone, I pulled the letter from my pocket. It was shaking like a dry leaf in my hand. 'If you would . . . give this to Jane for me?'

'Of course.' He took the letter. 'You mustn't over worry. I'm sure it's just the whirling prospect of Whitsuntide. It brings out—'

'The worst in everyone,' I cut in. 'In me, anyway.'

I could tell he didn't know what to say. How could he? Instead, he cleared his throat, picked up a book from his desk, and handed it to me.

'*Essays on Friendship?*' I said.

'I brought it down from the dusty shelves for Jane. But you're a faster reader.'

I knew then that Jane had shared our encounter with him. I held the book to my chest. 'Do you think I've lost her for ever?'

He gazed over the mantel at the portrait of his wife, then looked at me.

'In my experience there are few things in life that are irrevocable. What one feels today, however awful, will not be the same tomorrow, or next week, or next year. Given time, everything changes. Usually for the better.' I nodded.

'I'm sure by the ball next week, all will be forgotten.'

I looked down at my shoes. 'I'm afraid, that is . . . Well, Mama isn't feeling herself just now. We have no chaperone.'

'Oh. I see,' he said. 'Is there anything I might do?'

I couldn't tell him that Mama had retreated to her bed, that my brother Henry was hanging on by a thread. That I was ashamed of my family, my life.

'There'll always be another Whitsuntide,' I said.

To my relief there was no school the week it began, as its various festivities captured Beverley's imagination. No one could sit still, or speak of anything else. I froze when I caught sight of

Jane in the street, surprised that she waved to me and crossed to my side. She even squeezed my hand.

'When Father caught the breeze of your dilemma, well, he seemed most concerned for your circumstance, and I've persuaded him to write a letter to your mother. She should have it this afternoon. You mustn't miss the ball, Mary, not this one. It will change everything, I promise you,' she said, as if all was forgotten between us.

Mama sat up in her bed and seemed oddly flattered by the letter when it arrived. John Arden, in his sincere, gentlemanly way, asked after her health, offered to chaperone me and Eliza, assuring her that he had a keen eye for virtue, and would guard it with his honour. She consented, having lost the will to object to anything at all, but so like her, thrust me a warning: 'I'm only letting you go in hopes you'll find you and your sister a husband.'

It was the best of all worlds. I wouldn't have to fuss about Mama or worry about her, make conversation. I would be with Jane. Now that Whit week was upon us, Father no longer cared what anyone thought. He didn't wash or change clothes, rushing off to the cockfights and horse races, early morning, late night, and drank in between, I supposed, at any inn that would have him. We were free of them both, just as I'd hoped to be, on our own.

Eliza and I, with Everina's keen help, began our dressing at half-three the day of the ball, in order to move about in our gowns and grow easy in our steps. My dress was too big in places, but Eliza pulled it tight and secured it with a few straight pins, making doubly sure they didn't poke me. We curled our hair and put on our gloves. We each had two dances we could be sure of pulling off: a Scottish reel and a minuet which struck terror, I knew, in many hearts, as it was usually the first dance performed by one couple alone, with everyone else looking on. It would show, more than any other, that we were worthy of Beverley society. Mama complained of a headache and retreated to her bed, which allowed us to practise our steps in the parlour, all three of us sisters merry.

But it wasn't to last. A light commotion outside the front door alerted us to Henry sitting on the steps with his bag of clothes at his feet, running dirty fingers through his mop of hair, blubbering.

'Henry! What are you doing here?' I pulled him to standing, a rag doll with a tearstained face. 'What's wrong?'

'The other boys,' Henry said. 'They told me to do it. I'm sorry, Mary. I'm sorry.'

'Do what, Henry? What have you done?' I saw the note pinned to his coat, pulled it off, and read it. The charity school had tossed him out; he was never to return. I felt my shoulders drop, and the letter fall like a weight in my hand.

'You threw a rock? Through a window?'

'The other boys said it was a science experiment.'

'Oh, Henry.' I pulled him toward me and let his forehead fall to my shoulder. 'Why would you listen to stupid boys?'

'They said we'd put it back together, all of us, like a p-p-puzzle. But then they ran away when the glass fell.' He twisted the buttons on his shirt. 'And it was only me left.'

'Never mind, Henry,' I said, stroking his hair. 'Never mind.'

Eliza and Everina stood in the doorway, now understanding Henry's plight, and our own. We traded stricken glances. If Mama found out, or Father, all hell might break loose, and the ball be forbidden, when we were as close as we'd ever been.

'What will we do, Mary?' Eliza asked.

Thinking quickly, I installed Henry in the kitchen with buttered toast and a pile of illustrated books, some paper and pencils to draw with, and made him promise to be quiet. Lucy, who had charge of James and Charles, agreed she would try to keep him occupied until he tired, then put him to bed herself. She would make Mama dinner, and if Everina could take it to her room, perhaps she'd not find out. Not until tomorrow, anyway.

'Can you do that, Everina?' I asked.

Everina shook her head. 'Mama likes me least of all when she's in a mood!'

'It's me she doesn't like.'

'But me next, after you.'

'You could offer to brush her hair,' Eliza said. 'She never refuses that.'

'When *you* offer,' said Everina, biting her nails. 'You're the one who brushes her hair. Not me!' She was crying now, afraid she would fail at her task.

Eliza looked at me, and I knew at once what she was thinking.

'No!' I said.

'I don't want to go, anyway,' said Eliza. 'I just wanted to have a dress, and put it on, and curl my hair, and imagine myself at Norwood, but I'm not ready. I wouldn't know what to say if a man asked me to dance.'

'You'd say yes!'

'No I wouldn't! I'd be too afraid. And then I'd sit the rest of the night pretending to be like the drapery, and hoping that no one talked to me at all.'

'You're going to the ball!'

'You can't make me, Mary. And Everina's right. Mama likes me better. I'm the one who should stay. I'll brush her hair. You go. Be with Jane.'

I looked across their faces: Henry confused, Everina crying, Eliza already pulling her gloves off by each finger, Lucy bouncing Charles on her hip.

'Go for us,' said Everina. 'Remember every detail, so you can tell us later.'

Henry turned to press his face against the window, excited by the sound of horses' hooves. 'There's a carriage. Stopping in front of our house!'

Eliza put my cape around my shoulders, and fastened it at my neck. 'Make some excuse for me. You know the rules. Your minuet is strong. It was always you who should go.' She kissed my cheek. 'You're the brave one, Mary.'

I remember every detail, little bird, as if living it again. Sitting in the carriage, fighting my own well of tears and pretending to smile, my mother's words ringing in my ears: if they found out who you are . . . But as our carriage proceeds, even I begin to believe. John Arden attributes my uncharacteristic silence to butterflies, 'the most natural thing in the world.'

'Never mind butterflies,' said Jane. 'Prepare to be dazzled!'

Dazzled I was, as Norwood came into view, elegant like nothing I'd ever seen: a fine country house, scaled to fit the town in front, but with a parkland at its rear. Its neat red brick, stone pediment and plinths, and torchlight welcomed the throng of people stepping from coaches, landaus, and chaises, including me, in my silk gown and white kid gloves, relieved to leave the truth of my own life behind.

The ballroom itself, with its powder-blue walls, pristine floor, marble mantel, boasted three chandeliers, each with a hundred candles blazing above us like galaxies unto themselves. And how glad I was to find Marmaduke Hewitt the master of ceremonies, with his cheerful red cheeks. He remembered my name – 'How could one forget a Wollstonecraft?' – and declared that he would make it his mission to introduce me to suitable partners, though he apologised that 'We've a surplus of ladies this evening, and a rare lack of men.' Something about a light influenza among the ranks.

Wanting to get my bearings, I stepped to a wall where I watched a sea of pale pink and off-white silks twirl amidst the scarlet wool of the East Riding coats. I recognised a few of the girls from school, poised at the front of the crowd, waiting, nearly desperate, to be chosen by a man – as they were, one by one. I was surprised how much it rankled me. I thought of our headmistress telling us all how we ought to walk, sit, speak, be, if we intended to attract husbands. The rules, all the rules, and Everina repeating them to me late at night, so I didn't forget. After all the anticipation, I now felt the spectacle and falseness of it.

Then I saw Jane, cheeks pink from dancing, standing under a chandelier in her robe à l'anglaise, cream satin brocaded with floral sprays, pleated robings, and striped ribbon rosettes, blooming like a peony in spring. I can see her, even now, turn to walk toward me with her beaming smile. That's when the idea possessed me.

'I would like to call a dance, Mr Hewitt. May I?'

'Of course!'

'A minuet, please.'

'But we've had our minuets. We're on to country dances.'

'I'm begging you.'

Hewitt looked around at the paired couples. 'I have no one free.'

'Jane is free.'

Jane, three steps away, looked at me, stricken. I offered my hand.

'Please, Jane. This is the dance we learnt together. And if there are more ladies than gentlemen—'

'I know the rules, Mary!'

The minuet was struck, the first chords of the violin. The dance floor emptied. Jane glared at me but took my hand. As we moved to the centre, I felt the crowd gape at us, but I didn't care. Step, together. Right, left, right, together. I played the man, but we were mirrors of each other: small, graceful steps in perfect time, the sink, the rise, the giving of our right hands, the giving of our left, never looking down or away, but into the other's eyes as we were taught.

Every fibre of my being stood at attention, our bodies one, our turns perfect circles.

When the last chord sounded, Jane curtsied politely, as all partners must, then picked up her skirts and fled outside. By the time I caught up with her, she was almost to the stream out back. She turned to me in the jewel light, lungs fanning against her bodice, her face on fire.

'How could you humiliate me in front of all the town?!'

I was winded too, and could hardly form words, but still hoped she'd felt what I had, or that I could persuade her of it. 'This ball is beneath you, Jane, beneath all of us. Can't you see it? Pretending to be something we aren't, all in service of securing a husband, enthralled by any scarlet uniform, forget what man inhabits it!'

'I've told you, Mary. There is no other life!'

On a wild impulse I pulled a straight pin from my dress and pushed its needle tip into the pad of my finger, drawing a dot of crimson blood.

'What are you *doing*?'

I turned my head to the clear evening sky and spread my arms wide. 'From this day I declare that I shall never marry, because there is no man on this globe to whom I will bow down and surrender my soul, not *ever*!' I turned my pricked finger to her, and held up the pin in a dare. 'Pledge with me, Jane. Please. Promise that you will never surrender *your* will, your happiness, to any man's.'

She stepped away from me.

'Enough, Mary. This is the end of us.'

'No,' I pleaded. 'You are my heart and soul.'

'You,' she said, 'are nothing to me.'

She gathered her satin and turned to cross the lawn back to the glowing rooms. I thought of running after her, to press my case. But when she was close to the door, a man came lumbering out.

'Miss Wollstonecraft! Come at once!' Marmaduke Hewitt's worried voice poured across the lawn, shattering the twilight. 'It's your father. Demanding to be let in!'

The rest, little bird, spins to nightmare. My father, so drunk he'd fallen into a bush, was slurring and cursing those trying to help him up. He even cursed Henry, saying the most awful things, and then turned his wrath on me. He wanted to fight the gentleman who'd refused to grant him entry, but only managed to punch the air. I don't know what John Arden said to calm him down, nor how he got us into a carriage for the short ride home, refusing my frantic apologies, while a small crowd watched. I mostly remember Jane on the steps of Norwood, distraught but still dignified, and the last thing I saw.

> My dearest Jane,
> I don't know how to ask your forgiveness. Your father gave me a book of essays that pictures the possibility of two people who would be guardian angels to each other and enjoy the benefit of a lifelong attachment that corrects our foibles and errors, refines the pleasures of sense, and improves the mind. You have now seen my 'foibles and errors' in vivid presentation, but I will forever dream of a world away from the degradations of my home, from my own father's violent temper and extravagant turn of mind, which I've been afraid to tell you are the principal cause of my unhappiness, with you my only respite.
> But now I must bid you farewell, without the hoped-for forgiveness and forever friendship I so desire. We are to move to Hoxton within a fortnight, where it is my parents' intention to commit my brother Henry to one of its insane asylums . . .

'I thought I'd have a stroll on the Common,' said John Arden, when I ran into him on my last walk, the day before we left. 'Are you going that way?'

We were soon passing a stand of trees that shimmered in the onset of evening. He seemed as taken by them as was I, though neither of us had said much to that point.

'Jane told me you know a good deal about trees.'

'Did she?' It seemed hopeful that she spoke to him of anything good in me. 'I know some of their names, at least.'

'The thing about a tree that I often marvel at,' he went on, 'is that when it's young, well, it's only natural that its first fragile branches die and fall off, buds don't blossom, but burls seal their wounds like a scar.'

'What wounds?'

'Insects, floods, drought, an axe. Trees suffer more than we know.'

'And survive all that?'

'Yes. But even more cunning, the tree grows up around the dead spots, around its own scars, and makes new branches that are better branches, and nearer to the sun. While the dead places get pressed upon, and grow stronger.'

I linked my hands behind my back and looked at the ground. There was always a sense when he talked about the natural world that he was talking about the inside of us as well, one the echo of the other.

'They're still dead places,' I said.

He stopped and faced me. 'Yet cut open a burl, Miss Wollstonecraft, and instead of straight grain one finds waves and swirls of wood, marbled and feathered, even "eyes" staring back at us. It's the most prized wood, above everything.' He waited for me to meet his gaze. 'Our knots are the strongest part of us. And our burls the place of our greatest beauty, if we but grow up around them, and reach for the sun.'

I willed away tears, grateful for his gentle wisdom. I understood that I was to let Jane go, and grow because of it. I'd decided as much myself. But in that final moment in his presence, I knew that as much as I would suffer giving her up, the absence of John Arden in my life would be by far the greater loss. I might never know such a man again.

'I have no right, no place,' I said, wiping my eyes. 'But may I ask of you one last thing?'

'He's not mad,' I told Marmaduke Hewitt the next day, moving day. 'He's not stupid. He can learn and do things. Maybe in his own way, not the way we would, but in a way that works somehow. And he adores the natural world, the bugs and birds and trees, the way you do.'

I stood in the middle of Hewitt's drawing room, pleading for my brother. We both looked out the window to where Henry was clapping at spits of rain that shone in a narrow glimmer of sun.

'John Arden says I should take you at your word. And your brother looks like a lightsome young man,' said Hewitt.

'He's always in good spirits. Always willing. And I know you to be a good man. Not like—'

He put up his hand to save me. 'I understand,' he said. 'You needn't say it.'

I shook his hand with both of mine, thanking him with tears instead of words.

When I went outside to fetch Henry, I explained the best I could.

'Where are my aggies?' he asked me. 'And my doll?'

'In your bag. I've given it to Mr Hewitt. He'll make sure you have anything you need. Just be helpful in return, that's all. You're going to be an apprentice!'

'But where are you going? I want to go with you, Mary. To Hoxton.'

'No. Hoxton is a terrible place, Henry. Not good enough for you.'

'Please, Mary. I don't care. I want to be with you.'

I couldn't remember when he'd become taller than I was, but I pulled him toward me in a fierce embrace, my chest heaving against his. Sweet Henry patted me on the back.

'Don't cry, sister. Shhh.'

Soon he was whistling a song in my ear.

'Where is he?' Father demanded, when I got in the carriage without my brother in tow.

'Safe,' I said. 'But I'll tell you nothing more. And will never speak another word of Henry. Not to you. Not to anyone.'

Mother sniffled once and leaned her head against the glass. Eliza started to wail, then stifled it with her kerchief. Everina bit her quivering lip. My face was stone as I looked at Father, expecting to see his bulging anger, the way it strained at his collar. But what I felt instead was his weakness. And I saw that what's as pitiable as a man who misuses his power is a man with no power at all.

I knew I had his anger in me, the hurry of my heart, my head sometimes on fire. This, my inescapable lot, my knot, my burl. But I wondered how I might grow around it, what good might I do, what bad *un*do, in myself, in the world? Even without that one perfect friend, or any friend at all, to ease my way.

All I knew in that moment, little bird, was that the buttering of toast is nothing compared to what we would do, what we must do, for those whose scars we share.

My brother would not be the last.

Mrs B

2nd September 1797

How she wished the little girl had a name. Mrs B found Mary next morning sitting up in bed, bright-eyed, with colour in her cheeks, asking for the infant, and for Fanny, wondering whether there might be some food for herself, and couldn't she sit in a chair now; she'd had quite enough of her bed, was eager to receive visitors, and so on. It was as if she'd returned from a long, difficult journey at sea, and had her feet beneath her once more. The midwife felt her pulse, and drew her breasts just enough to tell her milk had come in. Mary wanted to try suckling again right away – to keep trying as long as it took.

Mrs B changed Mary's linen, settled her into a chair, pulled her shawl around her shoulders, and went to gather the little one into her arms. The poor babe was light as a twig in her swaddling cloth. The midwife couldn't help but return to the notion that newborn children were like young trees scarcely raised out of the soil, with nothing but their cries to tell their sufferings. Her pulse was feeble and slow, as if as her mother gained strength, the child's drained away.

Mary coaxed the babe to her nipple. She rubbed the top of her head, stroked her cheek, but still she wouldn't latch. Mrs B worried that she'd soon lose the will to nurse at any breast.

'I could make up a thin gruel boiled in beer with a little honey,' she said. 'I've brought my own pewter bubby pot. Lots of babes have suckled from its nipple.'

'I'm afraid if she did, she wouldn't want mine.' Mary looked up at Mrs B with crinkled eyes. 'My own mother didn't nurse me. She did my oldest brother but thought it too much trouble for the rest of us. I was sent away to a wet nurse my first two years of life. I've no memory of her, and I doubt she has any of me. But I've always thought it's why my mother and I were strangers to each other. I've seen the way a sucking newborn sees herself in her mother's eyes, nourished by a love that can be found nowhere else.' She ran a finger across her daughter's forehead, as if to soothe her scowls and frowns. 'That's why I made you promise, Mrs B. I mean for her to have no nipple but mine.'

Mrs B was used to making promises to women in the throes and never knowing why, but this one, well, she'd seen it herself: breast milk started a child right in the world, helped it along with a robust and healthy constitution, and prevented ailments of all kinds. She'd never considered that love might pass between mother and child through milk, though she'd seen that look between them, lots of times. She felt a sting of regret that she'd never known it herself.

A knock announced shy little Fanny, who, Marguerite explained through the door, missed her mother terribly, and insisted on seeing her with her own eyes, in fact, refused to eat or drink until she did. When Mrs B let them in, Fanny clung tight to Marguerite's skirts, almost frightened of the bundle in her mother's arms.

'Do you want to meet your sister?'

Fanny nodded and tiptoed to her mother, wedging herself lightly between her welcoming knees. Mary pulled the cotton cloth lightly away. The baby's fists were tight up against her furrowed face. Fanny gasped, with both hands to her mouth.

'She's so small, Mama. And quite ugly.'

'She's had a difficult journey.'

'But why is she so wrinkled?'

'It means she's lots of growing left to do.'

'When can I play with her?'

'Soon, Fanny, darling.' She blinked at Mrs B. 'We must have a little patience.'

'I don't know how to think about patience,' said Fanny, with a scrunched-up nose.

Mary swept a lock of hair away from her little girl's face. 'Well, then, think about spiders.'

Across the veil of her own weariness, Mrs B wanted to hear about spiders. She herself never killed one in the house, remembering the nursery rhyme from her own girlhood: 'If you wish to live and thrive, let a spider run alive.' It wasn't superstition so much as a 'do unto others' way of being good to all living things.

Marguerite stepped near to peek at the baby, and without a word between them, Mary placed the bundle gently into her arms. As soon as she saw the little face, Marguerite's eyes glossed with tears. She turned away so Mary wouldn't see.

'Do you remember that we watch spiders sometimes, through my quizzer,' said Mary, pulling Fanny onto her lap. 'How steady and careful they are, silk by silk, one stitch at a time, knitting their home just right?'

'I remember, Mama,' said Fanny, throwing an easy arm around her mother's neck.

'That is a kind of patience. And we must admire it very much.'

Fanny nuzzled her mother's neck, and twisted the indigo fringe of her shawl in her fingers. Mary rested her chin against Fanny's fine hair and breathed her in.

'Does she have a name?' asked Marguerite, fretting over the wee one in her arms.

'Not yet,' said Mary. 'Maybe Mr Godwin and I can discuss it at dinner. Will you tell him I'll be down to join him, as promised, only one day late.'

'Something light, mind you,' said Mrs B. 'A little boiled bread pudding and vegetables, fresh fruit. And could the missus have some dry toast and chamomile for now?'

'I'll see to it,' said Marguerite, walking close to Mrs B.

While Fanny whispered and giggled into her mother's ear, Marguerite leaned into the midwife, carefully passing her the swaddled child.

'Should we pray for her?' she whispered.

'Sooner the better,' Mrs B whispered back.

Marguerite let out a small sad sigh. 'Tell your Mama goodbye until later, Fanny.'

Fanny kissed her mother on the lips, natural as could be, and took to Marguerite's arms. When they'd gone, Mrs B helped Mary change into a clean muslin gown.

'Sweet girl, Marguerite,' she said.

'Oh, even sweeter than Fanny. Worries over every little thing.'

'Not all worries are wrong ones,' said Mrs B, settling Mary back in her chair.

'Let me try again?' said Mary, reaching for her child.

Mrs B settled the babe into her mother's arms, while Mary freed her bosom. The child was still, with so little breath.

'She ought to have a name,' said Mrs B, ginger on the subject. 'You can't call her "little bird" for ever.'

'Why can't I?' Mary said, soft-pressing her lips to the crown of her daughter's head. 'What name could possibly contain her?'

Mrs B couldn't bear to bring up baptism. A baptism at home could mean only one thing. The midwife had seen monsters born of normal people, and normal babies born of monsters, but the desperation of a mother to preserve and nurture whatever issued from her own body she had seen everywhere. If the child was loved before it was born, as this one was, its death was inconceivable. Even when she knew it was no use, Mrs B had done everything to revive expiring life: light tobacco and hold onion juices under a newborn's nose, frictions with hot cloths, rub cold brandy on the chest, and on and on, as parents grew frantic, peered over her shoulder, paced the room, or buried their heads in their hands.

At the sound of Mary's cooing, the little one finally opened her beak, but turned away from her mother's nipple, too weak to search for it. Mary lifted her chin to the midwife, her brandy-coloured eyes deep with tenderness. 'Don't give up on us, Mrs B. One more day.'

The way the light played, Mrs B could see the room reflected in Mary's eyes.

'One more day,' she said, and then under her breath, 'God willing.'

* * *

When Mary took visitors in the parlour that afternoon, the midwife tried to rest on the settee while the child slept in its cradle, but her old legs throbbed and crawled with pins and needles. Her eyes, too, stung with tiredness, but she feared that if she closed them, the child might take a final breath and be gone. Mrs B had faith, but she also had experience. She'd always thought it her duty to preserve the life of mother and child however she could, but she knew that death keeps no calendar. She felt desperate to baptise the little girl, before it was too late. An innocent babe, baptised, could alight straight to Heaven only if she had a name, so that God could hear it. But it wasn't her place to do it.

As a way to pass the time, she tried to remember the why of names, the honouring, the order. The first son should be named for the father's father, second for the mother's, third for the father himself, fourth for the oldest uncle, and so on; for daughters, first for the mother's mother. Is that who Fanny'd been named for? Second daughter, the father's mother? But Mr Godwin, not a believer, might choose never to baptise the child, and wouldn't be bound by custom or rules, she thought. And the way her mind was all mixed up and weary, she couldn't be sure she had them straight in any case.

How many hundreds, maybe thousands of namings had she witnessed in her time? Some with great forethought, some under duress, some that'd come from dreams, a handful by whim alone. Mrs B had seen babies named for kings, the Henrys and Georges, and names that would change four times in a night, even before she'd left her post. She'd seen husbands and wives argue, especially over first and second children, who would carry forward whatever legacy they believed theirs was.

Wives, weak in body but strong in cause, often won the day. She could always tell a man who doted on his wife by the deference he gave her in naming the child. It still surprised her that parents thought nothing of replacing one dead child with another, but took it to be a sort of honouring in itself, a way to remember: Johns and Janes, till one survived to give the name full life. But it was the naming of dead children, and the near dead who needed a name to be baptised, that moved her most.

Mrs B took the child into her fleshy arms. She carried her to the freshly filled water basin in the far corner of the room, and held the baby on the length of her forearm, the small head fitting like an apple in the palm of her hand. She pulled off the cap and cradled the little head over the basin, cupped her other hand into the water, then held it over the baby's forehead.

'Who are you?' she whispered to the child. 'What legacy is yours?' She knew no names of relatives; it didn't matter. The child's eyes opened wide.

'Mary,' she said, dripping the water onto the baby's forehead, slow and careful, 'I baptise thee in the name of the Father, the Son, and the Holy Spirit.'

Mary W

Hoxton meant to end me. No more of John Arden's lectures, no school, no walks on Westwood Common. Living in a village of lunatics. At least I had saved my brother, but I had no way to save myself. My gloom was excessive, and grew worse by the day. My head ached all the time, I had unexplained fevers, bit my nails to the quick. I barely ate, or washed my hair. For what? I thought. Why bother? Even the young men of the Hoxton Academy, in their drab frock coats, buffeted me when I took my turn around the square each afternoon. They were thick with ideas and each other, and couldn't see me. I didn't blame them; I envied them. I had wanted to be in the world, as they were, but the world shut its door in my face.

Then, one afternoon, our neighbour invited me for tea. I knew little of Mrs Clare except rumours that her husband had worn the same pair of shoes for twenty years, and didn't go outside. Having never set eyes on him myself, I assumed he was one of those lunatics better kept at home. But their parlour was surprisingly cheery, with its woodland chorus wallpaper and rose-coloured sofa, same colour as Mrs Clare's cheeks. She was easy to talk to and asked good questions that brought me out. When the Reverend Clare walked in, by contrast, he looked severe in his minister's clothing and wig, a dried-out reed of a man who hadn't seen the sun in far too long. She must have seen my eyes go wide and fly to the shoes on his feet.

'It's fourteen years, Miss Wollstonecraft, not twenty. And he's really quite proud of it, aren't you, dear?'

The reverend snorted an answer and sat down with his nose in a book. Nervous, I made a solicitous comment about the weather.

'Weather comes and goes,' he said, waving my words away. 'I do not care for it. But if you want to tell me where you stand on John Locke, that's another thing.'

'Now, Reverend,' said Mrs Clare. 'Leave the poor girl alone.'

He took off his glasses and studied my face, my hair tied back simply, no curls, my plain dress.

'I do not know John Locke,' I confessed. 'I'm afraid my education has been somewhat suspended.'

'Suspended how?'

'I went to school in Beverley, where we learnt frivolous things—'

'What frivolous things?'

'Well, I can manage a minuet, and ask for tea in French. Little else. I don't go to school here. I'm not learning anything at all.' I looked down at his shoes again. 'It's left a sort of gaping hole.'

'Ah,' he said, 'an *horror vacui!*'

I looked up to see his eyes flicker to life, an instantaneous glee.

'Yes, exactly!' I said. 'Nature abhors a vacuum!' (Thank you, John Arden.)

'Because the denser surrounding material would immediately

fill the rarity of an incipient void.'

'I believe it would,' I said.

'And if a void is by definition nothing, nothing cannot rightly be said to exist.'

I could feel myself come alive. Losing John Arden had created a hole in me, with nothing in Hoxton to fill it. I was the void, the gap, a hollow container. I felt I was nothing, and if nothing cannot exist, *I* no longer existed. Until that moment when Reverend Clare saw my nothingness as something worth filling.

'No learning, you say? For a mind like yours?'

'No sir.'

'Well, we ought to fix that, don't you think, Mrs Clare?' Mrs Clare smiled into her cup of tea.

Little bird, my life began anew. But of all the gifts the Clares gave me, none was greater than introducing me to the woman I have loved more than all creatures on this earth, save your sister and you. She was two years older than I – eighteen – when we met. I remember just staring at her, in her family's modest cottage in Newington Butts south of the Thames, where the Clares had brought me. While they visited with her mother in their narrow parlour, I sat in a corner of the kitchen and watched how she moved seamlessly from one task to another, giving her siblings food, cutting it into pieces where need be, kneeling down to meet their gaze when they spoke, and really listening, subtle corrections to their grammar, mimicking their facial expressions, and ending with a nod and a loving kiss on the tops of their heads. I felt I was looking at another self, a better self, a gentler soul, more complete. I cared for my siblings too, but frenetically so, sometimes sharp and impatient, sometimes resentful and then guilty for it. Fanny Blood moved in her world like a minuet.

'May I get you something, Miss Wollstonecraft?'

She woke me from my reverie. 'No, no. You've worked enough. You needn't attend to me.'

She took off her apron. 'This isn't work, but a prelude.'

'A prelude?'

She took me by the hand (oh, the warmth of her touch, I feel it still!) and led me to a small room with windows on two sides and light crisscrossing everywhere. On a table, neatly laid out, were specimens of flowers, many I knew the names of, others I didn't. And on the wall behind, a gallery of drawings pinned to the wall, each a flower in exact detail, its intricate parts punctuated with washes of paint, some in colours I'd never seen, not even in Nature.

'A flower sometimes looks small and simple at first, but then you look closely, and see a world unto itself.'

'These are beautiful,' I said, looking across them.

'I love the idea that one with only male or female parts is an "imperfect" flower, but one with both, that can reproduce on its own, has achieved the status of a "perfect" flower.'

She was standing beside me with her hands on her hips, surveying her own drawings. She blew away a lock of hair that had fallen across her forehead, and pointed to the topmost part at the centre of one of her flowers.

'They call this female part the "stigma." It's where bees and insects drop the pollen in. But why a "stigma," I often wonder? I think of a stigma as a stain or scar.'

'A blot, a disgrace,' I said.

She looked at me. 'A taint, a mark, a blame.'

'Yes,' I said, turning back to the drawing. 'Females take so much blame, don't they, for everything, and deserve almost none of it.'

'I think I would call it the "vessel" instead.'

'The blessed vessel.'

'The blessed vessel,' she repeated. 'Yes.'

And like that, somehow, I knew that Fanny Blood would be the truest friend of my life.

She had better handwriting than I, better writing altogether, was calmer, neater, more precise in her thoughts and words, more disciplined and demanding in her thinking. Yet she possessed a sense of wonder; she laughed easily, at even the silliest things, and was capable of whimsy. Like me, she had a father who drank and gambled, but she didn't resent him, and had found, through her drawings, a way to support herself and her family. She loved Nature as much as I did, taught me the names of more flowers than I knew – the perfect and imperfect alike. In public we observed a personal reserve, but in private we were better than sisters, brushing each other's hair, talking through the night, arguing over petty nothings, just for the fun of it. Every step I took toward her was rewarded with a step closer to me.

We soon began dreaming aloud of a life together. We would read and study without interruption. She would teach me the German and Latin she knew, and we would teach ourselves French, some days converse in French alone. We would take turns making meals, or stand side by side and cook them together; we'd share books, clothes (our simple taste); she might teach me to draw, I might teach her to dance, and if we could only afford one bed, we would share that too. We would make, the two of us, a perfect household, where we would be the male and female parts together, whole unto ourselves, without a man.

Reverend Clare had imbued me thoroughly with a reverence for the ideas of John Locke, and Fanny was my ardent pupil. I read to her while she drew, and we talked of it, even on the pillow. Creatures of the same species, we agreed, had a natural equality, and no husband should have more power over his wife's life than she had over his. I told her of my pledge never to marry, but now, all my resentment about my father's cruelty, the favouring of Ned, had a basis in thought. It was unjust. It was my right, my human right, to shape my own future, just as it was for her and everyone else. It was an obligation to overthrow tyranny wherever it was found. That was our pledge to each other. Together Fanny and I would be free from the despotism of men, whether at home or in the world.

There was only one man who stood between us. His name was Hugh Skeys. He was portly and self-satisfied, and had courted her patiently for a year, though she was lukewarm at best. On the eve of his departure to Lisbon, where he would solidify his business, he handed her his own portrait, with a vague promise to return in one year to marry her once he'd secured his financial future.

'It's a terrible likeness of him,' I said. 'And what sort of man has his own portrait painted who does not love himself mightily?' Fanny only laughed at me.

'Clearly he's left because he doesn't love you,' I said. 'Not like I love you.'

'You do not like Hugh Skeys, that's fine. But my feelings for him have no bearing on mine for you.'

'I think him beneath you.'

'I think him the only way my family will survive, Mary. It falls to me. I cannot keep them on what pittance I make from my drawings. Love does not enter into it. And I may come to care for him.'

'Love cannot be forced.'

'But it may be earned.'

'And haven't we, you and I, earned it of each other?'

'Yes, my darling Mary. But love won't feed us, or our families.' She pulled my hand to her lips and kissed my knuckles. The translucent slice of carnelian on Fanny's ring – her singular ornament – burned fiery orange, as if from within. She often threatened to give it to me, as the ancient Egyptians believed it cured bad tempers, hatred, jealousy, and anger, all of which I felt in that moment.

To prove to Fanny that we didn't need Hugh Skeys, didn't need marriage at all, I took a job as a companion to a widow in Bath, who was old and wealthy, ill-tempered and arrogant. By then I was nineteen years old and keen to earn my own way, if not enough to support our future life together. I knew Fanny would have done the same but for her weak constitution, the responsibilities of running the Blood household, caring for her mother and siblings. The money she earned from her drawings had to suffice until Skeys returned to take her hand. Mama took my leaving for Bath personally, furious that I would abandon *our* household, which she relied on me to manage. Father had all but disappeared, dropping by to pay the occasional bill and visit his drunken threats on us all, which it fell to me to fend off. Eliza and Everina, too, felt abandoned by me. I realised they were resentful of my freedom and ill-equipped to take on my duties. I should have taught them, but I hadn't. I couldn't stomach preparing them for wifely duties when I wanted them to know about the workings of gravity and the birth of human rights. They called me selfish for going away, and perhaps I was.

One year; that's how long I had to persuade Fanny against marriage.

Bath was my first introduction to high society, but I soon realised my widow and her friends, even the young women of the town, were everything I rejected. They were frivolous and frenetic, wore striped taffeta, tight corsets, and on their hips stiff panniers too wide for most doorways. A curtsy was almost enough to tip one of them over. Their faces were coated in white powder, with rounds of rouge on their cheeks, their frizzed hair built up in steep towers finished with feathers and ribbons, stuffed birds, and fruit. All their world felt false to me, the opposite of my life with Fanny. Out of contempt, and on principle, I made myself a monk among them, dining on grapes and bread crusts while they stuffed their mouths with pastries and succulent roasts. I wore a few simple dresses in rotation, and no make-up at all, my loops of reddish-gold hair unpowdered. I read epic poems, took long walks, finding solace in the variegated light and shade, the gorgeous palette the sun's rays gave to the hills around town. I could almost hear my dear Fanny gently lecturing me on the relative merits of ochre and umber.

One year turned to two. Hugh Skeys made more vague promises but had not returned to claim Fanny for a bride. I cut short my sojourn in Bath when Mama's health declined and she demanded that I return home to nurse her, echoed by my helpless sisters. I was not surprised to find them chafing at the cruel smallness of their lives, and their dim prospects for finding husbands, with no dowry of any kind.

Hope stirred when Ned, now apprenticed to a firm in London, reached the age of majority and announced he would marry. Father had long ago squandered his part of grandfather's estate, but now Ned would have his, a remarkable five thousand pounds. I hated the injustice of the eldest son receiving everything, but it was customary that on marrying, a brother might offer his sisters a dowry to increase their marriage prospects. It would have changed everything for Eliza and Everina, and for me, even a small nest egg would have made my life with Fanny possible. But Ned gave us nothing, not a guinea among us.

Right before Mama slipped into a coma, I sat at her bedside, desperate for some simple gesture of feeling. I had wiped her drool, held her bedpan, brushed her hair, but all she had to say to me was this: 'A little patience and all will be over.'

And then it was.

Grief mixed with bitterness is a powder keg. I travelled to London alone to find my brother, and when I appeared on his doorstep to demand he take our sisters in, Ned was so taken aback that he agreed.

'Not for ever,' he said. 'A few months at most. Then you're to come back for them.'

I wanted to spit in his face. 'I don't wish upon them a life with a man who's never cared for anyone but himself. But it's not them I pity.'

I was relieved when Eliza married soon after, and left for Bermondsey. Meredith Bishop was a suitable match, a respected bachelor, a shipwright – a path to security. Eliza flung herself into his arms, and he caught her, quite willingly. I still believed that marriage was a prison for a woman, and yet I knew it might also be her only means of escape. She'd grown into a vivacious, handsome young woman, who believed in marriage to excess, and begged me not to object. How could I blame her?

Father married the latest housekeeper, and retired to Wales. Some part of me was thankful to be rid of him, though he never missed the chance to ask me for money. Charles, now ten, went to stay with them. Everina was with Ned, still writing me desperate letters begging me to retrieve her. James, not yet fourteen, had gone to sea.

At Fanny's insistence, I moved in with her family in Walham Green, a pleasant place near Putney Bridge. The Bloods were warm and easy with one another, and with me. Fanny's mother was 'our mother,' a modest, gentle woman who must have seen the wounds my own mother had inflicted on me, and healed some of them with simple kindness. When she and Fanny opened a small needlework shop, I helped where I could. I didn't mind the punishing hours, the strain on the eyes sewing intricate stitches by candlelight. It was a way to piece together a life, scrap by scrap, stitch by stitch. I wanted to spend my life with them. This was poverty, yes, but there was bliss in it.

Fanny improved me in all ways: the quality of my writing, my thinking, my feeling, perception, manners, even my sense of humour. She taught me what it is to love, and be loved. Out of necessity we did share a bed, but it was as we'd always imagined, and even things we hadn't. We lay awake nights, recounting the high and low points of our day, making fun where we could, whispering our worries. In winter we piled on the bedclothes and made our own warmth under the covers. In summer we lay atop them in our light linen sleeping gowns, tracing the outlines of our bodies, touching each other fondly, naming our flower parts: pistil, stamen, sepal, petal, leaf.

She dared me to be happy, without caveats, to claim it out loud.

Not happiness in retrospect, she said, that was too easy. We must know it here and now. I promised her I'd try.

And then one day my dear Fanny coughed blood.

Her health was stable, her case mostly mild for now, but Fanny had bouts that frightened us all. They seemed worse when she had a letter from Skeys, anchored in Lisbon, putting her off yet again. He asked after the fluctuations in her lungs, as if a bellwether of his intentions. She'd come to feel disappointed by his hesitation, his courtship more off than on, and however relieved I was by it, I knew that her heart's longings must also be mine.

Marriage had not been kind to Eliza, who wrote me a month after the wedding to say the honeymoon rapture was over. I took it as more proof of my position, but to Eliza I suggested patience and forbearance. She'd wanted money and status, and got it the only way she knew how. She had sealed her own fate. It was hers to bear.

In August she gave birth to a daughter, Elizabeth Mary Frances Bishop, a nod to our mother, Fanny, and me. The birth had been hard, but what followed was worse. Eliza, it seemed, had fallen into a melancholia that erupted into fits of frenzy. Bishop, at his wit's end, begged me come nurse my sister back to health, her right mind. What I found when I arrived shocked me. My sister seemed to be wasting away, never dressing for the day, not washing without help, rarely sleeping, never settling, sometimes waking with a scream. She spoke what can only be described as gibberish. Her eyes were vacant; she didn't see the world quite right, or look anyone in the eye, except her little babe, Bess, whom she clutched to her breast like a doll.

I knew that women sometimes lost their senses after lying-in, but usually recovered with time. I thought Eliza just needed rest and relief. I held her in my arms, rocked her like a child. I washed and dressed her, took her for a drive in a coach. Sent the baby across the river to Everina, with instructions to send Bess home before dark, when Eliza would panic, going room to room if she couldn't find her. The ravings seemed to lessen, but in their place was a wandering mind with disjointed ideas, like strange dreams in another language.

Bishop paced in front of me, out of her earshot, asking what happened to his wife, where did his Eliza go, how could this happen?

'A little patience,' I said, 'is required of us all.'

'But it's as if her madness moves about, with no discernible pattern, and certainly no improvement. I cannot continue to live this way.'

'We must think of Eliza—'

'We must commit her, Mary.'

'No!' I stood abruptly, a book falling in a thud from my lap. 'You must believe in her.'

'Do you believe in her?' he asked me.

I felt sorry for him, I did. He seemed sincere in his concern, grieving the loss of the wife he knew, unsure if she'd ever return, and if not, what would his life be then?

'Please,' I said. 'We must give her more time.'

I had saved Henry from the asylums in Hoxton. I didn't know whether I could save Eliza. I couldn't leave her alone, except at night when Bishop took her to bed. I was glad for the respite, but alone in my own room, felt her madness creeping into me.

Then one day, when I was drying her after a bath, she grabbed her breasts and squeezed them hard in her fists, grimacing. 'This-this-this,' she repeated.

'Stop, Eliza.' I reached my hands for hers, but she took my wrist like a vice, pulled me close to her face, and looked at me, lucid.

'It hurts, Mary, hurts.' She pulled a handful of her own hair as hard as she could, beat her fist on her pubic bone, thrust her hips back and forth, making noises like an animal in heat.

I stroked her wet hair. 'What hurts, Eliza? Tell me what hurts.'

'He makes me. On my knees, on the rug. I have burns.' She rubbed her red knees with her knuckles. 'Pulls his pants down. Pound-pound-pound. It hurts, Mary, it hurts.'

'Meredith?'

'Pulls my hair, pound-pound-pound. Every night. Till I'm dead.'

'You're not dead, Eliza. You're alive. You're here with me.'

'Not safe, Mary. Not here.'

How reluctantly I walked her to her room that night. I put the babe to her breast to suckle, which was the only thing that seemed to calm her. She twirled a ribbon on the little one's cap, and whispered, over and over, 'Sweet girl, sweet girl.' Until Bishop came to join her. He stood beside her in the chair, stroked her hair, but it seemed like petting a cat. She closed her eyes and let her head fall back, but I couldn't tell, was it relief, or surrender?

I retreated to my room and wrote Everina to say I couldn't

help pitying Bishop, but his misery was a small portion of our sister's. I wrote to Fanny that Eliza seemed to think she was maltreated by him, but couldn't bear to say the rest. What she was describing, whether true or false, was the same fornication my father had visited upon my mother for most of my remembered life. I had never seen it, but I'd heard it, lying on their threshold, imagining the worst things Eliza was now giving voice to. And while I thought my brothers and sisters didn't know – that I was shielding them from it – they *must* have known, all the children, the walls, the windows, the doors. The whole house had borne witness. Was it possible that Eliza, in her madness, was conflating her married life with theirs?

When each day continued like that, whether I was dressing her or sitting just holding her hand, she'd begin again, describing awful scenes, some words I'd never heard, some I wish I hadn't. These were things Eliza could never have seen with our parents, and could not have made up. Despite her agitation, the nail-biting, the nonsense talk, I began to believe her.

'Why would you suggest such a thing?' Bishop asked when I tried to broach the subject as delicately as I could.

'I only wonder if perhaps there's a . . . roughness in your relations that makes her feel ill-used.'

'What would you know about the sharing of a marriage bed? You're a twenty-four-year-old spinster, Mary.'

'Quite by choice, I assure you.'

But Bishop was right, and maybe right to be offended. I know now what a chilly prude I was then, believing that carnal appetites, whether women's or men's, were deplorable inside marriage and out. And once children arrived, I was sure, the only passion between husband and wife should be whatever reproduction required. Indulging sensual gusts, I thought, was incompatible with the duties of parenthood.

Bishop moved close enough that I could see the sweat on his upper lip, and something between hurt and cruelty in his eyes. 'Your sister is mad. And the sooner we come to terms with it, the better we'll all be. The child most of all.'

I doubted him, my sister, myself. I knew that because of my father I assumed all men to be despots until they proved otherwise. I saw no change in Bishop, no willingness to bend to her plight, to feel compassion for his wife. But was I being unfair?

I missed Fanny desperately, wrote to her every day, about the vicissitudes of Eliza's madness, the precipice of my own. We were only in Bermondsey, but it felt a world away, and leaving Eliza, even for an afternoon, seemed dangerous. What she might do to herself, what Bishop might do to her.

One night I woke from a troubled sleep, twisted in my bedclothes. My nightmare compelled me to throw the covers off, put a robe on, tiptoe down the hallway and around the corner toward their room, without even a candle to light my way. When the floor creaked under my bare feet, I froze, until it felt safe to creep some more. When I neared their door, I heard it, what I'd heard so many nights of my youth. Him, grunting, groaning, clipped commands telling her what to do, how to lie. Her muffled shrieks, moans, sobs.

This, if not the first cause of my sister's madness, was the fuel to its consuming fire.

'Eliza,' I said the next morning, sitting her down and kneeling at her feet. 'I need you to listen, Eliza.' I took her face in my hands. 'I believe you. Everything you told me.'

She put her hands over my hands, and leaned closer, sheer

terror in her eyes. 'I will die if you leave me here. I'm begging you, Mary.'

I tried to talk to Bishop, to suggest that he try gentleness with her, or put his own gratification to the side, at least until she regained herself.

'Of course you take her side. She's your sister.'

'She's a woman in pain, of course I feel for her. Why can't you?'

'I house her, feed her, clothe her. Those are my husbandly duties! And what are hers to me?'

'She doesn't feel safe here.' I knew, from my own father, the look of a man on the verge of hitting me. I saw it in his face but didn't cower, didn't move.

'I own her. Our house. Our things. Our life. Our daughter. All are my property. Never, for one minute, forget that.'

When he stormed out of the room, my mind was made up.

I concocted a plan for our escape. Eliza had no right to divorce, no right to any shared property, or to custody of her child, who was five months by now, and had worked her way into my heart as well. Bess cooed and smiled, nestled contentedly in our arms. I had to believe we could come back for her. I knew that at first Bishop would be furious, but I hoped he would soften with time and return the little girl to her mother's bosom. I told Eliza just that. 'Thank you, Mary, thank you,' she said, weeping into my shoulder.

'We who would save her must act and not talk,' I wrote to Everina, imploring her not to share our plan with Ned. I scraped together what little money I could, with Fanny's help, and rented rooms in a modest lodging in Hackney as 'the Miss Johnsons.' Everina took supplies there, a change of linens, a few morsels to eat. We waited for Bishop to leave the house, and when he finally did after lunch one day, I quickly packed a change of clothes for each of us, and bade Eliza say goodbye quickly to her daughter, then hailed a coach outside. I waited by its open door, holding my breath as each second ticked by. When she finally appeared, Eliza froze in the threshold.

'I can't leave my baby. I can't do it, Mary.'

But it was now or never. Bishop might be back any moment. Not knowing what else to do, I grabbed her arm and nearly lifted her into the carriage, she weighed hardly a feather by then, and implored the driver to go as fast as he could. He couldn't help that a snarl of other coaches kept stopping us at first, but each time I looked back expecting to see Bishop hot behind us. For caution's sake we changed coaches twice to throw him off our trail. Sensing my agitation, Eliza rocked back and forth, gnawing at her thin wedding band until she nearly chewed straight through it, but with each mile closer to Hackney, a sort of calm came over my sister as I hadn't seen in so long.

'Ah, the Miss Johnsons! We've been expecting you,' said the housemistress when we arrived, bedraggled but whole. She led us to our room, two small beds, simple curtains on the windows. I pulled them closed at once.

'Don't like the light, that it?'

'No, it's just – it's been a long journey. I thought we might have a rest.'

'Where've you come from, then?'

I hated her questions. But our lives, our futures, whatever they were to be, needed this refuge now. I named a place, as far from Bermondsey as I could think of.

'Mmm,' she said, looking Eliza up and down. 'Well, your

poor sister looks like she could use a bit more than a rest. Is she all right?'

I feigned a relaxed smile. 'She'll be right as a line, you'll see.'

The woman hesitated. 'Well, never mind, then. There'll be a nice tea waiting for you when you wake up. Just come down to the parlour when you're ready.'

'Oh, no!' I blurted. 'It's just – my sister, she's rather shy. I wonder if we might take tea in our room.'

She screwed up her mouth. 'Suit yourself,' she said, then turned to go.

'Is there a lock on the door?' I had to know.

She jiggled the old knob, a half-broken latch. 'Not sure what it can hold back, but it's worth a try. Anyway, you're safe here. Haven't had any trouble at all for going on twenty years.'

When she'd gone I leaned a chair up against the knob, took off Eliza's cape, and mine. We fell onto our beds with our clothes on and slept like bears in winter.

Bang, bang, bang on the door. I woke with a start, trying to get my bearings. Where were we? What time was it, what day? We were in Hackney. In the lodgings. But had Bishop found us out? I peeked out the window to see that it was late morning by the looks of it, which meant we'd slept nearly fourteen hours. Another bang on the door. I crept to it in my bare feet, trying not to make noise, and leaned my ear against it.

'Mary, it's me,' the voice said in a whisper. I opened the latch, the door, and nearly fell into Fanny's arms.

'Thank God you've come,' I said, and swept her into the room.

'Have you heard from Bishop?' Eliza was still fast asleep.

'No. But I've had a letter from Ned, just this morning. He being Bishop's willing emissary.'

'Do you think they had you followed?'

'I made sure I was not. But Bishop is serious, Mary. He will find a way to destroy you.'

'Destroy *me?*'

'He blames you. And Ned says the Wollstonecraft name is forever sullied, says you've ruined Everina's chances of ever finding a suitor.'

I sat on the edge of the bed, sagging. 'I suppose I give him that.'

Fanny sat beside me. I felt the warmth of her hip resting against mine.

'What have I done?' I asked her.

'Saved your sister, that's what you've done.'

'I tried, for so long, to save my mother. I live with the weight of that. How could I leave Eliza to suffer the same fate?'

'You didn't, Mary. You did save her. You have rewritten the fate of your family.'

'But what fate have we to write now? What can I will into the world with no money at all? And Eliza's sweet, innocent babe. How could I have left her behind?'

'Because your sister begged you to save her life, and you had to choose. For the time being.'

I took her hands in mine and faced her. 'How I've missed you, Fan. I do not want to, cannot, simply refuse to live without you. Ever again.'

'I refuse the same,' she said, touching my hair, my face, as if to make sure I was real. 'What can be done? Because whatever it is, we must do it as one, and quickly.'

'Never be weak,' I said. 'Never submit. Never cower. Not let small difficulties intimidate us. Struggle to the death with any obstacles rather than fall into a state of dependence.'

'Yes. But what will we *do*?'

Fanny was paler than usual, and thinner than I'd last seen her, but her eyes were vibrant and steady.

This is the next knot in the tree that is me, little bird – when I wipe my eyes and find in my sight a narrow gap between the curtains where a small slice of daylight shines in.

'Start a school,' I say, with a clear-eyed confidence I still remember. 'That's what we'll do.'

Mrs B

3rd September 1797

The midwife woke with a start in the morning to find the child gone from her cradle. She hurried to lace her corset with clumsy fingers and fiddled to right her hair, remembering the whispers she'd heard yesterday that they were to build a coffin for the poor little dear. But as she reached for her spectacles, she heard Mary's voice waft in through a crack in the open door. Mrs B peered into the bedchamber, where the outline of the missus came clear. She was settled in the chair by the window, smiling and cooing to the baby latched onto her breast, who sucked as if she'd discovered the fount of all life, that miniature fist unfurled, pink fingers holding to her mother's roundness as if she might never let go. The curtain at their back lifted and fell on the morning breeze, breathing for the whole house. The thinking part of Mrs B thanked merciful God that her prayers, or someone's, had been answered. But there was another nagging swell of tears behind her eyes, for soon it would be time to go.

Mrs B didn't know herself this morning. She was always quick to pack up after a birth, as soon as any danger passed and things were set to rights, eager to put the kettle on at her own house, simple as it was, take off her shoes and rub her tired feet, then begin a soup for her husband, a rough bread. She liked the feel of dough through her fingers, the push and pull of the knead, the shaping of the loaf. Her husband always kept the embers live in the great ash bed of the kitchen hearth, providing ready light for a candle, a quick boil of water, and warmth most of all, for her creaky bones. She relied on him for it.

Not wanting to disturb the serenity of mother and child, Mrs B felt her skirts for the diary tucked in a pocket. She hadn't managed to write in it for two days, and that part of her itched to record the time spent. She sat quietly at Mary's writing desk, fashioned from walnut, the midwife knew (her husband was a cabinetmaker), with one simple drawer, nothing showy about it; a plain top, no leather, no marquetry, no veneer – but French, she judged by the fancy turn of the legs. A botanical drawing in a simple gold frame hung right above it, love-in-idleness, and a pinchbeck quizzing glass, cracked in two places, hung on a faded velvet ribbon over the frame's edge. Mrs B pushed a pile of loose letters toward the porcelain inkstand, and opened her little diary. She always started one fresh at the New Year, keeping records of births, deaths, remittances, expenses such that she might add them up at the end of each month to have an accounting of the year, and then ten years, and now forty, come and gone. She tried to say something of each birth to remember it by: the weather, inside or out, the health of the mother, the child, which tinctures and remedies were useful, what difficulties arose, which had been overcome, and which had done the overcoming. But what was it all for?

'Cloudy and cool. The missus is comfortable. Little Mary is cleverly, and, no doubt, as fine a babe as I've ever seen.' She hesitated. 'I am not so well as I could wish,' she wrote, and then scribbled it out. Mrs B set her pencil down and rubbed her face. When she took her hands away, her eyes darted to the pages she'd pushed away, stacked willy-nilly, the deep black ink of the letters peeking out, written not in one hand, but two. Where her own writing was small and considerate of space, not calling attention in any way, these words wanted reading. She always prided herself on keeping the privacy of her patients, not listening to gossips, or at least not spreading their spew. But this had a pull of a different sort.

'I have felt considerable anxiety about you these past days . . .'

Mr Godwin's hand was neat, even, and tight, with a few good round curls here and there, but always the same letters in the same way. His lines sat close together, and out near the margins, but you could feel the weight of his hand.

'We love as it were to multiply our consciousness even at the hazard of opening new avenues for pain and misery to attack us . . .'

Mrs B picked up a second letter, a third that stuck to it.

'I must tell you that I love you better than I supposed I did, when I promised to love you for ever – and I will add what will gratify your benevolence, if not your heart, that on the whole I may be termed happy.'

Mary's hand was taller and thinner than his, with jagged loops, slanted and in a hurry. But there was air between the words and lines, and clear space around them.

'How much tenderness for you may escape in a voluptuous sigh. . .

'A pleasurable movement to the sensations that have been clustering around my heart . . .

'It is not rapture – it is sublime tranquillity I have felt in your arms – hush!'

Mrs B remembered, as a girl who read better than her peers, that she once happened on a conduct book that advised any woman, if she loved a man, never to reveal the full extent of that love, even if she were to marry him, which would show preference enough. A good man, the book told her, would ask for no stronger proof, and a young Blenkinsop had taken it to heart. No other possibility had ever occurred to her.

She picked another letter from the pile. It fluttered in her hand.

'These confessions should only be uttered – you know where, when the curtains are up – and all the world shut out. You are a tender, affectionate creature, and I feel it thrilling through my frame giving, and promising pleasure – Ah me!'

Mrs B felt her heart thump behind her bosom. This was not who she was, nor how her life had been. When she was a new-married woman, unable to produce a child of her own, she'd determined to wake each day with a short prayer and to count three blessings, then go along her business, whatever it was. She ended each day the same, on her knees, worshipping Him, whom she relied on to make sense of whatever suffering she didn't know how to hold. She gave succour where she could, and counted that she saw far more good births than bad. Happiness, love, desire – these were never hers, or hers to judge. And yet, here they were, flooding her with feeling.

'Yes, I guess you must go,' said Mary, when Mrs B appeared with her satchel at the ready, her cape fastened at her neck, rubicund cheeks, like she'd sat too close to a fire. 'There's someone who needs you more than we do, I'm sure. You must go to them, and do what you've done for us.'

'I've done nothing but let Nature—'

'I know what you've done, Mrs B. I've seen it.' Mary was sitting on the edge of her bed, radiant. The baby was laid on a pillow, mewing and stretching her limbs, already filling out her own outline, cheeks right and full. 'I am sad to see you go. But I suppose your leaving is a good sign, a return to life, new life, where I will do almost everything for myself and my little bird.'

Mary looked down at her newborn, who seemed to look back, enthralled by her mother's face.

'I don't think we'll need that coffin after all, Mrs B.'

'I should think not,' she said. 'Why, you might even give her a name.'

'A name,' Mary said.

Mrs B wanted to confess about the baptism. It would sit hard on her conscience if she didn't. But she wasn't sure how to say it, and what offense it might give. She didn't want anything wrong between them for the leaving.

'I hope you don't mind, but I've called her "Mary," to myself, of course. You'll call her whatever you like, but I did wish her most fiercely to have a name.'

Mary looked at her little girl, and drew the shape of her face with the light touch of a finger. 'Is that who you are, little bird?' Then she turned to the midwife with a quizzing look. 'Have you children, Mrs B?'

'Wasn't blessed, I'm afraid.'

'I'm sorry.'

'Wasn't God's plan for me. He gave me a calling to get others

116

into the world.'

'But married?'

Mrs B shifted her satchel and looked Mary straight in the eye. 'Forty years.'

'Forty years! That's nearly as old as I am.'

'Feels like the blink of an eye, just now.'

'Yes, well, I know not all years can be happy ones, but I hope you've had your share.'

'Passing years,' she said, and then hesitated, wanting to speak something for him, now that he was gone. 'A good man.'

'I've a good man too.'

'Yes. He is.'

'I once believed that happiness was not to be mine,' said Mary. 'And that everything denied to me, that I denied myself, would be rewarded in the next life.' She looked back at her new baby. 'But here I am, Mrs Blenkinsop, twice-blessed, and happily married. In this very life.'

She stood from the bed and took Mrs B's free hand in both of hers. 'Would you do me the kindest favour, and drop a note to Mr Godwin? He has writing rooms twenty doors down. He'll get you a carriage from there. Unless you're dead on your feet.'

Mrs B knew the surge of energy in certain women who'd just given birth, as if they'd climbed to the peak of a mountain, and, surprised by their own strength, were eager to go again. Confinement for women like that was foolish. On this she and Mary agreed.

'A walk would do me good,' said Mrs B.

Mary scooped up the child and walked into the study, put her gently down in the cradle, and sat at her writing desk. Mrs B followed her to the threshold. She had tried to right the stack of letters as she'd found them.

'Hope I've left things in good order.'

Mary surveyed her desktop. 'Never mind, Mrs B,' she said, taking out a clean sheet. 'I've been rereading our letters to each other, Godwin and I. It is, in a way, an epistolary history of our struggle.'

Mrs B didn't know what to say in return. This place, and these people, showed no signs of struggle, not a one that Mrs B could name.

'I don't remember, in all our years,' Mrs B said, 'ever quarrelling, not really.'

'I don't know if I mean quarrelling,' said Mary. She looked at the midwife thoughtfully. 'I have spent my whole life fighting for all women to be equal to all men. But I've found that for one woman to be equal to one man, and for him to be equal to her, that is another thing. At least for us.'

Mrs B had a fleeting thought that she ought to have struggled more in her own marriage, though for what she didn't know. Never mind. It was too late now.

'Do you know the strangest thing, Mrs B? Mr Godwin and I recently discovered that we were in Hoxton at the same time, years ago. I was sixteen, dreadfully unhappy. He was a student at the academy, only a half a mile away.' She gazed out the window.

'To think that our shoulders might have brushed in the street.'

'I s'pose the good Lord didn't think it your time to meet.'

Mary laughed, and began to write her note. 'Well, when "the good Lord" ordained that we should, Mr Godwin detested me, and I him,' she said. 'He thought me domineering and difficult. I found *him* full of his own ideas and fixed in his ways.

But time softened our harder edges, and when we met again, we found each other changed. We still agreed, wholeheartedly, that marriage is a disaster for men and women both.' She turned her gaze to her little girl. 'But when the creature announced itself, it was I who insisted. Having suffered one child out of wedlock, I was not eager to do it again.'

'People can be awfully cruel.'

'And yet the cruellest experience didn't eradicate my own foolish tendency to cherish, even expect, romantic tenderness, above all else.'

'Well, then,' said Mrs B, 'I'm glad you and Mr Godwin found each other when you did, and a way to end your struggle.' Mrs B couldn't think what else to say, unaccustomed as she was to this sort of talk.

Mary signed and folded the note, no seal at all, stood, and handed it to Mrs B. 'Oh no,' she said with twinkling eyes. 'Our struggle has only just begun.'

'Seventeen Evesham Buildings.' Mrs B gripped the letter in her hand, finding it hard to take her leave. 'I'll see he gets it.'

Mary W

There were mostly two opinions on the future of our school: one, that it had none, and two, that it would fail before we opened our doors. True, we didn't have any doors, not even a town that we knew would welcome our venture. But we had a sense of urgency, Fanny and I, and the vigour of our beliefs. It would be our mission to teach girls to cultivate their minds and bodies so they could become independent, thereby helping to create a world in which wives could defend themselves against the tyranny of husbands, or if they didn't wish to marry, live their lives on their own terms. Eliza missed her child terribly, but began slowly to recover her mental and physical strength. She would join the effort. Everina too. But our zeal was not enough. We needed money, backers, a building, and I had no idea how to get them. I had three guineas in my pocket and no experience at all.

The thoughtful Clares, when they got wind of my plan, offered to introduce me to Hannah Burgh, the wealthy widow of a Reverend James Burgh, himself a prolific writer and schoolmaster on Newington Green. Until his death some years before, Burgh had advocated for free speech, universal suffrage, and educational reform, all things that gave me hope. There was little I could glean about his widow in advance, except that her current mission in life, according to Reverend Clare, which she believed had been bestowed on her by God, was to educate young women to be good Christians and useful citizens. Reverend Clare loaned me a copy of her dead husband's treatise, *Thoughts on Education*, but I was alarmed to find in its pages everything I was against. To his thinking, radical reform extended only as far as the world of boys, for whom he believed education should block any tenderness as a form of weakness. A girl, according to Reverend Burgh, should know only enough arithmetic to do household accounts, and whatever geography would allow her to converse with her husband and his friends. She was to ask questions more than answer them, being incapable of novel thought.

I prepared for the worst.

When a servant ushered me into the rather grim parlour with its heavy curtains, Mrs Burgh was already parked in what looked like an uncomfortable chair, in what looked like an uncomfortable dress, widow wear, though her husband had been dead nearly ten years. She had hooded eyes that were hard to read, and greeted me without a smile. After a few pleasantries, which weren't pleasant at all, tea was brought in. She wasted no time in beginning to quiz me, as she poured steaming hot tea into plain porcelain cups. I could see she had a slight tremor.

'Tell me something of your qualifications,' the widow said, taking a bold sip from her own cup that I was sure burned her lips.

I had no qualifications, of course, and paused to concoct an answer that was at least somewhat true.

'French?' she interjected.

'Not to speak of.'

'Fancy needlework?'

'No.'

'What about skills in music and drawing?'

Here was my chance. 'As for my part, no, but I've a friend, a colleague, Miss Blood, who makes her living in botanical drawings, and I must say, she is first-rate.'

'That's fine, but I'm asking about *you*, Miss Wollstonecraft. What do you bring to an endeavour of such scope?'

I picked up my teacup, trying to still my hand. 'I suppose I bring my own thoughts on education. The education of daughters, that is.'

'Ah, then you've read my husband's book?'

'I have. Twice.'

'As have a parade of potential headmistresses who have sat just where you are sitting now,' she said. 'But let us take *your* measure, shall we?'

I took my own sip of burning tea, trying to think of something safe to say. 'I believe young girls ought to live more meaningful, more virtuous lives.'

'I quite agree,' she said. 'But what is meaning? What, virtue?'

'I would have them cultivate their minds . . . and their bodies,' I said.

'Their bodies?' said the widow, blowing into the black ruffled neck that came all the way to her triple chin. 'Do you mean dance steps?'

I set down my cup. 'I mean running, Mrs Burgh. Jumping.

Climbing trees. Feeling the grass between their naked toes.'

'Naked toes?'

'For how can one know the natural world, or one's place in it, one's true self, without seeing it from on high *and* up close?'

The windows rattled just then. I glanced outside at the gust and whoosh in the treetops.

'Does the wind frighten you, Miss Wollstonecraft?'

When I turned back, she looked dismayed. 'No. I draw strength from it.'

'I can see that you are fine-tuned,' she said. 'And, I suppose, a devotee of the current "culture of sensibility." It is the fashion.'

'It is not fashion with me, Mrs Burgh, but nature.'

'A Rousseau follower, then? My husband abhorred Rousseau.'

'With me it's not all nature, but it comes close. I am fine-tuned, but only as it exhilarates my sense and exalts my sensibility. I don't want girls to be artificial beings, the sum of custom and manners, without reason or feeling, when they ought to have both. If only I could give them the education I wish I'd had—'

'Go on,' she said, her spine stiffer.

'You see, in my relatively brief experience of a girl's education, I found not much to recommend the tinkling on a harpsichord, spouting a few well-placed words of French, and parading around in unnatural protuberances, hoops and corsets and such, that have no relation whatsoever to the shape of the female body.' Widow Burgh furrowed her brow, but I moved closer to the edge of the settee. 'I believe young women have minds that are the equal of any man, yet they're taught to develop the merest aspect that would attract a husband, and nothing more, lest they scare said husband away.'

'Are you against marriage, then?' she cut in.

'For myself, yes.' I sat up straighter. 'I should like to see marriage not the only hope of securing a woman's future, but a choice she might make if she could find the right partner, though I doubt he exists, and lead a more meaningful life than being just a wife. Meaning being itself a virtue.'

'Say more,' she commanded, 'about how one teaches that.'

'The child's mind must be left to itself. I might nurture it, that's all. Feed their bodies with nourishing, healthy food, allow them the freedom to explore. Teach them to think for themselves, not memorise what other people say they ought to. Quite frankly, I'm sick of hearing about the sublimity of Milton, the elegance and harmony of Pope, the original, untaught genius of Shakespeare.'

'You don't think Shakespeare a genius?'

I leaned toward her. 'I do, of course. But they must find their own genius. Not read from primers but compose their own stories, in their own words, for there's nothing as true as the genuine emotions of the heart, before they've learnt *not* to feel them, *not* to think their own thoughts – I want them to follow the path of their own minds, even if it leads them off the beaten track. To make their own way.'

The widow drained her cup, revealing nothing. But I was unbridled and couldn't stop.

'Integrity, creativity, self-discipline. If they could learn to value their own minds, not the minds of others, of men, they might refuse trivialities in favour of depth, and true human purpose, a new society, made by them, reflected *in* them. That, I believe, is the highest virtue.'

The widow poured a long, thin trail of tea into her cup,

and then mine until it nearly overflowed, her tremor more pronounced. 'And you believe my husband would approve?'

Here it was, the question I dreaded most. I cleared my throat.

'No, Mrs Burgh. I feel sure he would most decidedly *dis*approve.'

Widow Burgh inclined toward the back of her chair. She studied her tea while I waited, terrified. Finally she clapped her eyes on me. They were clear as a bell, and blue. 'Then we quite agree,' she said.

'That he would disapprove?'

'Quite,' she said, setting her cup onto its saucer with a punctuating clink. 'But Reverend Burgh is dead, and has been for some years. And I am the one with the money now, Miss Wollstonecraft. And have been waiting for you for a very long time.'

My lungs expanded, as if taking my first breath in a new world, little bird.

'And I've been waiting for you, Mrs Burgh. For even longer.'

We quickly came to agreement on the particulars. The widow found us an enormous empty house in her own village, Newington Green, north of London, and a handful of families who would send their daughters, ages seven to sixteen, including two families who would board them, which would pay for our extra expenses. I prepared to leave London, taking Eliza and Everina with me, sure that Fanny was set to join us. I could see in her face that she wanted to, desperately so, but her lungs had taken a turn for the worse over the winter, the tuberculosis lodging inside her.

'I don't know what I'll do here without you, Mary. You are the weft and warp of my life.'

'And you mine,' I said, brushing a stray lock from her face. 'You'll join us when you feel stronger, promise me you will.' I pressed my forehead to hers.

'I promise. When I'm stronger.'

When we sisters arrived at Newington Green, we found a second paradise, after Beverley. It had the feel of a rural hamlet, but with handsome Georgian houses lining the old Roman road, circling a shady green with steepled churches and pretty gardens. Our house was cavernous, without a stick of furniture. That first day we skittered up and down the stairs, let our laughter bounce against the walls. Fanny had taught us her favourite Scotch song, 'There's Nae Luck about the House,' and we sang it, full lungs, at least four times, like an incantation to bring her there. I had enough money from Mrs Burgh to buy furniture, desks, books, hire a cook and two maids, and begin to prepare for our first girls (and even a couple of boys). I was twenty-five years old, living, for the first time, a life of my own choosing, my own direction, my dreams.

By the end of summer Fanny felt some surge of strength and joined us. She would help teach where she could, especially botany and drawing. Mrs Burgh approved of her almost to senselessness. They talked like young girls; Fanny was disarming in that way. She could make an old widowed woman, almost without realising, confess that hers had been an affectionless marriage, her husband believing that 'supporting the species' was the sole aim of marital relations, which should be curtailed otherwise. She told Fanny that she'd been beautiful once, many men had thought so, her dance card was the first to fill, but that Reverend Burgh thought beauty 'a mass of flesh, blood, humours, and filth covered over with skin.'

'How awful,' Fanny said. 'For you.'

We were walking on the Green, but they thought I was farther behind them and couldn't hear.

'Yes, well, I suppose I hoped his passion would overcome his prejudice. But he believed that to admire me was to deny that possibility. He called his thoughts "filthy," and believed it his prime duty to eradicate them. And so eradicate them he did.'

'Without supporting the species?'

'I'm afraid, yes,' she said, making clear that it was a sadness to her. 'And so I must do so much more to advance the cause now.'

'Well, you've picked a good one to advance it. Mary does whatever she sets her mind to.'

Mrs Burgh took her arm. 'I think of her, more than anyone, as a kind of daughter.'

'What kind?' Fanny asked.

'The very best,' said the widow, patting her arm. 'Like me. But without the giving in.'

I had to stop on a bench to gather myself. What I would have given for my own mother to see me that way. My world felt complete.

She took me to church with her one Sunday, a Unitarian church 'full of Dissenters,' and led me straight to the front pew. I had set foot in many churches, felt the exaltation of high ceilings, but this was new to me. Dr Richard Price was short, thin, and dour looking, with thick eyebrows angled like arrows, a stiff black coat, and full-bottomed white wig. I half expected a speech on damnation, hellfire, and brimstone, but when he opened his mouth, his voice was so soft and quiet, I had to lean forward to hear him. To my surprise, he spoke affectingly of individual conscience and reason, the habit of attention, patience of thought, the sagacity of mind that protects us against error. America had just secured a victory over us, and he pointed to it as progress. Freedom from tyranny; this was his subject!

The widow made a point of introducing us after the sermon, and I was gratified he knew who I was.

'Mrs Burgh has spoken to me of your originality, and a passion for reform, that's what she said, which naturally endears you to me. We need someone to school our future torchbearers. We won't be around for ever, you know.'

I hadn't thought of it as a torch to be carried, but over the weeks, through his sermons, our deepening conversations, I came to understand where we two saw the world the same. For Dr Price, as for me, education was the path to a more perfect future. The great American experiment was his ideal, the best example we had of the potential of an enlightened citizenry who might govern themselves. And if it failed, he said, what a tragedy that would be for humankind.

He knew Benjamin Franklin, the Adamses, both man and wife, Thomas Jefferson, Thomas Paine. I asked him everything about all of them, each conversation they'd had, every letter written. But we had Locke in common, who had given me a new vocabulary to express what had always been my intuitive sense of injustice, my rage. Even before I'd read Locke, I'd felt the feelings, which had given me the strength to fight for myself and others, to challenge my father, save my brother, my sister, start a school. It was personal for me, and the stakes high – our very lives and futures – but Dr Price gave me a politics that made it whole. My own life was the life of the world; my own struggle, the struggle of all people simply to be free.

Fanny, who took her Sundays to rest, rarely came with me, but she would insist that I sit on the edge of her bed and recite his sermons, our conversations, word for word.

'Your eyes shine when you speak of it. I do believe you're happy, Mary.'

'Oh, that cannot possibly be,' I said with a wry smile.

'Why shouldn't it be? You ought to have every expectation of happiness.'

'I wasn't born like you, Fanny. Or had it drummed out of me. Happiness was not my family's creed.'

'Well, that's over now. You have your school.'

'We have *our* school.'

I smiled and lay on the bed beside her. Without a word, she put her arm out to let me rest my head in the nook of her shoulder.

'You see?' she said. 'This, here. This is our creed.'

Eliza and Everina didn't share our enthusiasm for any of it. They hated the long days and hard work of teaching and keeping up the school. Eliza regained her senses over time, seemed more like herself, if a fragile version, but she pined for her little girl. We took turns writing letters to Bishop, imploring him to let her see Bess, if not surrender custody altogether. He never wrote back, but word came to us, through Ned, that he would never forget what Eliza had done to him, never forgive her. The daughter was in the care of wet nurses and maids, which was hardly reassuring.

As her daughter's first birthday neared, in August, Eliza became more agitated, more desperate. She couldn't focus, often didn't finish her sentences, would walk to the window to watch any mother and small child in the street, following their every move.

One day I took delivery of a letter from Ned. In a final act of cruelty, Bishop could not even bring himself to deliver the news that little Bess had caught a fever and died. There were no details, not how long she'd suffered, whose arms she died in, if she'd called for her mother. Knew that her mother loved her.

Eliza lay down on her bed and clutched a pillow to her chest. She stayed there for three days, wouldn't eat, slept in fits. And then one morning she appeared at the breakfast table in a crisp dress, hair swept neatly back. She expressed no regret for her decision, but her eyes told me that she knew she had sacrificed her child to win her freedom.

Her stoicism didn't last. Everina was struggling with her responsibilities, and the two found common cause in their resistance to me.

'We must all live up to *your* standards, Mary. What is just in that?' Everina asked me.

'I seem to be the only one *with* standards. If you have something to contribute, Everina, by all means.'

'You've always had to have it your way, all our lives.'

'Don't be ridiculous.'

'Because of you, and the scandal with Eliza, I will never find a husband.'

'Go then.'

'You know I have nowhere to go. I serve *your* will, *your* wishes. We all do. We must grind away to remake the world in your image. Not God's, not our own, but yours!'

'I thought we were one on this, all of us.'

'Why must we all remake the world, Mary? What if I just want to live in it as it is?'

'I thought I was making a life for us, a life of independence—'

'Yes, we can be free so long as we are subservient to *you*. Even Fanny.'

'What about Fanny? She is here of her own will, we all are.'

'She is devoted to you beyond all reason.'

'We are the ruling passion of each other's hearts and

minds, no less.'

'And where does that leave us, your sisters? You treat us like children.'

'You behave like children! You want me to take care of you, while you do as little as possible on your own behalf, much less anyone else's.'

'You go off to your lectures and discussion groups, your precious Dr Price.'

'You want no part of that world. You've told me so yourself.'

'But did you know that Fanny stays behind to smooth our ruffled feathers? *She* is the sister we wish you were, Mary. And you seem not to see it at all. Not even to see *her*.'

'I see Fanny above all.'

'Then why haven't you seen that she's getting worse? Her coughing fits, her weakness? She cannot bear this damp, chilly England. It's killing her. And yet you would work her to the bone. While she is the one keeping peace in this house. Behind your back.'

'Fanny is her own master.'

'Is she? Then ask her about Hugh Skeys.'

'You've had a letter from him, and didn't tell me?'

It was her Sunday rest, of a sort. Fanny sat on top of the covers, propped against a pillow, shawl around her shoulders and thick wool socks on her feet. A piece of vellum on a makeshift easel rested against her bent knees; cloudy water and brushes in jars populated her bedside table, with pens and India ink, her paints, and a single flower, her subject. She still used her botanical drawings to earn money for her mother and siblings. This was her one day to do it.

Fanny's ink-stained fingers slipped Skeys's letter from under her pillow. 'Two months ago.'

I sat on the edge of the bed with an offering of tea. She took it, set it on the table, along with the letter, but kept her eyes steady on her drawing.

'Words are not Hugh Skeys's friend. Honestly, a cow could have written it better.'

I knew this was her way of dismissing the subject, so I kicked off my slippers, spun around, and sat on the bed beside her.

'Looks like a common pansy,' I said, studying the fine ink drawing she was just starting to fill in with touches of purple, both subtle and bold.

'Love-in-idleness is the name I prefer, but lady-in-waiting, kiss-her-in-the-buttery, heartsease, if you must. Though there's nothing common about the pansy.' Fanny commanded a room when she talked about her plants. 'Even Shakespeare exploited its magical power to alter the course of true love.'

'What a terrible affliction,' I said.

'But it's also its own cure, strangely enough. And my favourite of all the flowers.'

I leaned my head on her bony shoulder. 'I like it for you. It's who you are. Delicacy, with power. But magic most of all.'

She sighed lightly. 'Wouldn't it be wonderful to be one's own cure?'

I thought she meant her illness, but we rarely spoke of it. She hated to.

'I think we're so often the cause of our own suffering,' she said. 'The things we let wound us, the indecencies that offend our beings, the injustices.'

'But those things are real, and outside of us.'

'I know. But what if our real power, the one we're born with, which we rarely assume, lies in altering our sensibility to the things that aggrieve us?' She tucked her paintbrush behind her ear. 'Imagine,' she said, 'if we could heal ourselves.'

I knew she was talking about me. She had none of my animus, even if she marvelled at it sometimes. Fanny accepted things I never could. She believed we could be content with the gifts we are given.

'What flower would you think for me?' I asked her.

She turned her head to study me, then leaned over and dug from a pile of discarded drawings on the floor. She handed one to me.

'The nigella?'

'Devil-in-the-bush, ragged lady, love-in-a-mist if you prefer. Can thrive in the most neglected patches of land.'

'Its leaves look like spiky thorns. Its petals have claws!'

'So do you, Mary. But in fact they're soft and delicate. And though they favour a brilliant purple, they can be every variety of white and pink, lavender and blue. Like your many moods.'

I studied the flower, trying to see myself in it as she did. Our silences were snug and easy. We had no need to fill the empty space with unnecessary words. But Skeys's letter still hung in the air between us.

'He says he's ready for marriage,' she said at last. 'That his business in Lisbon is secure enough to support a family. To support me.'

'Why didn't you tell me?'

'I feel humiliated by him. All these years, waiting, hoping. And then losing hope. And how many years has it been since I've set eyes on the man? I don't even remember what he looks like. Probably old and fat by now.'

We laughed, but Fanny dissolved into a coughing fit. Her shawl fell away. There was blood on her kerchief. I'd pretended that Fanny was invincible, now that we had the life together we'd dreamed of, that she would naturally gain strength and health from it. I pulled her shawl back over her shoulder, waiting for her lungs to settle.

'And I would hardly call it an inspired proposal.' She reached for my hand, braided her fingers with mine. 'But more than that, I don't think I can leave you, Mary.'

I looked down at her hand, skin so thin it seemed barely to cover her bird bones underneath. I spun the silver band of her carnelian ring around easily with my thumb, and remembered her telling me that the Egyptians thought the stone protected the dead in the journey to the afterlife. I felt my stomach tighten, and wanted to cry.

'We have no choice, Fanny,' I said. 'You must write to him, and accept.'

She retrieved the paintbrush from behind her ear.

'Portugal. A world away from you. I can no longer imagine what it could possibly hold for me.'

'Hugh Skeys,' I said. 'Remember, you told me you might come to love him?'

'I don't remember, Mary. I hardly remember the why of anything, but certainly not the why of Portugal.'

'Health,' I said. 'Life.'

She squeezed her kerchief in her palm. It was always tucked into her sleeve, at the ready. Coughing was her constant companion, and messy.

'What is my life without you? Without my family, who need me?'

'I'll look after them,' I said. 'I give you my solemn word. But you're of no use to any of us if you continue this way.'

'You mean dead. Just say it.'

'You need dry air, hot breezes, sunlight.'

'It was you who tried to persuade me against it! Against Hugh Skeys altogether.'

I was aware we'd changed places, each adopting the other's view. But that's how it had become between us. Merging easily one into the other, a united soul, if sometimes a divided heart. I didn't want to lose her, but the choice was stark: accept Skeys's proposal and sail for Portugal to be married, and recover her health, or refuse him, stay in London, and die.

For me the answer was simple. I would rather lose her to marriage than to death.

Mrs B

4ᵗʰ September 1797

A loud bang on the door, like a thunderclap. Mrs B heaved
herself from the sink of her own feather mattress, between a
groan and a sigh, strung a shawl across her shoulders, reached
blindly for her spectacles, and pushed them onto her face. It
was still dark in the house; the fire in the hearth had expired,
but she had a sense of dim first light when she opened the door
to a driver in livery, who wasted no time.

'Blenkinsop, yup?'

She pulled her shawl closer and peered over his shoulder at
the waiting carriage.

'You're to come at once,' he said. 'Get your things.'

'Come where? The Lying-In? Who sent you?'

'The Godwin house. Been a terrible turn in the patient.'

'The child?'

'Don't think so. He said, "Tell her it's the missus," for he
knew you'd come at once.'

Mrs B heard a great sucking in of breath, and realised it was she who'd gasped. It was the same sound that'd startled her a fortnight ago, when she woke in her feather bed to find her husband cold beside her.

She dressed, squeezed her swollen feet into her brogans, and replenished her bag as quickly as she could. How could it be? she kept muttering to herself. She'd left Mary standing and smiling on the very threshold where they'd met, radiating good health. She'd dressed simply for an expected round of visitors, read a book to her sweet Fanny, planned a dinner menu, and nursed her new girl for the third time since they'd risen. Mrs B would not have left had there been any doubt, reluctant as she was to go.

On the galloping ride to the Godwin house, in the back of the carriage, Mrs B felt the rattling deep in her bones. She'd arrived to her cottage the previous evening, wet and toilworn, to a thin layer of dust on the sills, stone floor like a mausoleum, crisp browned wildflowers in a small pewter jug. Exhaustion did odd things to the mind, she knew, but she felt herself standing in a strange house, or she the stranger. She relived those first minutes as if dreaming them, an uncanny awareness of her every movement, doing each thing again: set down her bag, lower the hood of her cape, wipe her fogged spectacles on her skirt. How she reached for the old elm tinderbox, lifted its lid, strangely soothed to find it intact and still neatly divided, steel and flint in the one part, tinder and damper in the other. Instead of charred rags her husband collected dried moss, leaves, and fungus, anything from 'God's great floor,' he'd say, 'to bring a bit of Heaven inside.' She let the hook-shaped fire steel hang over her fingers, marvelling at how it conformed to the human hand, and in the other, held the sharp-edged piece of chalcedony her husband had chosen just for this. With a few quick strikes on the steel, she coaxed a spark, caught it on a piece of dried moss, then a splint of wood, blowing on it to help the spark become a flame, then flame to candle, candle to hearth.

She had avoided going home as long as she could, said yes to all the births since he'd passed, slept at the Lying-In and then the Godwin house. What a blessing that this new deadness inside her had been kept at bay by life there.

'Please God,' she whispered, alone in the dark cab. 'Watch over her.'

Which is when Dr Poignand skirted across her memory, and his unclean hands in Mary's womb.

Marguerite greeted the midwife at the door, her young face pinched with worry. Mrs B stepped inside and looked up to the ceiling. She could feel it even there, the convulsing house, and heard the iron bedstead strike the wall. There was no mistaking a racking fever.

'Poignand is seeing her now. And there's a Dr Fordyce as well.'

'Fordyce?'

'I don't know. Seems to be a friend. But Mr Godwin said you should go straight up.'

Mrs B climbed the stairs, already short of breath, a hand on the wall to brace her way.

Godwin, pale as fright, opened the bedchamber door, holding the mewling baby to his chest. 'Thank God,' he said.

Poignand was at Mary's bedside, trying to feel her pulse,

while her whole body shivered and shook.

'Please make it stop, Mrs Blenkinsop,' said Godwin.

Mrs B glanced at the older gentleman leaning against the far wall. He seemed to be holding up that side of the room with his own corpulence. He balanced a gold snuff box on his palm and took a generous pinch, watching Poignand out of slitted eyes.

'Fordyce, Mrs Blenkinsop.'

She nodded to him and brushed past, set her bag down, and tossed her cape onto a chair. She wrung out a cloth from a bowl of cool water, put her elbows on the bed, and mopped Mary's damp brow, her eyes were fevered and high up in her head.

'I'm here,' she whispered. 'We'll get you through this.'

She wasn't sure Mary could hear her until she gripped Mrs B's sleeve with her hot hand and clung to her hard.

When the shaking finally subsided, and Mary slept, Poignand continued his examination. He felt the pelvis, the joints, for signs of swelling and heat. 'I ought to have a look at her tongue,' he said.

'Let her rest,' said Fordyce in a Scottish brogue, with the grumbling slur of a man well into his cups. 'None of that helps, anyway.'

'Fordyce is a lecturer,' Poignand said to Godwin, ignoring his rival. 'In chemistry.'

'And the practice of medicine,' said Fordyce.

'Oh, do you see patients?' said Poignand tartly. '"Put out your tongue – there. Let me feel your pulse – that will do."'

'All that business tells us nothing of the sort of fever it is. Have to let it run its course, see what shape it takes, whether it resolves on its own.'

Mrs B pressed the cool cloth to Mary's forehead, attentive to

139

the squabble. Fordyce was big-headed, puffy-faced, with heavy eyelids and protruding lips. He wore his white wig askew, and looked as if he wore the same clothes he'd slept in.

'I'm told no one knows fevers better than Fordyce,' said Godwin, in the man's defence.

'What about bleeding her?' said Poignand, who stood and wiped his hands on a towel. 'I think it's called for, under the circumstances.'

'Of course, *leeches*! Why not call in the snails, toads, and staghorns while we're at it, shall we?' said Fordyce, spitting each syllable.

'A lancet will do fine,' said Poignand, losing patience.

'Ah, the lancet! Fever, sore throat, stubbed toe – what isn't it good for?'

'You're drunk!' said Poignand.

'Not too drunk to think the lancet's any improvement on the guillotine.'

Poignand looked to Godwin to officiate, but it was no use. The midwife could see the terror in Mr Godwin's eyes.

'I want both your opinions. Anything that will help my wife,' he said, looking between them. 'But *are* you drunk, Fordyce?'

The doctor took another pinch from his snuff box. 'Well, if it's before noon, which I think it is, likely drunk from the night before. But after lunch, which I take precisely at four o'clock – my one meal of the day, at Dolly's Chophouse on Paternoster Row, the usual ale, brandy, port wine – also drunk. So, in a word, yes.'

Mrs B had always been thankful that her James never took to the bottle, but was surprised to find herself drawn to Fordyce. She liked his blunt instincts.

'Never mind. Tell me what you can about the extraction of the placenta,' he said to Poignand, changing his tone. There was

140

no accusation in it, only inquiry.

'He's not trained in midwifery, obstetrics!' Poignand said to Godwin. 'I won't be in the same room with him.'

'Please,' Godwin begged. 'We've got to do something for her.'

The newborn started puling again. Mrs B got up from Mary's bedside and took her from Godwin's arms. She had more experience settling a hungry child. An agitated Poignand punched his arms into his coatsleeves, preparing to go.

'No visitors,' he said. 'And the child should be put out of the room. You ought to send it to a wet nurse straightaway.'

Poignand and Godwin turned to Fordyce, expecting him to weigh in.

'Mary won't want a wet nurse,' said Mrs B. All three men looked at her. 'She'll put up a terrible fuss.'

Poignand snapped his bag shut and marched to the door. Godwin grabbed him lightly by the elbow.

'I'm sorry, Poignand. I'm desperate.'

'Don't risk the child's health as well,' he said, and left in a huff.

Fordyce walked to Mary's bedside, studied her sleeping face.

Mrs B watched him wring out the washcloth in the water bowl and press it lightly to her forehead.

'I agree with Poignand,' he said. 'She can nurse if the fever breaks. But not until then.'

'But will it? Break?' said Godwin.

'Let's give it another day,' said Fordyce with a sigh. He looked at the midwife. 'And if she has the strength to put up a fuss, we'll take that as a good sign, won't we, Blenkinsop?'

'That's right, sir. Mary Wollstonecraft is stronger than us all.'

Mary W

Fanny was pregnant within two months of the voyage to Lisbon and her long-anticipated marriage to Hugh Skeys, despite his being, in fact, 'much fatter and at least ten years older' than the portrait he had left her long ago. She wrote often to me and my sisters, 'her dear girls,' with brave humour, assuring us that her Skeys was a good sort of creature, with the good sense to let 'his cat of a wife follow her own inclinations in almost everything.' She claimed he even relished when she was well enough to 'coquet' with other men. Fanny, in turn, didn't seem to mind learning that he'd been a dreadful flirt with the ladies of Lisbon, who were disappointed by his marriage. She had tamed him already into a plain man now inclined to pay more attention to his wife than any other woman. I thought she was pretending at contentment, and for myself, remained sceptical of his worthiness. How could he possibly appreciate her marvels, as I did?

Fanny promised to send 'our assemblage of irresistible

charms' at Newington Green at least two men from Lisbon who she assured us were tolerable flirts, and one in particular, her very own physician, whom she thought would be a good match for me, though she feared his shyness and sincerity would impede his getting forward in a world where arrogance and dishonesty seldom fail to succeed. I didn't pine for a man, and Fanny knew it. But it was her way, I knew, to avoid the subject of her health, though she did admit that, on the good doctor's advice, she'd quit the country for the dry, hot air of town, and had already found the spitting of blood arrested, and her cough, most days, trifling. Her letters went on like that, with seeming high spirits, regaling us with stories of playing the bon vivant, a crowd of visitors every night, but it seemed she was hiding the truth of things. She sometimes signed them 'Frances (Heigh-ho!) Skeys,' which seemed overzealous, even for her.

I wanted to go to her, of course, nurse her through her confinement, knowing that she might not have the constitution to see a pregnancy through, and that it might kill her if she did. But without Fanny the school was on even more precarious footing, and Eliza and Everina showed no inclination to take on more responsibility. My only consolation was the students themselves, who awakened in me a deep well of patience I didn't know I had. I treated them with respect and tenderness, not shame, not punishments, and they returned it all with keen attachment. Every day I reminded them to have the curiosity to learn, and the courage to say what they knew. No feigned raptures, haughty words, fake manners, and piddling accomplishments. I wanted them to write as much as read, trust their experience of the world, their truest feelings. They were like twenty Fannys in the making. I didn't want them to be me;

I wanted them to be her, at least until they could be themselves.

I tried to distract myself with the demands of the school, the students, counting our pennies in hopes of making ends meet one month to the next, even week by week. If we lost a single student, we'd have to close. Though I missed Fanny every day, I found stimulation in an ever-expanding world of ideas. I was often invited to Newington dinners, where men and women talked openly about childrearing, schools, education, women, marriage – all subjects near to my heart, and quick on my tongue. It was June when the Green was abuzz with news that John and Abigail Adams were in London and had chosen Dr Price and his church for their visit rather than one in the fancy West End. Londoners were aghast that these American heroes would choose an old Dissenter instead of a more fashionable minister, but Price had won the Adamses over by being one of the longest and loudest champions of the American cause. And now they were in our midst.

Price himself saved me a place near the front. When I thanked him for the privilege, he told me that I had a way of angling toward him when he sermonised, as if I were about to leap from my seat and throw in for the cause right then. He believed my enthusiasm contagious to all. When John and Abigail Adams walked in and sat in the pew in front of me, I thought my heart would pound out of my chest. Mrs Adams was known for her homemade bonnets, he for his awkward manners (the West Enders would have laughed at him), but I was drawn to their native simplicity, taking it as a sign that they preferred liberty to fashion, and ideas to trifles. Once, during a hymn, I could just see over the pew, the husband squeezed his wife's hand, and she turned to him with smiling eyes. It was a small gesture, but I never forgot it.

I saw Abigail Adams in deep conversation after the service with Mrs Burgh, who rarely came out these days, but of course she wouldn't miss this. She leaned heavily on her favourite malacca cane with the painted porcelain female bust for a handle. Her tremor was worse, but her blue eyes gleamed like one of our girls at the school. I stopped a few steps short, not wanting to interrupt their conversation too brazenly. I was surprised to hear Mrs Adams waxing poetic over the 'simple charms' of Scotch songs. They always called up a memory, she was saying, of when her husband had been away in Paris, while she and her youngest sons were fending off a bone-cold winter in Braintree.

'Picture me, surrounded by a mountain of snow, sure that winter would begin and end me, my days as lonely as my nights were solitary. I missed my husband as if my own soul had flown away. A young friend found me in the worst melancholy, and sang me a song to cheer me up, about a wife greeting her seafaring husband after he's been "awa." I still sing it to myself when I feel that hour upon me: "His very foot has music in't/As he comes up the stairs—"'

'"And shall I see his face again/And shall I hear him speak!"' I couldn't help cutting in. It was Fanny's song, the one she'd taught us.

They both turned to take me in. 'Yes! You know it too,' Mrs Adams said to me. 'It has beauties in it an indifferent person wouldn't feel!' She offered her hand to me. 'And you are?'

'This is Mary Wollstonecraft,' said Mrs Burgh, beaming. 'Not an "indifferent person" at all. She's got a school for girls. Teaching them how to think for themselves. Reform the girl, reform the world! You would approve, Mrs Adams.'

'I very much approve,' Abigail Adams said to me. 'And always tell my husband, as the men busy themselves writing the new laws of the land, that they ought to remember the ladies, with a little less unlimited power for husbands.'

'All husbands would be tyrants if they could be,' I said.

She laughed heartily, completely at ease.

'You see what I mean,' Mrs Burgh said to her with a wink.

'Well, there are a few good husbands, but I like to remind mine that if care and attention is not paid, the ladies will foment a rebellion not bound by any laws in which we have no voice.'

'Then America has won my heart!' I said. 'Perhaps it's my rightful home.'

'Oh no.' She hadn't let go of my hand, but now had it between both of hers. 'We need you right here, Miss Wollstonecraft, doing what you do, one precious girl at a time.'

Our encounter renewed my vigour and purpose, but a week later I received a letter from Fanny that altered my course. She tried to be buoyant. Hugh, she said, was working hard at being a good husband, though he was of little use or comfort. Still, she admired his effort. It was so like Fanny to find some cause for optimism, but there was misery between the lines. She included her now-finished botanical drawing of the *Viola tricolour*, the wild pansy, heartsease, her love-in-idleness, a 'small token of her love,' and urged me to gaze often on its happy face. I sensed the underneath of it, that while accepting her fate, Fanny feared for her life and the life of her child, and thought she and I might never see each other again.

I could stand it no longer. I set a plan in motion to sail to Lisbon as soon as possible. Eliza and Everina accused me of abandoning them, of caring for Fanny more than I cared for them. A few of the parents had no faith that my sisters could continue to uphold the ideals of the school, much less the day-to-day of it, and threatened to withdraw their daughters if I should go. I tried to assuage their concerns, but mine had a greater hold on me.

I went to the widow Burgh, my only hope for passage.

'What about our school?' she asked. 'I thought *this* was your purpose. I fear without you it will fail. And there's Mrs Cockburn down the way who has her eye on three of our very advantageous lodgers we might lose if you go.'

Here I was again, staring into a teacup hoping to make my case. 'I once abandoned a little girl, not one year old. My sister's daughter. I thought, at the time, that I must choose between them. That it was the only way to save my sister's life.'

'Perhaps it was.'

'Our little Bess died one month shy of her first birthday. I left her to be neglected, without a mother, without motherly love at all. With no one to protect her. I still lie awake at night, sometimes, wondering what else I might have done to save her. I cannot live with myself if I do that again.'

'Yet our Fanny Blood, however dear to us, has her own fate. And is not a child at all.'

'We were, all of us, children once,' I said. 'I think of who Bess might have grown to become, to full flowering, if I hadn't left her there. So while Fanny lives and breathes on this earth, her fate is entwined with mine, the child she once was, the woman she is now, and may yet become. I cannot abandon her.'

Mrs Burgh put her cane between her knees and leaned her chin on the tiny porcelain head, thinking. Her breathing was laboured, her eyelids drooped low. Finally she looked up at me. 'I will fight off Mrs Cockburn as best I can,' she said. 'Go to our Fanny. Leave the rest to me.'

I had never travelled by sea, a woman alone, with little experience of the wider world. I left on the first of November, All Saints' Day, knowing that thirty years ago that very day, Lisbon had been crushed by an all-consuming earthquake and tidal wave that swallowed the city, first by crumbling it, then drowning it, and then setting it all ablaze, due to the many candles lit to celebrate the day. I had an ocean to cross to get there, in three long weeks, during which time I prayed every day, on my knees, that Fanny would wait to give birth till I arrived, not even sure any more if God was listening. I shared my cabin with a man and his wife, she seasick the whole time, and he a consumptive so oppressed by his complaints I never expected he would live to see Lisbon.

A November sea in that part of the world is an angry one, slapping and tossing our ship, daring it to stay afloat. For thirteen straight days the boisterous water came at us, into every cabin and crevice, and almost rolled the ship over. We had such hard gales the captain was afraid we'd be dismasted. The sea was so rough I couldn't write, couldn't read, sometimes reduced to staring at the chopping waves, trying to steady my jangled nerves on the straight line of the distant horizon. The last three days we were surrounded by a fog so thick and dark I thought we might disappear in the miasma.

And then one morning, as if by some miracle, the air cleared and magnificent Lisbon came into view, a sparkling new city built on a series of hills, with its grand boulevards and plazas, white buildings, tall windows, red roofs, a vast harbour full of every variety of vessel, masts billowing and full.

I was bedraggled but elated at the prospect of soon being with Fanny in this magical new world. I put myself together as best I could, said my goodbyes to my traveling companions, and clambered into a cab. It took me up a long, winding street lined with young trees, then turned into a small courtyard off a narrow lane.

Skeys met me at the door.

'Thank God you've come, Miss Wollstonecraft,' he said, a mess in his unbuttoned waistcoat, hair fallen across his forehead, and a beading brow beneath. A servant took my things. 'Her labour started in earnest some sixteen hours ago, but I fear she's too weak to be delivered.'

He took me at once to Fanny, who looked as if she herself had been tossed by an angry sea: stringy hair, skin pale as whitecaps, liquid cough, blood on her pillow, her gown. Thin as I'd ever seen her, cheekbones protruding, sunken eyes. And yet her face came alive when she saw me.

'I'm here, I'm here,' I repeated, springing to action, but calmer than I expected to be, obeying the commands of the midwife (who was no Mrs B, I assure you). 'Mop her brow! Rub her back! Squeeze her hand!' We stayed like that for four hours, while Fanny had not even the strength to scream, and suffered the worst of her labour in silence. I had never seen a child born, had no idea what to expect, but a woman so enfeebled, too weary to push her baby out, a woman I loved as I did her, was a terrible thing to watch.

And then, without one peep from Fanny, not even a whimper, he slipped out of her, a little boy. Skeys was called into the room and held the swaddled babe in his arms, but he looked at Fanny, asleep on her pillow, as if she were a corpse already.

The child was puny but had good lungs for wailing and a strong desire to suck. Fanny was in every way his opposite, so reduced and worn out her recovery would be almost a resurrection. She held her child, said loving words, tried to suckle him, but every vain attempt ended in a coughing fit. It was no use at all. I wondered how there could possibly be milk in her breasts, but found myself praying there would be; even a few drops would be a sign that her body could sustain and provide, that she might regain her strength. Skeys wasn't in his right mind. I tried to console him, but he was so sure of Fanny's imminent demise, he wouldn't listen when I suggested a wet nurse. It would be as if we were giving up on her, he said.

Wednesday night. Friday morning. Monday noon. Pounding rain and a dead stillness in the house. Time meant nothing any more, the days all being one. Fanny continued exceedingly ill, without the strength even to lift a spoon. I tried to feed her myself, but she couldn't hold her head up, could barely muster words to speak. I began to think it was almost wrong of me to hang on to her, but if I gave up it would be as good as signing her death warrant. When she finally had a comfortable night, her symptoms seemed a bit better in the morning. There was something almost sanguine in her mood.

She consented, at last, to bringing in a wet nurse, and Skeys at once sent for one, but Fanny's little boy contracted a sudden fever that night and died in my arms. Skeys didn't want to tell Fanny. He wanted to say that the child had been sent to a wet nurse and was doing well, in hopes the subterfuge would be enough to revive her.

'He's gone, isn't he, Mary, my little boy?'

I took her hand in mine, as she so often did for me. 'Yes, darling Fanny. But I held him to the last.'

'Do you think he could have known that I loved him?'

'I think all the world, and everything you've ever touched knows your love, Fanny. You shine with it, and all of us feel its rays.'

'I'm so very tired,' she said. 'I think perhaps I'll go and live with my little boy, wherever he is.'

'Must you, Fanny?'

'Will you forgive me if I do?'

'Forgive you?' I pressed my lips to her palm; even its lines seemed to be fading, as if she was being erased before my eyes. I studied both sides of her hand, trying to commit her to memory. The carnelian ring was the only colour about her, burning, as it always did, like a warm fire. With tremulous fingers she slipped the ring off and pressed it into *my* palm, closed my fingers around it.

'With this ring,' she whispered, 'I *thee* wed.'

Choked with tears, I couldn't speak, but touched my forehead to hers, kissed her softly on the lips. She asked that I climb on the bed with her, and I did, offering my arm so that she could rest her head in the nook of my shoulder. There I stayed, holding her close, until she took her last rasping sips of breath.

In my grief, my spirits flown away, I didn't have the strength to board a ship again so soon. And leaving her alone in the cold hard ground of the cemetery just beyond the city seemed a second abandonment too cruel to exact. Skeys was inconsolable, and wanted my company in his anguish. How could I leave when each day began with him crying over his toast, clutching

Fanny's shawl to his chest, and ended in a bottle of port and a recitation of his regrets at having taken so long to marry her? He'd lost everything, how would he ever go on without her, rebuild his life? I had to bite my tongue.

I haunted the streets of Lisbon by day, like a woman made of air. I would have been willing for even the lightest wind to lift me, all the way to Heaven if possible. I could think of nothing that would tether me again to this bitter earth. Maybe another great quake would come, reduce Lisbon's new elegance to rubble, and swallow me with it. Despite what my eyes could see, the optimistic rebuilding of the city into great wide boulevards and grand buildings, parallel lanes named for their purposes – Gold Street, Silver Street, Leather Street, and so on – I had a sense at all times that the ground beneath my feet was not what it seemed. This alluvial soil so easily churned into unstable mud. For an earthquake is the collapse of the most basic trust in the world: that the very ground upon which we have built our lives can hold us.

The weather on my passage home to London, little bird, had teeth and a temper both. The ocean was like a monster with a thousand hands that slapped against our boat, heaved us up, and threw us down. We felt in imminent danger all the time. Even the captain's hard face showed it. Day in, day out, and through each night, the grey brutal sweep of ocean waves pounded us, a storm furious and unrelenting. Our vessel rose and tilted on squalls, then descended into yawning gulfs. I wondered how we would ever hold together.

Then a respite came one morning, and a few of us, desperate for air, went out on deck to see what we could, while the captain inspected for damage. I saw it first, and pointed to it – a shredded French flag appeared like a mirage out of the thinning fog, and then the vessel below it off our starboard bow, dismasted and drifting. Part of it already submerged. Soon we were close enough that we could see the sailors' emaciated faces. There were maybe twenty of them, waving their arms at us, calling out through cupped hands. 'Rudder broken! We drift for days! No rations! S'il vous plaît! We starve! Mon Dieu, mon Dieu!'

'We must take them on board,' I said to our English captain.

'We've rations barely enough for us, with at least a week more at sea. We sail past, that's all we can do.'

'I'll not have it!' I could hear their cries on the wind, fading in and out. 'While there is food to eat we'll share it, and all land safely. All of us live! Take them on board, I demand it.'

'Who are you to tell me how to run my ship?'

'I am the person who will report you first thing upon landing to the maritime office, if you do not take these men on board, now. You would leave them to starve or sink? It's a floating coffin! They have no rudder!'

'They're not our countrymen!' he said, now red at his collar.

'They are fellow human beings who need our care.' I turned to see another wave batter their boat, and for three seconds obscure it from view. My desperation fuelled my ire. 'I will not be a witness to such cruelty! Take them on board, now!'

A handful more of our fellow passengers had scrambled to the deck, plus the parson, the cook, the boatswain among them, watching me fight with the captain, not coming to my aid or his. This, the battle of our two wills. I don't know where I found the strength to stand such shaky ground, no ground at all, but undulating boards beneath me. We, too, had survived for two weeks on salt beef and hard biscuits, with barely enough ale to wash it down, if we'd the stomach for it, and little sleep. But I knew that once we slipped sight of shore, we became a floating island, unto ourselves, dependent on the integrity of our ship to withstand these beating storms, and the integrity of one another through moments of peace *and* terror. We make our own society, are responsible one to the other. And those French sailors pleading for their lives: they were us too.

I can still hear their cries of joy mixed with the roar of the waves as we took them, one by one, on board. I joined the rescued men in a prayer of thanks, but later, all alone staring into another coming storm, feeling the spray like a thousand pinpricks on my face, my soul mounting and sinking with the waves, I knew that *I* had saved them too. I felt my own insignificance on that vast ocean, yes, but also what power I have, we all have, to force the human heart. And I knew that to let that ship drown to the bottom of the ocean with all its sailors would have been to let new Lisbon die by sea again, and my dear Fanny be buried twice.

Mrs B

5th September 1797

Poignand didn't have the nerve to show his face again, and wasn't asked. Dr Fordyce returned after his lunch at the chophouse to sit by Mary's bedside through most of that first night. Mrs Blenkinsop would have said that he slept in a chair and snored, while she kept watch, with strict instructions to wake him if there was any change. She was glad of being in charge. No one had said it out loud, for Mr Godwin's sake, but childbed fever was everyone's worst fear. It was said to be caused by foul, noxious air that arrived on the wind, or came from a woman's own body. For Mrs B's part, the more that doctors were about, intruding on the business of childbirth, the more women died of it. She didn't need science; she had experience.

As for remedies, she had rarely seen more applied with greater diligence and less success. Bloodletting was one thing, early and often, according to Poignand. Others preferred Peruvian bark, an emetic for vomiting, or an emollient clyster

– a mix of linseed tea and new milk, cream of tartar, rhubarb, or castor oil – to help carry off the morbid matter. If the patient was truly sinking, doctors often advised throwing everything at her: strong infusions of the bark, wine, and cordials, applying blisters to the abdomen, even injecting antiseptic solutions into the uterus. Mrs B believed her only duty was to keep Mary comfortable and give her strength for the fight, whether this was an ephemeral fever or not. Only time would tell.

When Mary's fever burned, Mrs B stripped her down to her chemise, threw open the windows, and kept a cool cloth on her head. When the cold shivering fits took over, she heaped on clothes and covers, gave her wool socks and bottles of hot water at her feet, offered sips of warm tea or broth, hot spices, and spirits. But she knew there was no amount of heat that could prevent the rigors in a puerperal woman. It was nearing twenty-four hours of fever taking turns with rigors for Mary; anything longer, after childbirth, was considered a terrible sign. There was little to do but keep clean linens about her and hope she would sleep. She tried to help Mary onto her side, then her back again, to give her a few moments of relief, but Mary struggled against each wave shaking her body. In the moments between she was thirsty and restless.

Her skin was translucent yellow, her eyes red.

'I thought I heard my baby cry,' she said when morning came.

'Yes,' said Mrs B, patting her hand. 'Your little girl is hungry.'

Mrs B had tried a few drops of thin gruel from her bubby pot when the baby fussed in the night, but of course she wanted the nipple and her mother's sweet milk, now that she knew it.

'Let me feed her, please, let me,' Mary said, hanging on Mrs B's sleeve.

Fordyce was awake now, rumpled but accounted for. He felt Mary's forehead, took her pulse. 'For Poignand,' he said with a sideways wink.

Mrs B, who hadn't slept all night, picked up the little one in her arms and lightly bounced her, trying to buy some time for them all. She knew what was coming.

'Can you hear me, Mary?' Fordyce sat on the edge of her bed, and waited for her eyes to focus on him. 'Yes, that's good. Now, I want you to listen to me. Your girl needs a mother's milk to grow strong.'

'I can nurse her. I want to.'

'I know you do. But your milk, just now, may not be healthy for her. It could even do her harm.'

'How do you know that?' It was an effort for her to think, to talk, Mrs B could tell. Her tongue was thick and white.

'We don't know that. In fact, we don't know very much at all. We are observers, really. Asking questions, writing down what we see, looking for patterns. I do not like to admit it, but each patient is a sort of experiment.'

'Then experiment on me!' Mary held out her upturned forearms. 'Bleed me. I don't care. Anything. If it will let me nurse my daughter.'

'We don't want to weaken your circulatory system, which may help to move whatever putrefaction you're suffering out of your body.'

'I'm begging you,' Mary said.

'I'm afraid I must forbid it.'

Mary cupped her breasts with her hands. 'They *hurt,*' she said. 'I need to suckle her.'

Fordyce looked anxious at the prospect of examining the

patient's breasts. 'Mrs Blenkinsop,' he said, 'would you mind?' He took the whimpering baby from the midwife's arms.

Mary began to cry too. 'It feels so cruel,' she said, 'to both of us.'

Fordyce didn't look to Mrs B like a cruel man. In fact he looked at home holding the infant, even as she puled and squirmed. He was older than most of the doctors she encountered in her work, but she suspected he would fall on the modern side of the wet nurse debate: mother's milk was better than animal milk, pap, or panada, and only a serious intractable illness could justify separating a mother and child. If the mother could not suckle, for whatever reason, a wet nurse was next best. It was said she should be between twenty and thirty, of good health, character, and manners, and no redheads, for their hot temperament, at which Mrs B took special umbrage.

She sat on the edge of the bed and loosed Mary's chemise. 'I know what it means to you,' she said, rubbing her hands together to warm them. She then felt all around Mary's breasts, pressing lightly with the flat of her fingers. They were hot to the touch, knotty in places, rock hard in others. A quick glance at Fordyce told him what he needed to know. She replaced Mary's clothing with a light touch. 'But for your little bird. We've got to get her to a wet nurse, today.'

Mary had sweated so much, wet through the sheets already three times, that she had hardly any tears to cry. Dry crying had no satisfaction in it, Mrs B knew. Though her face showed all the same pain. A keening pain.

Mr Godwin walked in quietly, wearing fresh clothes. Mrs B understood that people, even in the midst of the most difficult things, and often without knowing it, perform small acts of optimism, as if a prayer. A clean, pressed shirt was of that sort, she knew, each button a rosary. But when the husband took one look at his wife, and the tableau around her, his whole being sagged. He walked to Fordyce and took the baby in his arms, then took Mrs B's place at Mary's bedside.

'Darling,' she said, with a brave face. 'We've got to send our little bird to a wet nurse.'

'Is that what you want?' he asked.

'It's for the best. For her.'

Godwin looked between his wife, his child. 'I will do anything you think right. Find someone nearby. Someone close, and kind. And our little girl will come back to us very soon, when you're well.'

Mary smoothed the tussock of their little girl's hair with her fingertips, pressing the feel of her into memory. 'When I'm well,' she said.

'Of course! It's only temporary,' said Fordyce, offering the only comfort he could. Mrs B sensed the lie in his voice, but hope was the only medicine there was.

'I do wish our girl had a name,' said Godwin, looking into his wife's eyes. 'Before we . . . send her away—'

'A name,' she said. 'Yes.'

Godwin held the child's cheek to his own, and pressed his eyes shut for a long moment. His tears were ripe as raindrops. 'I want to call her Mary,' he said. 'After you.'

'Mary?'

'What else could she possibly be?'

'A thousand things,' said Mary, beginning to fade, whether into fire or ice, no one knew.

'Then let her be a thousand things,' said Godwin, 'but Mary first of all.'

Mary W

Grey is the colour of grief. Not black, not white, not colour at all, but bland nothingness. Days that are dark all the time. Water, frozen in the washbasins of our school, the furniture pulled up, all of us hovering around our one meagre fire in the large drawing room, the one we could afford. I'd been gone only two months, but our world had changed in my absence, and I didn't have the will to correct its course. Eliza and Everina showed me little empathy, instead blaming me for having gone to Fanny, my leaving having prompted several parents to pull their children, others now planning to leave. How could I argue otherwise? Without Fanny, I didn't care.

'I'm sorry, Mrs Burgh. I know I've let you down,' I said, when she called me back to her parlour upon my return, greeting me with a warm embrace. She sat close beside me on the settee and asked after Fanny without reserve, her final moments, my state of mind. I didn't tell her about my recurring dream, Fanny calling me to join her, and how sad I was when I awoke to still be alive. 'I can scarcely find a name for the apathy that's seized me,' I said instead. 'I am sick of everything under the sun.'

'With time, it will change. Everything does.'

I thought of John Arden, when he'd looked upon his wife's portrait and said the same thing to me. But the now pressed on my heart.

'I blame myself, even still. It was I who persuaded her to marry Hugh, go to Portugal. She might still be with us if I hadn't. The school would be thriving, our girls – our grand project, yours and mine.'

She patted my knee in the most motherly way, something my own mother had never done, not once. 'There, there,' she said. 'There's nothing in it to blame yourself. We must look forward, not back.'

'I'll find a way to make it right, Hannah. I promise you.'

Mrs Burgh took in a deep breath and considered the ceiling. I had not the heart to tell her that despite her substantial backing, the trip to Portugal, the school's expenses, including for me and my sisters, had far exceeded what we were taking in. I'd had to borrow money before I left, and now had creditors chasing me.

'I think we have no choice but to close the school,' she said. 'As soon as the academic year's done.'

There was no disagreeing. It was the practical thing to do. For the next three months I watched the students leave one by one, prefaced by last walks and long hugs. Each parting was for me another loss.

'What would Fanny want you to do?' our friend John Hewlett asked me when he dropped in for a friendly visit, and instead found me in despair. Dr Price had introduced us when we opened our school, as Hewlett had done the same in Shacklewell, in Hackney. Aside from running his school, he was working on a chronology of ancient Greece, translating a book on algebra, and writing his own collection of sermons on various subjects. Fanny and I were fervent in our admiration, and revelled in his company, as he did in ours when we pounced with questions, bandied about ideas, and finished each other's sentences. But now all I could do was shake my head. I didn't know almost anything, least of all what Fanny would tell me.

'She would want you to learn from her loss, grow from it, remember the transient nature of human life,' he said. 'But also remember *your* purpose – yours, Mary – here on this plane, before God calls you home.'

'My purpose was Fanny.'

'No, that's not what I saw. Fanny exemplified your purpose, mirrored your highest ideals.'

'*She* was my path to virtue. Fanny made me better in every way.'

'But don't you understand what she saw in you?'

I shook my head.

'I think she saw God in you, the way she did in her plants. Trying to understand their separate parts, admiring the whole.'

'I don't know about God any more. Except that he decided to forsake me.'

'You're thinking about it all wrong. Think of pure intelligence, a perfect brain, but without our human weakness. And you, Mary, you make the purpose of your life the urgent improvement of your own intellect, and the thinking powers of those around you. There's no higher calling. All we have, each of us, is our own perfectibility. I think that is the gift we return for the one we are given. If we are sparks of His great Creation, then we must make of those sparks a fire, and with that fire light the way, that we might be worthy, and made whole again in His eyes. Make the world whole with us.'

'How do I do that? By spring I'll have no school at all.'

'You must write, Mary. Write it down. Tell the world what you've learnt.'

When we said goodbye to the last student in May and shuttered the school, I felt like the drowning French sailors, cast adrift with no ship on the horizon. Not knowing what else to do, I did put pen to paper, pouring out my anger and resentment, railing against the injustice of women like me, like Fanny and my sisters, unable to make our way in the world. Fanny might still be alive were it otherwise, and sitting next to me now, drawing a wildflower and all its intricate parts, joking with me, appealing to my better self, running her fingers through my hair. Whatever I was writing, I wanted to dedicate it to her. I told Mrs Burgh I was calling it 'The Unfortunate Situation of Females, Unfashionably Educated, and Left without a Fortune.'

'Why so glum?' she said with a mischievous smile. 'Why not call it "Thoughts on the Education of Daughters"?'

Hewlett, when he read it, rushed it to his personal friend Joseph Johnson, one of the most famous publishers in London, a radical reformist. Hewlett thought my 'original voice' might appeal to him. Johnson invited me to come to London at once. I washed my hair, considered what to wear, decided on exactly what I wore every day (what good would it be pretending to be someone else?) and took the next coach for the city, arriving at his offices near St. Paul's.

163

'I like the way you think and write, Miss Wollstonecraft,' he said at our first meeting, sitting with my pages stacked on the desk in front of him.

Johnson was small and tightly made, with a sharp-cut jaw and slender nose. He wore his hair with two stiff curls above his ears, and a neatish mop on top. He had long fingers and fingernails, as I'd never seen on a man. Dressed in austere black, he welcomed me with the warmth of our mutual friend, Hewlett, but it was just the two of us now. I found it harrowing to have my future once again in someone else's hands, even if I had less than nothing to lose.

'It's direct and to the point,' he said. 'No unnecessary flourishes.'

'I abhor flowery writing.'

'And flowery women, it would appear,' he said, looking me a little up and down.

'I mean to be hard on simpering society misses—'

'Who apparently raise spoiled, selfish children?'

'Well, who simply raise children in their own image. It is no fault of the children,' I said.

'Of course not,' said Johnson, breaking into a smile that seemed to put all his colours on display. 'They prefer to make girls into creatures too delicate to think for themselves.'

'Yes, we must hammer their bold, creative spirit out of them as early as possible.'

'Never lead, but obey! For they are created for pleasure and delight alone!'

'As long as it isn't *their* pleasure, *their* delight,' I said.

'What? Women having their *own* delight?'

I heard myself laugh out loud, and it startled me, for it was a sound I hadn't heard in many months. To be deprived of one's own laughter I knew in that moment to be a cursed thing. I felt delight as my right, my connection to the wonder that the world contained. I'd relied, for so long, on Fanny to provide it. But here instead was a near stranger, a man with tight-curled hair and plain dress, the opposite of Fanny in every way, making a twenty-seven-year-old spinster laugh. I realised I had tears in my eyes, and hadn't spoken for some time.

'I'm sorry. Did I offend you, Miss Wollstonecraft?'

'No, Mr Johnson,' I said. 'You amused me. And I'm grateful for it.'

He looked down at my pages, his brow heavy. I prepared for the worst.

'Well, I would be grateful if you would take ten pounds for it, your manuscript.'

'Ten pounds?'

'With one condition.' I held my breath.

'That you will send me anything you write in the future, give me first chance at it.'

I wanted to throw my arms around him and bless his good face. The whole way back to Newington Green, I felt the wind lift my sails. An important publisher, who had high regard in the world I wanted to be regarded by, would publish *me*. But Johnson's ten pounds, though I was elated to have it, wasn't enough to dig myself and my sisters out of the hole we were in, not to mention do something to help the Bloods, who had lost their primary source of income with Fanny's passing. I'd promised her I would never abandon them, and promised myself. I would find something, anything, to right my ship.

I would not fail my friend again.

* * *

Robert and Caroline King, Lord and Lady of Kingsborough, Mitchelstown, Ireland, were in need of a governess, and liked the sound of me. I was the right age, a spinster, and now an experienced schoolmistress. Lady Kingsborough had been impressed by my book, or at least that I'd written one. But more to the point, they would pay forty pounds for a year's service, which, if I could suffer it that long, would give me twenty to pay off my debts and give something to the Bloods, while the rest I would save to help me and my sisters begin a new life. One year, and then I would be free.

The Kingsboroughs were the largest landowners in all of Ireland, English overlords who'd stolen Irish land for the Crown, and been rewarded for it. After a long, incommodious journey from London, I found myself in a carriage hugging the northern slopes of the Galtee Mountains. It was better than the Ireland of my imagination, a landscape of peaks and valleys, preternaturally green, drunk with water, birch and whitethorn trees. The road took us over a hill, opening onto a vast plain bounded to the south by the Knockmealdown Mountains, thick with evergreens, and in the middle of it, Mitchelstown Castle, surrounded by a twelve-foot wall.

It was a large Palladian thing with wings, but two towers carefully preserved from the old castle, I guessed, as a reminder that it was once a fortress. The house looked to be trying very hard to impress, with classical gardens, terraces with statues, a conservatory, and even vineyards, as if it had been plucked out of Renaissance Italy. But entering its gates felt like going into the Bastille. We passed the hovels of tenant farmers, where dirty-faced children in tattered clothes, even the littlest ones, worked outside in the cold.

We turned onto a long road leading to the grand entrance, and I felt the unhappiness even of the yews lining the way, trained and upright, not as a wild yew grows, with curling, reaching arms. This whole place was the opposite of Nature, and everything I hated.

'Where's the village?' I asked the driver, when I disembarked.

'Oh, Lord Kingsborough didn't like the view.'

'So, obscured by trees?'

'No, miss. Took the whole village down, board to nail, and moved it over there,' he pointed over a far hill, 'where he don't have to see it at all.'

A butler, one of eighty people (I soon learnt) in their service, led me into the great foyer, more like the entrance to a museum than a house. I looked up at the cupolaed ceiling, painted with the Rape of Proserpine; the fleshy daughter of the earth goddess, breasts pressed against Pluto's hairy chest, hanging her head in dread and disgust. We continued to the upstairs drawing room, where I was greeted first by a half dozen of Lady Kingsborough's constant companions – not her children but her yapping dogs, followed by Lady K herself, examining me as if with a quizzing glass. I thought high society in Bath would have taught me what to expect, but was ill-prepared for the ghastly chalk of her face and heavily rouged cheeks, the tower of frizzed hair atop her head (I wondered if mice might have taken up residence). She wore gondola-like protuberances beneath her taffeta skirts containing enough fabric to curtain an entire room. She could pass through doors only by turning sideways, though she didn't walk so much as sashay.

Her lisp was extreme, her voice grating and high. She giggled when she told me she found me 'quaint' in my simple dress, my hair gently swept back, no make-up, no embellishments at all, which seemed to please as much as amuse her. I soon came to understand that the governess before me had been seduced by Lord Kingsborough, and unceremoniously dismissed. She took me, apparently, as no threat whatsoever.

The older sons were away at Eton; the three daughters were to be mine alone. She called them in and introduced them with no motherly pride, but more curiosity as to how these girls could have issued from so fine a womb as hers. There was Margaret, fourteen, tall, and built squarely. She had a pointy nose and brown hair that fanned around her face in fashionable disarray, which didn't suit her at all. With arms crossed firmly across her flat chest, and a militant frown, she looked both miserable and fierce.

'Just look away from her spots if they bother you,' said Lady K, moving on to Caroline, twelve, and Mary, seven, with big blue eyes and abundant brown curls. Though stuffed into French dresses à la mode, they struck me like the wild yews outside, unhappy in the same way. Their manners were rough, nothing polite about them, and they seemed almost bored to meet me.

'You'll be gone before Christmas, trust me,' Margaret whispered in my ear when she gave me her hand and curtsied, her gaze fearless.

'No need to curtsy for me, Miss Margaret,' I said. 'I am not your master.'

'Yes, you are! And they must curtsy,' said Lady K. 'I'm trying to teach them manners. And so must you. Anyway, make something of them, won't you, Wollstonecraft? Not too much. Just enough.'

'She means, to get a husband,' said Margaret, rolling her eyes.

'As soon as possible, yes! I know it won't be an easy task. But do your best. We're counting on you.'

The girls, united in their cause, plotted and played tricks on me, presenting me one day with a bouquet of dead flowers, the next putting a live beetle in a hollowed-out apple, and the coup de grace: a dead worm in my tea. When I seemed unimpressed, and told them about the Beverley girls and their tricks, I had their attention, at least for a moment. On our first day of lessons in a bleak, airless 'schoolroom' – though I'd prepared over the summer, improving my French, music, and art – my own restlessness equalled theirs. They fidgeted. I shifted in my chair. We couldn't find a rhythm.

'Put on your coats,' I said. 'We're going for a walk.'

'A walk?' Margaret groaned. 'Outside?'

'For walking, I prefer outside to in,' I said.

'But we might catch cold,' said Caroline, 'and then mother will scold us!'

'Mothers do not scold over niggling colds. And it is a lie that the outside will make you sick. It is the outside that keeps us well,' I said, trying to raise a window that was stuck.

'Mother makes them paint them shut,' said Margaret.

'Well, it's this stuffy air that makes one ill. So, coats please.'

And so we started each of our long days together with a walk, no matter the weather. They resisted at first, walked single file behind me, griping at the ground, answering my questions with grunts. I'd stop to pick up stones, moss, fallen bark, and leaves, make them close their eyes and describe what I put in their hands. On one unseasonably warm day I made them take off their shoes and socks, to feel the grass between their toes.

On another we walked all the way to where the tenant farmers lived. They didn't seem to know who 'those strange people' were, or how they were connected to their own estate, or how kept down by it. They only knew them as 'stinking Irish,' and didn't seem to care.

That I *did* care, and wanted *them* to, was the only evidence I had that there was a world outside this pretend one. And that I was still of it.

By mid-October they were climbing the yews, begging to go outside, asking questions one on top of another: why are some stars brighter than others? Why do things die? Why do the French hate their king? In the handsome, well-endowed library that no one seemed to use, I cracked the spines of books and found all the knowledge I needed, each lesson designed around a question the girls asked. They were astonished that I detested needlework and eschewed French pleasantries, all of which, I told them, amounted to a heap of rubbish. If they wanted to learn French, it must be to speak of ideas. They soon began, as I did, to refuse eating sugar, which was linked to the slave trade, and to forgo the eating of meat whenever possible. They were surprised I coddled them when they were sad, and that I wanted to know why. Slowly they began to tell me, and I formed a picture of a house where love was banished.

When they fell sick six weeks after I arrived, one after the other, they were baffled that I tended to them closely, instead of quarantine, on which their mother insisted. I felt genuinely sorry for the girls, put warm rags on their chests, made them hot drinks of elderberry juice and gin, and told them stories, until at last they were better, and told stories to me.

Margaret, who held out the longest, came to me one day

before Christmas with tears in her eyes. She had blood on her dress and stockings, and the look of a girl who was sure death was near. With calm reassurances, I helped her change her soiled clothes, explained what was happening, what to expect in the future. I could tell she was relieved, not just that she would live, but that someone would tell her the truth of things. She hugged me for the first time before she left my room. I felt her arms tight around my waist.

'You don't wear a corset, ever?' she asked me when she pulled away.

'I don't care for them,' I told her.

'Why do I have to wear one, then?'

'Do you?'

'Mother says it's a practice corset, and that I must. But it seems the only thing I'm practising for is not being able to breathe.'

I smiled, seeing my young self in her. 'Have you told her so?'

'She scares me. It would appal her if she knew my real thoughts.'

'I was afraid of my mother too. She was cold and distant—'

'And featherheaded?'

'I sometimes thought so. But I feel sorry for her now. I'm not sure it was her fault, her choice, to be that way.'

'But you tell us we must try to be true to our nature, fashion our own choices.'

'I wish that for all women, and yet feel compassion for those who don't know themselves, and can't find words for what they wish for, which seems to me a prerequisite for trying to get it.'

She licked her lips – for Margaret, a prelude to thought. 'Well, I don't like girl clothes at all. Mother dresses us like bonbons. I wish to wear boy clothes, in fact.'

171

'Hmm. I do see the difficulty of convincing your mother of that. But when you are grown, you should dress exactly as you wish, not as the rest of the world demands you do.'

'Then I will,' she said. 'Dress as a man someday.'

'I have no doubt you will,' I said.

Margaret was devoted to me from that moment on, and I to her, to Caroline and Mary. The Kingsborough girls became my reason to live.

The rest of my world was a cruel desert, my room a prison, the loneliness crushing. In the first month I refused dinner every evening to rush to my room and cry in torrents. I thought it was Fanny I was lamenting, but it was also my grief for the fact of her fading, becoming less vivid, less near. I could no longer call up her voice, her laughter, no longer close my eyes and feel her finger trailing the length of my arm. And I was so far from everyone who loved her as I did. I wrote the Bloods, sent them money, but it wasn't the same as having them near, to remember Fanny together.

I reviewed my whole life and found, apart from a few smatterings of joy, a catalogue of calamities, disjointed as a dream and impossible to decipher. Despite being treated by everyone in the house as a gentlewoman, I had fallen so far, lost the only independence I'd ever known. I was an exile in a new land, trapped in a strange netherworld that held nothing for me. All the comforts of life weighed nothing against the liberty I longed for.

'Why are you sad today, Mary?' Margaret asked me one day when we were walking.

'Do I seem sad?' I didn't want her to worry.

'I can see it in your eyes, the way you see it in mine sometimes.

It's a faraway look, but I don't know where you are.'

She waited for my answer. I thought I ought to protect her from the darkness I felt, but if I urged them to speak from the heart, mustn't I do the same for them? I took her hand tightly in mine. 'Sometimes I am nowhere at all, sweet Margaret, but I feel frightened and alone.'

'Don't be frightened, Mary. You have me. You have us.'

'And I count myself fortunate for that. But this is your place in the world, not mine.'

She thought for a moment and squeezed my hand back, her shoulder leaning into mine. 'Sometimes I don't know if it's my place either.'

Lady Kingsborough, through all of it, vexed me entirely. The clearer the girls became to me, the more obfuscated she was. There was no humanity in her that I could see, not even love for her own children. She cradled her yipping dogs in her arms, talked to them like babies, laughed when they skittered across the marble floors, chewed up pillows, and said nothing when they pissed in the middle of the foyer, right under poor Proserpine. She seemed to hate her husband, of whom I saw very little, and was often confined to the company of women who gossiped and tittered, not real laughter or talk. When I tried to tell her about the girls' progress in various subjects, she talked over me with news of last night's party, who wore what, who flirted with whom, which men flocked around her, which friends were in, which out, whose love affairs were the most scandalous.

Out of desperate need for adult company, I accepted an invitation to one of those soirées, and soon found myself in animated conversation with a handsome man who caught my eye. His name was George Ogle. He was in his forties, married, successful, suave, but deeply unhappy in some way, and alert to another melancholy soul. He didn't bother with small talk or gallantry. We found we were both reading Rousseau's *Émile*.

'I find the hero a bit moody,' said Ogle.

'What if moods aren't a symptom of weakness, but greatness?' I said. 'I would certainly be relieved to know my aches and inner torments aren't for naught.'

'"Aches and inner torments"? We are made for each other,' he said. 'Honestly, I find women far more sensible, on the whole, than men. Even Rousseau's poor Sophia.'

'Who matters not at all except as she exists to be desired, attract, and charm, no real thoughts of her own, no autonomy of any kind.'

'How would you have written her?'

'My heroine would have thinking powers. And not be governed by fear.'

'No weeping and sighing, then?'

'Just enough. As I weep and sigh, just enough.'

We put our heads close and laughed. 'I hope you do write it. You ought to.'

Having seen our tête-à-tête, Lady K insinuated herself between us, irritated at our easy intercourse.

'I'm so pleased you've discovered each other. Isn't Mary novel in her . . . plainness?'

'I find her novel in mind and spirit, actually,' he said, not taking his eyes off me. 'Frankly, I thought this evening might be dull, so I congratulate you, Lady Kingsborough, for your good taste in guests.'

'She's not a guest, she's our governess!'

'Well-chosen all around, then. Excuse me, ladies.'

174

'I thought you would be a wallflower,' she said to me in the carriage home. 'Not thrusting yourself into the arms of men who are far above your station.'

'I take it you've chosen George Ogle for your flirt of the moment?'

'It's harmless, after all. I relish his good looks, his strong shoulders.'

'I'm sure. For I doubt you're able to relish his depth and humanity.'

For the first time I saw hurt on her face. But she turned up her nose and didn't speak to me for a week. For that I was thankful.

When we moved house to Dublin in anticipation of summer, I felt some movement inside me, some change of season for myself. I had better apartments, a proper schoolroom, and the use of a private drawing room where I could receive visitors. I glimpsed a new form of life. Like daffodils pushing up through softened ground, ideas burst open inside me, so many I could scarcely arrange them. I read whenever I could, metaphysical sermons and philosophical lectures, and began to write the very novel Ogle and I had discussed, loosely based on my own life.

One night Lady K took me to a concert where we ran into George Ogle and his wife, an unexpected treat for me. I was surprised to find Elizabeth Ogle open and warm, almost proud of her husband's own acute sensibility. It seemed she was not the source of his melancholy, nor did she believe it needed curing. She liked me simply because he did, with no jealousy at all. But seeing us in deep conversation, Lady K pounced at once. Now that I was something between her show toy and her rival, she couldn't bear any intimacy between us, insisting the Ogles come around to visit her. Instead, separately and together, they visited me often, trying to arrange it when Lady K was on her social rounds. Occasionally I supped at their house for a lively hour or two of wit and rational conversation, and could hardly pull myself away. I liked his great faults, and her little ones. It was a place to air my heart, to express my sometimes crumbling yet grasping faith, my attraction to my own demise.

'Speaking of demise, how fares your Gothic heroine?' George Ogle asked of my novel in progress.

'Well, I've decided, after some deliberation, to call her Mary.'

'Your life is just like a novel!' said Mrs Ogle. 'Why, the pages of your life seem to turn themselves.'

'And I've given her a mother not unlike Lady K.'

'Mmm. A revenge well-deserved,' she said.

We three found communion in railing at her flaws, laughing at her puerility. Condemned her for wanting the patina of high-mindedness and the flush of deep feeling without any of the effort. But even as I said the words, new sympathies started up inside me.

'I can't help it,' I said. 'I'm tied to my fellow creatures by our shared weaknesses. Do you know that once I walked into her steward's closet, and felt something like envy, touching her silks, taffetas, and crêpes, the ribbons and feathers, spangles and pearls, let them glide through my fingers, and burst my eyes with their bouquets of colour. It was a feast of sensation, and I felt the cost of my chosen plainness.'

''Tis these whims that render you interesting, Miss Wollstonecraft,' George Ogle said. 'These ups that tumble into downs, and the downs that rise to ups.'

'And still I own that I dislike her.'

'As we all do,' said Mrs Ogle, with a supportive pat on the knee.

Then one day I found Lady K in a taffeta puddle on the drawing room floor, tears like rivulets through her powder and rouge, her hair half falling down from its tower.

'What is it?' I asked, helping her to her feet. 'What's happened?'

She pulled a paper from the bust of her dress. 'This!' she said, poking the air with it. 'I intercepted it from our former governess. The one before you. A letter to my own husband, after I banished her from our house!'

She handed it to me. I scanned it quickly. 'An annuity of fifty pounds? But that's more than I will make—'

'And for doing nothing at all!'

Lady K plucked the letter from my hand and melted into a chair, trying to breathe. I had never seen her so distraught.

'How could he do this to me?'

'Has she had some injury to her reputation that makes it impossible for her to . . . find another position?'

'Injury to *her* reputation? What about *my* reputation? What about his betrayal of me?' She splayed her knees, all decorum disappeared, put her head in her hands, and wept, real tears.

I knelt in front of her, feeling her pain genuinely. 'I'm sorry,' I said. 'It was insensitive of me. But you must know I am ever aware of the plight of a woman who has nothing, no options, no choices. And you, Lady K, you have everything.'

She looked at me, defeated. 'Yes,' she said, 'I have everything you do not. And nothing that you do.'

As the make-up washed away, I could see her more clearly, her pretty oval face, large, slanted eyes, creamy lids.

'I was only fifteen years old when I was presented with my

future husband, only one year older than I was. Our pairing made us the largest landowners, the wealthiest people in the country. But we were children, Mary, terrified children, forced into each other's arms, and beds, with no regard, no real desire; I could have been a post for all he cared. I was well pregnant by the time we were married, bore him three children before I was nineteen, without love, or sincere affection of any kind, while he has dalliances with whomever he pleases, wherever he likes – even under our own roof. All I have is my money, and the occasional attentions of good-looking men, who at least are acknowledged to be clever, so that their light might reflect on me, though it is harder and harder to get them to flock—'

'You have your children,' I said.

'Who do not love me.'

'Maybe they don't know how to love.'

'How could they know? I was never loved one day of my life. Except by my dogs, who need me, lick my face, sleep in my arms like little angels, and follow me everywhere.'

'It needn't be that way.'

'But it is. This is my life.'

'And you think mine is better?'

'I know what you think of me, Mary. That my femininity is factitious, my intellect blunted, my heart stupid. While you wear what you want, think what you like, say what's on your mind.'

'You overestimate my freedom. I cannot move about in the world as a woman alone. My options are . . . circumscribed.'

'As are mine, Mary. As are mine.'

She wiped a tear, gathered her skirts, and stood. She walked to the door, unsteady, pulling her shoulders back, as if to remind her head to stay high. When she got to the door, she turned to me.

'I'm not an idiot. I know that George Ogle visits you when I'm away.'

'And sometimes his wife.'

'Yes, I think they're both quite in love with you.' She made a pouty face, like the fifteen-year-old girl she must have been. 'But why not with me?'

I tossed through the night, wondering if I'd misjudged her, but the next day she greeted me in the hallway as if the day before had never happened. She had the light of an idea in her eyes, and fresh rouge on her cheeks.

'Mary, when I woke this morning, I knew precisely what would cheer me, what would cheer us all. I'm to host a ball, in honour of my own Margaret. It will be her coming-out!'

I stuttered at first, unprepared for this turn. 'I do not think Margaret wishes to come out, not yet.'

'I am her mother, and I deem her sufficiently accomplished, thanks to your efforts, in the skills she will need to be an asset to a husband.'

'At fifteen you would send her off to market? When you yourself just yesterday decried your deep unhappiness—'

'Oh, that was me being self-pitying. I've had a think on the pillow, and reminded myself that we Kingsborough women are not made for happiness, but breeding.'

'Why not wait until she's sixteen, at least?'

'Because Caroline is prettier! Much prettier! It will take time to find a suitor for Margaret. We cannot risk Caroline being spotted first.'

Margaret was desperate when she found out. She buried her face in my collar and wept like a squall. 'I don't even like boys.

Why would I wed one? Please, Mary, can't you stop this?'

'I'm afraid she's quite determined.'

'Why can't Caroline go first? She's prettier; everyone says so. I want to be a spinster, like you.'

'"Spinster" is a cruel word, said in that way. I *choose* not to marry.'

'Then why can't *I*?'

Margaret had become like a daughter to me, my favourite of the girls, the one most like me, every bit as headstrong. But there was no way to stop the ball, planned with all the precision of a military campaign. The week before, even the kitchen maid and I were drawn into the important business of preparing wreaths of roses for Margaret's dress, stitching her fate prick by prick. We had no time for our morning walks, our lessons. Margaret and Caroline were consumed with dancing, singing, and piano lessons, all in preparation for the grand event. I expected Margaret to become more adamant and fiery as the day approached, but instead she was taciturn, almost tame, and I worried that she felt I'd betrayed her.

She made me promise I'd attend her coming-out. I had refused all of Lady K's invitations to balls and masquerades of the season, arguing I could afford neither the expense of a gown nor the hairdressing, Dubliners being expert in the fashions of Paris and London. But when Lady K offered me a present of a poplin gown and a petticoat, I couldn't refuse. Margaret needed me, if only to bear witness to her public humiliation.

On the evening of the ball, I visited Margaret in her bedroom. She was suffering through the finishings, the tying of her corset, her hair being tightly curled.

'I cannot breathe, Mary. How can I be expected to dance? To speak?'

She looked at herself in the mirror, lamenting her fate. I put a hand on her shoulder and assured her that her suffering would soon be over.

'I'm afraid,' she said, putting her hand on mine, 'this is where my suffering begins.'

When guests began arriving to the new Dublin Assembly Rooms at quarter past ten, Lady K, decked out like a wedding cake, took her position at the entrance to the ballroom to greet them, but Margaret had not yet appeared. It was required in a coming-out that she stand by her mother's side to welcome guests, and take their compliments. Lady K grabbed my elbow and commanded me to go find her at once. But as I turned to take the flight of marble stairs, I heard a collective gasp rise behind me. I looked up to see Margaret on the landing above, posing like a statue, head in profile, nose turned to the ceiling, shoulders thrust back, a hand on one hip. Her hair was braided in a queue, tied with a simple black ribbon. And instead of her dress, she wore her older brother's fancy suit of breeches, waistcoat and frock coat in blue damask moire, a cravat at her neck, and a frill of sleeve at her wrist.

Margaret King had arrived.

When we returned to Mitchelstown abruptly the next day, Margaret was banished to her room for a month: no walks, no lessons, no books, no company, and gruel for each of her meals. She could look out the window if she liked, but only because Lady K believed it would punctuate her isolation. The cruelty of it was hard for me to bear. Of course Lady K blamed me, accused me of plotting with Margaret to ruin the ball, which was the same as ruining her future prospects, which, she said, was my clear intent from the start.

'She has a mind of her own that is not mine at all,' I said.

'But you have taught that her mind is her own to make up, in contradiction to everything her family stands for.'

Lady K barely spoke to me or looked at me for the first two weeks of her daughter's exile. I took the opportunity to finish my book, little by little each night, after I'd finished pinning up Caroline's and Mary's hair, and washing them in the customary milk of roses. We had been told we weren't allowed to speak Margaret's name. The girls were desperate to know whether their sister would survive her ordeal, but terrified to disobey their mother. Instead I invented a governess named Mrs Mason who had the sole care of two young girls, an amalgamation of the three King sisters, but the eldest most like Margaret in curiosity and temperament.

'But what about their parents?' asked little Mary.

'Oh, no parents,' I said, making a sorry face. 'Both dead.'

'So Mrs Mason, then, she can do whatever she wants with them?' said Caroline. 'Teach them all sorts of things, have adventures outside, and never has to worry that they will be struck with a switch or shut up in their rooms eating gruel for an entire month?'

'Oh, Mrs Mason is not that sort of person, no. She believes in kindness and patience above all.'

With that, Mary climbed into my lap, and Caroline looped her arms about my neck. I told them stories inspired by our life together, about learning not to stomp on snails, who are God's creatures, too, or kill a spider, who might be the only friend a prisoner has, how the prettiest girl visits a poor family and takes money from her purse and the scarf around her neck to give to them, as Caroline had. I never mentioned Margaret's name. But we all knew, and were soothed by remembering what we had learnt together. I felt the warmth of motherhood for the first time in my life.

Being forbidden to see each other was awful for me and, I knew, the worst part of Margaret's imprisonment. I also knew that she visited my room while I was with her sisters for our night-time storytelling. Sometimes things on my desk had been moved, or there would be a little gift of a stone or a seashell, maybe a note under my pillow. She'd sign her own name to it, in clear, strong letters.

In the final week it seemed that Lady K was softening. She invited me to the drawing room two or three times, tried hard to be civil and temperate, even invited me to another concert. I think she was surprised Margaret hadn't buckled, hadn't come to her begging for forgiveness. I wondered if some part of her even missed her daughter. Perhaps she saw me as at least a tenuous connection to her, even as she asked for reassurance that I had stayed true to my word.

'I have not gone to her, not set eyes on her, as I promised. But perhaps *you* would go to her.'

'I will not.'

'Do you not miss her?'

'Miss her disobedience? Her disregard? Her unkindness toward me?'

'Margaret—'

'Do not speak her name to me, or to anyone. That, too, you have promised.'

'Your daughter is more than those things, just as you might be more than she assumes of you. If only you'd show her. That is how children learn, by seeing. By feeling. You try to govern with a rod, when she responds best to the simple touch of a loving hand.'

'I am resolved,' she said, looking away from me. We spoke of it no more.

I wrote the last pages of my novel late that night. It had been a catharsis to conduct my heroine through a disappointing world, where none but the doomed or dying, like my Fanny, are fully worthy of love. Perhaps I couldn't save Margaret from marriage, but I could save my Mary by killing her off to hasten her to a better world where there is neither marrying, nor giving in marriage. I stacked the pages, tied them with a string, and put the whole of it in a drawer.

Two days later, on the eve of Margaret's release, I was called from my rooms to attend to Lady K in her bedroom. I found her pacing the room in a dressing gown, hair down, the dogs reclining on their cushions, watching her, back and forth. Her face was crimson, eyes livid, holding pages of some sort in her quaking hand. As soon as I stepped into the room, she read from it aloud, without looking at me.

'"She bestowed on her dogs, but never her children, the warmest caresses! . . . It proceeded from vanity! . . . Lisping out the prettiest French expressions of ecstatic fondness!"'

I took a step toward her, furious and mortified at once. I could see now that my entire manuscript was strewn across the bottom of her bed.

'"In accents that had never been attuned by tenderness—"'

'You went through my things?'

'"Her voice was but a shadow of a sound, and she had, to complete her delicacy, so relaxed her nerves that she became a mere nothing . . ."'

Lady K threw the pages at me. 'How could you do this to me, write these horrid things? Make me so . . . ridiculous. A laughingstock!'

I knelt down and gathered the scattered pages. 'How dare you go into my rooms! This is my private writing! Not for your eyes, not for anyone's. It is my right!'

She swept the rest of my pages off the bed onto the floor, and sat on the edge of her silk coverlet, watching me on my knees picking them up, one by one, both of us fuming. When I finished, I stood, clutching the mess of papers to my chest. She looked at me, deflated.

'I didn't go in your rooms,' she said. 'I went to Margaret, as you told me to do. She was standing on a chair, her corset tight around her bedclothes, powder on her face, disks of rouge on her cheeks, and hair pinned up in a great pouf, with ribbons and feathers, willy-nilly. Caroline and Mary sat on the edge of the bed, in stitches, while Margaret lisped her way through my words, acting out what you've written. My daughters . . . were laughing at me.'

By dusk I was leaving Mitchelstown in a carriage, my hastily packed bags on top. I hadn't been allowed to say goodbye to the girls, or to Margaret. I could feel my heart beating through my homespun shift, my jacket. When I turned to take one last look down the avenue, there she was, lifting the skirts of her dress, hair flying, face streaked with tears, running after me, legs and arms pumping as hard as they could, bare feet on gravel, yelling

185

over and over, 'Please, Mary, don't leave me! Don't leave!'

I opened my hand and pressed it against the glass. She held hers in the air up to mine, fingers splayed, until the distance between us was too great a gap. She slowed and then stopped, straining for each breath, nostrils flaring like a racehorse, spent. I couldn't bear to take my eyes away, even as she grew smaller. But even then, I could see her strong jaw set, like her hands on her hips.

Margaret King, I knew, would save herself.

Mrs B

6th September 1797

'Wet nurse engaged to give the Poor Babe suck. Puppies brought in for the missus.'

Milk fever, caused by stagnation, was to be avoided at all costs. Mrs B had become dexterous over the years in drawing off an engorged breast, with the aim of more pleasure than pain. If the breasts grew knotty, she rubbed them softly with an oil-moistened hand. But the midwife, much as she tried, couldn't keep up with Mary's abundance. She used cabbage leaves to ease her discomfort, but it was Fordyce who finally ordered puppies brought in. He recommended that poor Mr Godwin be spared the sight of it – in fact, spared the truth of most things.

Midday, Godwin led bright-eyed Fanny in by the hand to deliver her mother a nosegay from the garden. Mary, blessed with a respite from the fever and chills, hid her feelings, closed her eyes, and smelt it in, the small bouquet. Mrs B could see that she fought through her fatigue to name the flowers with

187

her little girl, always teaching. She drew each letter in the air with her finger: 'P is for "poppy." L is for "lavender." Y is for "yarrow." And C is for—'

'Cosmos!' Fanny shouted.

It brought delighted tears to Mary's eyes, quickly followed by sad ones. The absent baby left a hole that not even Fanny could fill. The whole house felt it. Strange, how quickly a baby's gurgles and cries become part of the furniture, a habit of being, the way you walk around a chair, even if it's been taken away. Or still feel a limb that's been severed.

'When will baby Mary come home?' Fanny asked her mother. 'I want to play with her.'

'Soon enough, Fannikin,' said Godwin. 'Soon enough.'

'Will you play with me, Mama? We can take my hoop to the field, like we do.'

'I'll do that with you,' said Godwin. 'I have the whole afternoon to do anything you wish.'

Godwin didn't look like a man who enjoyed playing games with children, but he wanted to be of some use, to show that he could, and would, do whatever was needed. Mary tilted her head and smiled at him. How little time they'd had these past few days to be alone.

Godwin turned to the midwife. 'You ought to get some rest, Mrs B, while you can. Marguerite's doing the same.'

'I got a few winks in the night, sir. 'S all I need. But a little walk round the garden might be good for the soul, if you don't mind.'

'I planted it myself, Mrs B,' said Mary.

'Before bookcases, or pictures hung!' added Godwin, taking his wife's hand in his. 'She insisted on it.'

'It's got hollyhocks and foxglove, and the most wonderful

love-in-idleness, but you have to look for it.'

'Mary granted me one little stone bench. Turns out it's my favourite place to read in the whole house,' said Godwin, with a light squeeze of her hand. 'But I didn't know it until now.'

It was a penny's worth of back-and-forth, but to Mrs B, said so many things.

'I wonder if Fanny would like to show me the way?'

Mrs Blenkinsop couldn't remember the last time she'd held a child's hand in hers. For a woman who'd helped birth as many babies as she had, she rarely got to watch them grow. She was struck how much affection lived in so small a grasp, and that it was offered without a thought, informal and natural, just like Mary's garden out back. It was humble in size, but she'd made every inch of earth count. Herbs and flowers, enjoying their first full summer of life, spilled their colours, mingled and flopped over the walkway, the little gate. The midwife was glad to let Fanny lead her along the narrow, meandering path, to feel plants brush against her ankles. At the end of it sat Godwin's bench, not much more than two rough plinths and an old sandstone slab that looked like it might've been pulled from a nearby field and pressed into service. It had an inviting carpet of mosses in greens and silvery greys, and a book resting open on its stomach.

Fanny wanted to sit and rest, so she could point to the flowers whose names she knew, the pansy being her favourite. Mrs B lifted her onto the bench, her little legs dangling, picked up the book, and set it in her lap, just as it was, so as not to lose Mr Godwin's page. It had walnut-coloured leather for a spine, and marbled boards for the back and front, in autumn hues.

Letters Written During a Short Residence in Sweden, Norway, and Denmark, by Mary Wollstonecraft. It was the first she'd seen her charge's name like that, not only on a book but embossed in gold.

Fanny insisted on taking off her shoes, and did it all by herself. 'I'm allowed,' she said. 'Mama likes me to feel the wind between my toes.'

Mrs B thought that sounded just right.

'Will you read it to me?' said Fanny.

'I don't think it's a book for little girls.'

'Oh, I don't like books for little girls. Well, I do, really, but I think all words are pretty. Especially big ones.'

Just then Marguerite appeared, rolling Fanny's hoop at her side and calling her name. The little girl leaped off the bench into her arms, wrapping her legs tight around the young woman's hips. 'How is she?' Marguerite asked.

'For the moment, comfortable,' said Mrs B.

Marguerite nodded and brushed Fanny's hair out of her eyes. 'What do you say, Fanny?'

'Merci, Mrs B-b-b . . .' Fanny couldn't quite remember her name.

'B is for "Blenkinsop,"' said the midwife, with a hand on her heart. 'But I'm the one should do the thanking.'

Fanny and Marguerite chattered away in French as they trotted off to the fields to play. Mrs B closed her eyes and turned her face to the sun, the breeze. Filled her lungs and swore she could smell the first tinge of autumn, then other things: hyssop and wormwood, catmint, delphinium, phlox. All the smells of her husband's flower garden; she could see it in her mind's eye, where once a week in summer and into autumn, he clipped

190

blooms for her, and left them in a pewter jug on the table. He told her they were his consoling friends on her many days away, and a welcome smile for her return. James never let them die; dead flowers in a house brought bad luck, he liked to say. She couldn't remember having thanked him for it. Maybe in the early days, when they still held each other's hands, when she knew the knobby parts of each knuckle, the scarred bit of his left thumb where he'd lost a chunk chopping wood, the shocking softness of his palms. It was she who'd stopped taking his hand and offering hers; she who'd turned away.

She felt a body sit beside her on the bench, heard the *whoosh* of a sigh. Was it James himself come to forgive her? She could almost see him sitting there, fresh-shaved the way he was on Sunday mornings, ruddy from a quick survey of his kingdom outside, drinking tea out of his good porcelain cup, reporting to her which flowers were waking this week, and which ones past their prime.

If only he would take her hand now, and tell her about the flowers, she would never let it go. But when she opened her eyes she found Godwin in a heap beside her, slouched with his fists in his pockets and staring at the ground.

'I would rather be fighting with her,' he said. 'About almost anything.'

'Some women,' she said, 'they come through it. We don't know why.'

'I think she *is* stronger than all of us,' he said. 'But only from being broken so many times. How much more can she take?'

'We mustn't give up. As long as there's still fight in her.'

'Fordyce tells me to keep faith. That from a man with more science than anyone I know.'

191

'He's right. You must believe.'

'I know, Blenkinsop. Of course I do believe. But not like you. Or Mary.'

'No sir. You're an atheist.'

He smiled, and looked to a distant stand of tall trees swaying in unison, clouds pillowing above them. 'Yet sometimes when I walk with her in the wide-open fields, I think I experience it the way she does – that I see Him in the clouds and hear Him in the wind – in every object, a living soul, and in Nature all that is holy.'

Mrs B was used to men wanting to talk in their weak moments, telling her their secret fears, regrets, their hopes. But she felt weak too. And no one talked like Mr Godwin. She found herself hungry for it.

'You know, I didn't like her at all when I first met her,' he said. 'I found her overbearing and brash, and frankly, unfeminine. Then our friend Johnson gave me this new book of hers, new then anyway, and thought I ought to read it.'

Mrs B handed it to him just as she'd found it. 'I saved your place.'

'Oh, I've read it fifteen times by now,' he said. 'Every page is as good as every other.' He ruffled the pages across his thumb. 'If ever there was a book calculated to make a reader in love with its author, this is it.' He closed it and passed his hand across the cover, a bible of his own. 'I love her imagination. Marvel at how her mind attaches so readily to the sublime and the good. Her sorrows fill me with melancholy, dissolve me into tenderness . . . but it is her genius that commands all my admiration. I am simply in awe of her.'

Godwin clutched the book to his chest, and bowed his head,

his pain palpable. They sat in silence, letting themselves be filled by Mary's garden, until Fanny's voice tinkled on the air in the near faraway, breaking their reverie.

'Well, I've got some playing to do. I believe hoops will be involved.' He planted his palms on his knees, steeled himself, and stood, like an old man might, though he was far from old. He left the book on the bench beside her. 'Why don't you read it, Blenkinsop. I daresay it'll make you a convert too.'

She held the book to her bosom. 'Thank you, sir. But I was a convert from the first.'

Mary W

Imagine me, little bird, sixteen hours in a coach, then stepping off in hot, stinking London, buffeted by the crowd, the fashionables and downtroddens, pushed and pulled along streets I hardly recognised, stepping through other people's sewage, and thinking I'd arrived in Paradise! My seclusion was ended, even if I was alone in the world. I wanted it that way. Never again would I let someone else dictate my terms, my station, my boundary as a human being.

I wanted to bathe, wash away the coach ride, Ireland, Lady K, and worst of all the memory of dear Margaret chasing after my carriage, both of us ripped away from each other. But I had nowhere to go, and no idea where I'd sleep that night. There was only one place I *wished* to go, where I would not be expected at all. So, in my homespun shift, thick-soled shoes and flat beaver hat, I took up my suitcase, bursting with more books than clothes, and headed for St. Paul's Churchyard through narrow dark lanes, as if they were birthing me, to the offices of the man who was my only hope in the world.

'Good Lord, it's Mary Wollstonecraft!' Joseph Johnson said when he answered the door, and found me, ragged and drowning in rain. 'You look like Miranda, tempest-tossed!' 'I always feel more like Hamlet,' I said.

He laughed and ushered me inside. Took the large bag from my hand and placed it neatly by the door, as if he'd been expecting me all along.

'Well, Hamlet is always welcome here,' he said. '"To be or not to be." As she wishes.'

He poured me a welcome sherry, put a blanket around my wet shoulders, and invited me to sit across from him at his desk, a hundred times more chaotic than I remembered, like the room itself. Hill after hill of books closed in on us; they were crisscrossed and stacked almost to the ceiling, even covering the single window and snuffing out the light. But that musty darkness in midsummer was as good as a warm fire in winter. The drink gave me courage, but I'd come already fortified.

'I have a new plan, Mr Johnson,' I said, perching on the edge of my seat. 'To live entirely by my pen.'

He opened his mouth to speak, but I wasn't done. The speech had taken shape in my mind all the way from Ireland, or maybe the whole last year of my life, if not all my years. And this, my one chance to say it.

'I must be independent. It is the project of my life. I wasn't born to tread the beaten track, it's the peculiar bend of my nature. And I know your sex generally laugh at female determination, but I never resolved to do anything of consequence that I didn't adhere to resolutely, improbable as it might have seemed.'

He sat back and considered me, folding his slender hands into a perfect steeple.

'First, I am known for not being the most accurate representative of "my sex." I am asthmatic and short, with a weakness for chintz. But I will say that nothing about you seems improbable, Miss Wollstonecraft. Still, how will you do it?'

I opened the haversack on my lap and pulled out my hastily tied manuscript, unrolled it, tried to straighten the pages, and set it on the desk between us, though there was scarcely space for it. 'I've written a novel. About a woman. Named Mary.'

'What a surprise,' he said, taking it in his hands. 'Not a wedding bells plot, I presume?'

'I'd say not. She is . . . a sort of genius.'

'Ah, so more reason than sensibility.'

'No! An exquisite sensibility, which is the fruit of her genius, or the seed of it. Not the derivative, prescriptive, imitative, affected, but the freshly seen – originality, independence, spontaneity, the natural, innovative, imaginative, and real, true feeling felt first hand!'

'All that, in this?' he said, riffling the pages. 'Does she marry at all?'

'Yes. But unhappily.'

'Of course. Live or die?'

'I do not strive for happy endings,' I said.

'So dies then.'

'But free. To love whom she chooses, in Heaven. For all eternity.'

He cleared his throat. 'Heaven is fine, but I am more for what happens here on earth.'

'But will you at least read it?'

'I will, but I don't need to. I'll give you ten pounds for it.' He paused while I collected my jaw from the floor. 'But keep in mind that a woman writing for her living must think what will make money . . . on a continuing basis.'

I felt my shoulders sag and a corner of the blanket fall away. 'I don't know what will make money. I suppose that is the flaw in my plan.'

'Already with the gloom?'

'I do have a tendency to despair and vexations.'

'Well, banish them. Will you write reviews? Translations?'

'I think I can.'

'What are your languages?'

'Well, a bit of English,' I said, in hopes of making him laugh, which he did. 'A smattering of French, pinch of Portuguese. But I'll teach myself. Any language you require.'

'What about conduct books, making ready for the marriage market, for the lady readers. Is that something you might do?' His eyebrows punctuated the question.

I hesitated, knowing he held my fate in his hands. 'Honestly, I should as soon throw myself off Blackfriars Bridge.'

He laughed again. 'Exactly what I hoped you'd say. Now, tell me where you're staying.'

How the heart soars and dips, little bird. He must've seen my panic because he stood abruptly and put his hand on a pile of books, as if taking a pledge.

'Here. That's where you're staying. Until we can find you something better. Unless, that is, you would be scandalised by a single man and a single woman sleeping under the same roof without supervision.'

'I have no worries how I'll be judged, as I've never considered myself on the marriage market, or intend to be. Surely I'm a spinster by now.'

'Then we'll be spinsters together,' he said.

He showed me the two floors above his print- and bookshop, where he lived. They were not elegant at all: tilting floors, low ceilings, rough walls at odd angles, with only books to anchor them, as if words and leather spines held the whole enterprise upright. Even the dining room had volunteered as a makeshift library, though the table and chairs looked well sat-in, and on one wall loomed a large painting I couldn't make out in the half-dark. I saw the occasional chintz, yes, but this was a home fashioned most of all for thinking.

He showed me a bedchamber and introduced me to a servant, an old woman, not unlike our Mrs B, who would help me with a bath, if I so desired. Oh, glorious bath! She poured warm water over my hair, my back and shoulders, cleansing me of Mitchelstown. It felt like a baptism. I missed my Margaret, but she would never be mine. I was twenty-eight years old. Unmarried by choice, without children. I had debts to repay, sisters who begged to be cared for, Fanny's family always in need, and guilt about all of them. But when that old woman scrubbed my body dry with a coarse towel, it felt like a new skin. For the first time in my life, and no one to care, I climbed between the summer bedsheets with nothing on, not a stitch, and slept like a sailor home from sea.

I woke in the morning to footsteps outside my door, threw on my robe, and opened it to find a small pot of steaming tea and a pitcher of cream on a tray beside my manuscript, with Johnson's corrections, gentle but exacting. I had never studied grammar, not really, and my style lacked elegance, but I could tell from the care he took that he was shepherding the book. I put on my spectacles and set to work at once, not even asking for water to splash my face, sending his woman away when she offered me lunch, never stopping until I was called down to dinner, when I realised how many hours had slipped by. Not lost hours, but found.

I can tell you, sweet daughter, that during those few weeks under Johnson's roof, I found the first true home I'd known in my life, apart from Fanny Blood, where I was not just welcomed but wanted, not just wanted but listened to, not only listened to but wondered at. When I wasn't at work upstairs, I followed him around his bookshop by day, peppering him with questions. We jousted on issues of grammar and merit, sported over ideas. By night I sat at his dinner table, often the lone woman, but an equal in his eyes, with as much right to be there as anyone. Joseph Johnson treated me as the person I believed I was, or wanted to become. There are good men in the world, and bad, little bird, but then there are other men altogether: the ones who hold up a light that we might all better see our way.

He found me a small terraced house, cheerful yellow brick, in George Street, a ten-minute walk across the Thames, and engaged a maid from the country part of his family to shop, cook, and clean for me. I was terrible at asking her for anything, in fact, shocked her when I said we should take our meals together when at home. (I had seen Lady K tyrannise her servants, and vowed never to do the same.) It wasn't the stylish side of the river, but I didn't care. I had no money for furniture. I didn't buy new clothes, didn't curl, puff, or powder my hair. But I had a place of my own, a bed, table, chair, paper, ink, and sharp-nibbed quills. What else could I possibly want?

I worked on the novel, and surprised Johnson by presenting him with a book of stories based on my 'Mrs Mason' and the

King girls, meant to teach morals to children and adults alike.

'So a conduct book, which you swore never to write?' Johnson asked.

'Only a sort of conduct book. To form the mind to truth, goodness, compassion.'

'Well, I like it. We'll come out with it first; our readers will eat up its piety and virtue, and then we'll hit them with your novel – the radical Wollstonecraft!'

What happiness was mine, daughter! If not writing, you'd find me walking through a gritty London fast becoming my city. I stalked the Thames daily, past the bustling waterfront, ships jammed in like stacked logs. I dressed simply, hair down my back; in cool weather my beaver hat, in warm my straw. If I was an oddity, no one cared. I'd begun to earn more money with less trouble, felt in better health than I'd enjoyed in so long – no headaches, stomach troubles, monthlong bouts of despair. I breathed in the fragrant spring, content, as if I'd found my soul again. Fanny was still with me, every day, but her loss no longer skewered me.

Each day at five o'clock I'd walk to Johnson's house for dinner, a daily pilgrimage along Great Surrey Street past Albion Mills, up to the start of Blackfriars, as if a bridge from my old life to my new, with its solid brick arches and girders under my feet, and a view of all London, from Westminster downstream to Billingsgate, and everything in between, the gilded dome of St. Paul's floating above it all.

I'd arrive, exhilarated from my walk, at Johnson's upstairs dining room to find a world unto itself, and the one I took most pleasure in. The dinners were neither vast nor elaborate, no drawing room drinks before or after, nor a display of courses, but everything on the table all at once, with instructions to help ourselves. The food was simple: variations of boiled cod, roast veal or beef, potatoes, vegetables, and rice pudding, in some rotating order, but the wine was extravagant, and the company always rich. Here was my old mentor Price, when he felt up to it, my friend Hewlett. Another night, John Bonnycastle, who wrote math and science books for the common reader. Another, William Blake, desperate for whatever engraving jobs Johnson threw his way, including my own children's book. Here, William Cowper, a sad young poet who needed loans to live on. Over there the naturalist Erasmus Darwin. They were high-minded and silver-tongued, believed ideas could change the world, and, like Hewlett, that reason would lead to the perfectibility of the human species.

At first I wasn't sure of my place at the table. But when Johnson published my *Original Stories* and the novel that autumn, with my own name on the cover, I felt their regard grow, that is, until the arrival of the much-anticipated Henry Fuseli – Johnson couldn't stop talking about him – just back from some Roman picture tour. He was Johnson's best friend, though they could not have been less alike. Fuseli was always last to arrive, like the legend he was, cutting a dash in the room, his silver-streaked hair going this way and that, as if he'd just come from a windswept moor or a ship tossed at sea. He was near fifty, gnomish and bowlegged, with a nose too grand for his small face, and a heavy brow over smart, piercing eyes that seemed to look straight through everyone. He sat opposite Johnson at the long oval table, a seat that was always his, in front of the very picture he himself had painted that dominated the room: a sleeping woman bathed in white light and loosely clothed, arms and head flung over the edge of a bed, hair falling like a fountain, with a demonic incubus crouching on her loins. The whole painting shone with blackness, the woman the only light there was. I couldn't help staring at it, now that the artist himself was present.

'Ah, my *Nightmare*. Does it shock, frighten, or titillate you?' Fuseli asked when he found me staring at it over his shoulder.

'It does seem she's having a horrific dream,' I said.

I caught a lightning glance from Fuseli to Johnson, as if to say, Ah, you've brought me new prey.

'Oh no,' said Fuseli. '*That* is a painful and soul-shuddering ecstasy. The incubus has made love to her in her sleep. She's been shaken to her core, deliciously depleted.' He shrugged. 'Or perhaps she ate a bit of bad pork.'

Fuseli was quick-witted and pugnacious, had eight languages and a degree in theology. He considered conversation a blood sport, could speak of the highest things, but preferred the lowest. Everyone adored him most when he recounted his sexual exploits, with men *and* women. I knew he hoped to shock me, but I wouldn't give him the satisfaction.

'Well, I'm not easily titillated,' I said, neatly quartering my potato. 'I'm no prude. I simply believe that sex oppresses women; it doesn't free them at all.'

'It certainly frees them of their clothes, and inhibitions,' he said, to laughter all around.

'Aren't you married, Mr Fuseli?'

'Indeed, I am. Quite recently. But Sophia Rawlins enjoys the same privileges, I assure you. Equality of *sex,* isn't that what you want?'

'Of the *sexes,* yes. But equality is difficult when gifted men so often mate with their inferiors, beauty coupled with a childish vivacity – like sporting lambs and kittens.'

'Oh, my bride has vivacity, all right, as well as beauty, and "sports" like the devil. Mrs Fuseli is no philosophical sloven. *Her* hair is not lank at all,' he said, cutting into his meat.

I set down my knife and fork. 'I should rather you spoke of my sentences than my hair.'

'Well, then, I find it all loose and informal, without structure.'

'My sentences, or my hair?'

He covered his smile by flourishing his knife in the air. 'You have a sort of disorganised, running style.'

'True to the way I think, and feel. I seek propulsion, an openness to experience, honesty. Not flaccid, love-fixated romances.'

'"Flaccid," you say?' interjected Darwin, an expansive, bulbous man of sixty, who wanted to play. 'Have you read my *Loves of the Plants*? It was deemed too pornographic for unmarried female readers!'

'In fact,' I said, 'one woman asked me whether she might read your book without losing her female delicacy.'

'And what did you tell her?' asked Johnson.

'That she could not. And by all means, should read it at once!'

Darwin threw back his head and laughed, then wiped his face with the napkin tucked in at his neck, suddenly serious. 'You know, every specimen *is* some combination of male and female sex organs, which has equality built into it, as Nature prefers.'

'Our Erasmus is only interested in the sex life of flowers, I'm afraid,' said Fuseli, flashing his dark eyes at me.

'I believe the canna lily boasts one male and one female in

each flamboyant flower,' I said.

'An ideal arrangement!' said Darwin. 'Our Miss Wollstonecraft is a proficient in botany!'

'I once cared deeply for someone who was,' I said, bringing a curious silence to the table.

'More pistil or stamen, your botanist?' Darwin asked, with a mouth full of roast beef.

Fuseli set his chin on folded hands, awaiting my answer. 'My guess is pistil,' he said, as if reading my mind. 'I take it from the Mary in your novel that she has a great passion for her female friend.'

'The point is having the freedom to love, not which gender.'

'The freedom to pluck each other's petals, shall we say?' He popped a potato into his mouth, getting laughs. 'Certainly your girl doesn't care much for men.'

'No man can offer the erotic satisfaction that Nature can. As I said, sex with men is uniformly a disaster because it's fundamentally unfree and chokes a woman's capacity for genius.'

This brought guffaws all around. I thought Darwin might choke on his beef.

'Sex with men,' said Fuseli. 'Have you had any?'

My cheeks flushed, I could feel it. I had never loved a man, it was true. I don't believe a man had ever loved me. But I had loved a woman, whose memory was the most precious thing I possessed.

'It's marriage I oppose, not men,' I said. 'It's a tyranny of its own for women, who make themselves silly, subservient creatures, the same way we all give away our rights to kings.'

Johnson raised his glass. 'You see!' he said. 'This is my specialty, finding genius in the making. Just wait for this one.

Mary Wollstonecraft will be remembered better than all of us!'

I felt Fuseli's searing gaze. 'A challenge, then,' he said under his breath.

When I lay alone that night, I had a sensation that my body was strange to me. It was frozen in time, while my head had carried on long ago without it. I was a museum piece now, a relic of some sweet past where pleasure was possible. When Fanny died, I'd made a choice to sacrifice my own feelings and comforts, my own pleasure, to what I fancied was purity of conduct, and caring for others. I wouldn't even read a book except to improve my mind. I thought I could rise above my earthly habitation, that there was no happiness to be had here and now, as Fanny had wished for me. I'd lived my life in my head since then, with straight up-and-down walls, the chairs hard-backed and stiff. Desire had no place at all.

Fuseli and I proceeded from there, fencing with each other on a regular basis. He was a constant at Johnson's table, wooing me, so often the only woman, in his goading way. I held my ground at first, kept my distance, but we stayed later and later, spinning from one idea to the next, like carding the rough wool of our thoughts, pulling, pinching, twisting them into taut thread.

'I want to paint you,' he said.

'What would Sophia Rawlins say to that?'

'I return to our marriage bed, every night, don't I? I would call her content.'

He did return to their bed every night, no matter how long we stayed at the table, till the candles burned to nothing, and we whispered in darkness, an intimacy I'd never known with a man, even as I refused his subtle advances. It surprised me when he brought his wife to dinner one night. I wondered if she'd come, according to their rules of engagement, to peruse her competition, or perhaps give her assent. She was much younger than her husband, an amateur artist's model, a coquettish beauty, the usual spilling breasts, a French silk gown with a hundred pale pink bows to match her cheeks. Her hairstyle was complicated and extravagant, almost an architecture unto itself. Jewelled earrings dripped from her lobes. I expected a Lady Kingsborough when she opened her mouth, but she was not afraid to speak her mind, and had the advantage of an upturned nose that gave her an air of superiority. Sophia Rawlins had come to spar.

'Fuseli tells me you're a good hater, Miss Wollstonecraft. Very hard on all us women you vilify and ridicule.'

'In fact, I've never met a woman so hard on her own sex,' said Fuseli.

'Or hard on novels!' said Johnson. 'She dropped a batch on my desk today, asking if I wished her to review any more sentimental rubbish this month! Why, her pen is as good as a knife. One for gutting a fish!'

Everyone laughed but Sophia. 'Why would you deny us the one indulgence that belongs to our sex alone, Miss Wollstonecraft?'

'I hold novels in high regard,' I said, 'except those by scribbling women whose tissue of pretty nothings sanctions the libertine reveries of men and makes *our* sex weak. The same review would do for all of them.'

'Do say!' said Darwin.

'Here are the favourite female ingredients for a novel: ridiculous characters, improbable incidents, vague fabricated feelings instead of opinion, women tremblingly alive all over – freed hair, fevered cheeks – who run, faint, and sigh, blown about by every momentary gust of feeling! Oh, and count on oppression and repression all at the same ball, and virtue rewarded with a coach and six!' I thought even Sophia stifled a smile.

'Best of all is a sad tale of woe, some dismal catastrophe, with dying for love the favourite theme. Moping madness, tears that flow for ever, and of course slow-consuming death!'

The men clinked spoons against their glasses, cheering my performance.

'Yet *your* book ends in a slow-consuming death,' said Sophia.

I was surprised she'd read it. '*My* Mary has knowledge of the human heart. She grows through her errors.'

'Then dies pining for the love of her life, who is a dead woman.' Sophia had put a finger in my wound.

'I believed they could meet in another realm. At least that was my hope.'

'I assumed, with your black worsted stockings and rough wool gown, that you aspired to nun, or milkmaid. But now I see. You're in mourning, is that it, for the love of *your* life?'

We sat across from each other, perfectly opposite. The men looked between us, not a muscle moved among them.

'I dress as I see fit,' I said, 'and not as some man would have me do.'

'Well, not much danger of a man having you in that getup,' she said, drawing awkward laughter around the table.

I caught a glint in Fuseli's eyes, a sort of pride at Sophia's agility. He had brought his wife to show her off, to let her loose, to point and laugh at me. Here was coquetry turned cruel.

I felt everyone watching me, almost pitying the way she seemed to relish eating me alive. Even poor Johnson pushed food around his plate.

'I seek higher things than being had by a man.'

'Spoken as a woman who has never been in love,' Sophia said. 'Do tell us what you seek instead.'

Words gathered like a storm in my mouth. 'To think and feel for myself. Observation, thought, imagination. A vigorous mind and finely-fashioned nerves that vibrate with rapture, and nature.'

I felt the power of my own voice, the men leaning in. Darwin stopped chewing. Johnson set down his silver. Even Fuseli was riveted.

'You say that I am hard on all women. But no harder than I am on myself. I want a serious and thoughtful examination of authentic human emotion and experience, not false sensibility that imprisons us, but a genuine one that empowers us. Not only for me, but for you too, Mrs Fuseli.'

She smiled with closed lips, but did not drop my gaze or say a word.

Fuseli raised his glass. 'Well, I for one hate clever women. They're only troublesome.'

'Here's to troublesome women! May they long live!' said Darwin, raising his wineglass over the candles.

Johnson joined in, quoting from my novel. '"Her joys, her ecstasies, arose from genius." Like *our* Mary. The best troublesome woman I know.'

Sophia looked at me squarely, the last to lift her glass. 'To troublesome women, then.'

I had much to occupy my days, writing for Johnson's new

journal, penning essays, reviewing novels by the cartload, but also books about children, education, women, travel, even boxing; translating books from Italian and German, teaching myself along the way, every inch of text a mile. But my nights transpired around Johnson's table, where I didn't see Sophia again. Fuseli was there as often as I was; we resumed our wrangling, though perhaps with greater care. He didn't give up his wooing, nor I my refusing him, but a friendship flowered between us, one closer to that of equals. He told me one night that my 'genius and cultivation of mind' roused his curiosity, which was the most Fuseli had ever granted me. How desperate I was for his approval, however determined I was not to show it.

And then everything changed overnight, life as we knew it.

We spilled out of Johnson's house (after staying well later than we should), the pile of us, still laughing and talking over one another, into the sheer light of a midsummer dawn full of exhilarating expectation. The sky was a painterly wash of lavender, the cool air on our faces bracing and pure. Right away, we saw that the streets were full for the early hour, people huddled in pairs or more, leaning toward some person reading to them from one of the morning papers. Hawkers on every corner yelled out – '*Flying Post! Daily Courant! Gazette! Examiner! The World!* By express from Paris Saturday evening!' their voices mingling with the chimes of St. Paul's, the smell of coffee, and coaches rattling by.

We searched our pockets for three halfpence to have a paper of our own. By now Johnson had heard the racket on the street and come out to find us gathered round Darwin, reading as fast as he could, skipping ahead, going back, all of us agog. "'The Comte d'Artois is fled! Messenger dispatched by the

Queen stopped by the populace! The Opera House cleared! The Bastille broken open, all prisoners at liberty!"' We listened with hands on our heads or across our mouths. "'Here, scenes as novel as history ever recorded! Friends long lost again met each other! Captivity regained its freedom and despair found instant consolation! A national revolution with no parallel in the history of the world!'"

We embraced, all of us, one to one, and then together. We stomped our feet, shouted '*Liberté! Fraternité! Egalité!*' till it transformed from a chant to a chorale on the street, everyone joining in. We raised our fists to the newborn sky. Johnson scrambled back upstairs and found a hidden reserve of French champagne we drank straight from the bottle, handing it around to anyone who passed, even the one-eyed beggar and his friend. None of us could believe that we were witness to the first turning, the surest sign that this might usher in a new chapter in the history of mankind, a freedom long imagined but not thought possible – the birth of a new age of rights for all. We laughed, cried, pressed our hands to our hearts, breathless and giddy.

In the midst of that madness compounded by joy, Fuseli came to me, put his hands on my waist, and pulled me close. His lips grazed my cheek as he leaned in to whisper, 'We shall go to Paris, Mary, don't you feel it?'

I felt everything – I feel it even now, that vivid moment – his warm breath on my neck, the strong grip of his fingers at my waist, the music in his voice. 'I feel it, Fuseli. I do.'

The French prisoners were free, and I could not help but feel my own freedom tied to theirs.

At last we retreated to our houses to sleep, but how could

one sleep? Soon we were back at Johnson's table, where we were often in those heady, dizzying days that followed. Johnson, Fuseli, and I would stay up long after everyone had retired, well past the port, the sherry, the return of the cold veal, the shrivelled potatoes, the finger-licking of plates. We plotted that we three would go to Paris together, stay such-and-such place, visit so-and-so, use our contacts and calling cards. We would bear witness. And when Johnson could keep his eyes open no longer, Fuseli and I drew our chairs next to each other, occupying one end of the great oval table, near enough that his knee brushed mine.

'What will become of all the fashionable women of Paris,' he asked me, 'from whom Englishwomen often take their cues?'

'They will have equality. Be citizens. Same as the fruit and vegetable sellers.'

He drained the last drop from his glass. 'I wonder sometimes if there isn't a certain self-disdain in your view of women. If you don't feel excluded in some way.' I looked at him, bemused.

'You, who grew up with nothing,' he went on, 'who suffered being born a girl, with no reward in it for you, no love, no warmth, no tender hand on your face. Would it be so bad to be Sophia Rawlins? I think she quite enjoys being exactly as she is.'

'I want more than a tender hand on my face,' I said.

'Does anyone want more than that, really?'

'Men want power. They *have* power. Over women especially.'

'So women should want power over men?'

'They should have the same power men have.'

'How can they, when you yourself say they aren't governed by reason?'

'I seek a poetics of change. For women *and* men. That joins sense with sensibility. But a sensibility governed by reason.'

'There's no such thing as reason between women and men. You fool yourself.'

'Then what governs you?'

'Sex!' he said. 'Isn't that obvious? The pursuit of it, thrill of it, its pleasures in all possible variations, with pistils and stamens alike, ending with transcendent satisfaction, and then begin again, with pursuit. The world would be a better place, for both men and women, if we just came out with it.'

I looked at the painting looming over his head. Fuseli was a master of light and shadow, but the light was fleeting, ephemeral; it was in the shadows that his true genius lay.

He always offered to drop me home in his carriage, but I remained a proud solitary walker, trundling home between brief stretches of darkness and oil lamps, the occasional clop of horses or call of a night watchman to keep me company, and thoughts swirling in my head. I knew the danger of saying yes to even a carriage ride. Not since Fanny had I felt anything like it. For the first time in years, I wanted someone to touch me.

The glad course of events across the Channel took a turn in October when a starving mob from the markets, mostly women, advanced on the king and queen, invading their apartments at Versailles, demanding bread. We all went to hear my old mentor Price preach at the Meeting House in the Old Jewry soon after. He was in his late sixties now, more frail than I'd seen him, but never with more power in his tremulous voice. 'Behold kingdoms . . . starting from sleep, breaking their fetters, and claiming justice from their oppressors!' He bade us all remember that our country owed its people the same liberties. It was a call for England to throw off its own fetters.

And moved us all greatly.

But when Edmund Burke, that vain, verbose, self-interested climber of a politician, attacked our beloved Price in print, our anger was unleashed. How dare he turn the fight for liberty in France into a warning against mob rule and a breakdown of civilisation that must never darken English shores! How dare he say there can be no new genus, in person or country, since our identity can come only from our past – an unbroken contract between generations across time, as if the Church and the monarchy alone reserved the right to tell us who we are! How dare he defend Marie Antoinette, and not the starving French people! But his greatest sin was his florid fakery; heaping words on words, dodges of rhetoric that I knew to be the most dangerous enemy of truth and justice.

Scores of writers set out to answer Burke, but no one expected me to send my pen darting across the page. I was a lady-author, essayist, reviewer, not a writer. But, like them, I wanted to take Burke head on.

When Johnson caught wind of it, he printed each page as frantically as I wrote it, hoping that my 'Letter to Burke' might be the first.

"'Where are Burke's tears for men taken by violence to fight wars, or people who hang for stealing five pounds?'" Johnson read aloud to the group gathered at dinner, the day we published. "'No, he thinks the poor must respect the property of which they cannot partake and look for justice in the afterlife! His tears are reserved for the downfall of queens!'"

"'In mourning the plumage, he forgot the dying bird!'" read Darwin, from his own copy. 'Nicely done, Wollstonecraft.'

Though we'd agreed it should be printed without my name

on it, my *Vindication of the Rights of Men* made me, among the dinner goers, an overnight philosophical peer. Suddenly I was no Miss or Mrs, just 'Wollstonecraft' to them.

'You've spoken for all of us,' said Johnson, with pride in his eyes, amid clinking glasses and raucous toasts. Fuseli sat back, yet to say a word, though I could feel it stirring inside him.

'The thing I cannot understand,' he said, with an elbow on the table and his temple resting on one finger, his thinking posture, 'well, you write like a man, or something, certainly not like a woman at all. I cannot place it, not according to class or gender. What are you, then, Wollstonecraft?'

I couldn't sleep that night, couldn't think of anything else. What was I, and to what end? I paced, looked out the window at nothing, tried not to think of Fuseli in the arms of his wife, and finally picked up my pen by the small light of my candle, and wrote the biggest thought I could conjure: 'A wild wish has just flown from my heart to my head, and I will not stifle it, though it may excite a horselaugh. I do earnestly wish to see the distinction of sex confounded in society.'

Confounded, ended, debunked. I knew that I'd only said half of what I'd wanted to, that I was ready, finally, to explain to Fuseli – to everyone – what I was, but more, what *all* women could be, if they had the education that men had. If revolution was in the air, why not one that would restore our lost dignity and make us part of the human species as we were meant to be? I would throw down my gauntlet: no, Fuseli, I don't want women to have power over men, but power, at last, over themselves.

I closed myself in my study for days, words tumbling out that had long festered inside me, but now, given light and air and ink, blossomed into fullness. Even when I struggled, I revelled in the glowing colours of my imagination, gleams of sunshine and tranquillity, right there at my desk. How rare it was to feel happy, all by myself. But I was, gloriously so.

I finally sent a batch of pages to Johnson with a note saying I had begun my second, bolder vindication, this one clearer and sharper. He devoured the pages as I sent them; in a month, I'd finished. I told him I wanted my name on it from the very first printing. I'd been told to be silent all my life, and this would be an end on it once and for all: *A Vindication of the Rights of Woman*, by Mary Wollstonecraft. My thoughts, my voice, my words, my name.

Johnson demanded I come to dinner soon after the book appeared to meet his friend Thomas Paine, fresh from America and his own *Rights of Man*, newly bailed out of jail by Johnson, and thinking of leaving for Paris. Paine wanted to meet the 'hyena in petticoats' who had dared challenge Edmund Burke. The guest list included William Godwin, a little-known journalist I'd heard of, but never met, who, according to Johnson, had pestered him for an invitation. A few others, and Fuseli, of course.

We all seemed to arrive straight from our writing desks, heads hot with our own words, parrying for a match if not a duel. I didn't like Godwin on first sight. He was slight, pale, with a high forehead and thinning hair, a long, Roman nose. Whatever mild handsomeness he conveyed was diminished by a mouth that seemed in a perpetual pout. He bristled whenever I opened mine, which I did often, trying to draw out the quiet guest of honour we had all imagined as 'fiery Tom Paine,' who spoke so little we hardly noticed him.

'Mr Paine,' I said. 'I found your "Occasional Letter on

the Female Sex" so to my own thinking, I wished I'd written it myself.'

'But you didn't, did you?' said Godwin, irritated, while Paine finished chewing his bite.

Fuseli jumped into the fray. 'Have you read her new *Vindication*?' he asked Godwin.

'Oh,' said Godwin. 'Was another necessary?'

'Only for the half of all human creatures who've been denied their God-given rights by the other half,' I said.

'God-given? I am more or less an atheist, Miss Wollstonecraft,' said Godwin.

'We just call her "Wollstonecraft,"' said Johnson, trying to create some amity between us.

'You cannot be "more or less" an atheist, Mr Godwin,' I said. 'And don't blame me for taking refuge in a deity, when I despair of finding sincerity or equality here on earth. I've seen enough to know that civilisation, run by men, has utterly failed us.'

'All of us? Or just you?'

'All women. All men.' I was incensed. 'But don't worry, my aim is to redeem us both.'

'I do hope marriage is not in the bargain. It is a tyranny for all parties,' said Godwin.

'Finally something we agree on! "Except tyranny, like Hell, is not easily conquered,"' I said, quoting Paine to the room but aiming daggers at your future father.

'She explodes a whole system of gallantry!' said Johnson.

'That oppresses women!' I said. 'That makes them nothing more than the object of male sexual desire.'

'I'm afraid Godwin still believes the ideal female is a delicate bird that warbles unmolested in its native groves,' said Darwin.

216

'That's it exactly!' I said. 'The problem isn't women, but how men want women to be.'

'Then how are we to know what to do?' Godwin asked.

'You mean, with a woman interested neither in sex nor in men?'

Godwin pulled at his collar and blushed. I felt Fuseli's eyes on us both. As always, he drew strength from disagreement, energy from enmity.

'Our Wollstonecraft is in the business of denying desire, which is the business *I* am in.'

'We all know your business, Fuseli,' said Godwin, dropping his knife and fork with a clank.

'Desire is delusion, leading to disappointment, leading to misery,' I said.

'You see?' said Fuseli. 'A hopeless case.'

'And yet I've never been more full of hope,' I said. 'That my sex too will breathe the invigorating air of freedom that tears down walls and breaches gates. Shouldn't our liberty matter to you too, Mr Godwin?'

Godwin looked flustered and frustrated, searching for an answer. I almost felt sorry for him.

'How much better the world would be,' Darwin intervened to save us, 'if we could accept men and women, and plants too, as equal citizens, with the same feelings and desires – worship the pistils and stamens in all of us, according to Nature's plan.'

'The most divine of all,' said Fuseli, putting a final point on it.

We emerged into a drizzling November night, the others still waiting for carriages, when Godwin and I found ourselves, walkers that we were, aimed in a similar direction.

'I should offer to escort you home, Wollstonecraft, but I fear you'd consider it gallantry.'

'I'm quite capable of watching out for my own welfare,' I said, putting up my hood.

'Well, then, I shall walk this other way.'

As he turned to go, I couldn't help but call after him: 'Why did you look irritated every time I opened my mouth?'

He turned back, and stepped closer. 'I came in hopes of hearing the great Thomas Paine,' he said, 'who never had a chance of opening *his*.'

'Because of me, you mean.'

'You do occupy quite a bit of space.'

'As a woman, you find me opinionated and domineering. If I were a man—'

'You are no Thomas Paine. I don't mean to insult you.'

'Ah, but you have.'

We were nearly shouting over the rain, dripping off my hood, his hat.

'I've read your first *Vindication*. Frankly, I found it dishevelled and rambling.'

'Says a thinker who sights a woman of no importance advancing on his territory.'

'I didn't say you had "no importance." But like you, I'm trying to earn my living by my pen. Hardworking at my own ideas of political justice. Johnson believes in me.'

'Yes, I think Johnson described you as rational to the point of coldness. How I look forward to reading you. Goodnight, Godwin.'

It was my turn to steer away, when he nearly shouted to my back.

'I must say, in the matter of your welfare, that Fuseli is

notorious. I would caution you to stay away.'

I stopped and turned, surprised he'd noticed whatever spark there was between us.

Godwin walked close to me. 'The man is a rake. A seducer. With equality in mind, but not the sort either of us is fighting for.'

'I can take care of myself. I've been at table with him for months—'

'Not everything begins with you, Wollstonecraft, though I do think some things escape your keen attention.'

I stood still, never losing his gaze. 'Do say, Mr Godwin.'

He searched the wet darkness before he spoke. 'You never wonder why Johnson saves a chair for him, sets his plate out, whether he comes or not? Don't you see the look in his eyes when Fuseli arrives, as if the whole room just came alive? And the look in his eyes when he goes?'

I pulled my heavy cloak closer around me, stung. We stood silent under a gas lamp that threw shadows across our faces, the night sky spitting rain. I couldn't bear him telling me what to notice, how to behave, with whom to consort. I was exhausted by being told by men, and women too, what sort of person I was and ought to be. But I hadn't seen it, he was right.

A coach rattled near us, then stopped at our shoulders. The door flung open, and Fuseli – of course, Fuseli – stuck his head out.

'Get in, for God's sake!' he said to us. 'You'll both drown.'

Godwin waited for my answer, but when I said nothing, turned to Fuseli. I could see the sharp line of his proud jaw. 'No, Fuseli,' he said. 'Thank you just the same.'

He looked back at me. They both did. Godwin and Fuseli, awaiting my answer.

Even as I took Fuseli's hand and climbed inside, I looked back over my shoulder to see Godwin turn and walk away. I knew mine was an act of defiance, of hurt feelings, a flash of anger. I couldn't see that my own revolution was just beginning.

I remember it now, little bird, as a sort of watery dream lit by a single chandelier, standing before a large gold-framed mirror in the middle of Fuseli's studio, green walls two stories high, dawn breaching the windows. I am drenched and worn out, but I want him to paint me. I *need* him to paint me. Without a single word between us, he lowers the hood of my cape, unties what ties I have, releases what clasps. I let him slide my wet wool cloak, limp clothes all the way to the floor. Let him dab my body dry with a towel, and drape a long indigo shawl loosely about my shoulders, push my hair from my face. I let him see me.

'You are a thing to behold, Mary Wollstonecraft,' he said, standing some few feet behind me, looking at my visage in the mirror. 'A thing of rare beauty.'

'Why rare?'

'Because your strength *is* your weakness. The part you guard most closely, deny most fiercely, is the part of you that most wants to be free. If you would only surrender to it.'

'Surrender. Is that what you want from me?'

'It's what I want *for* you, Mary,' he told me. 'I have observed you, heard you, felt you, these months we've dined together, and I know that when you part your full, rosy lips, pearls of wisdom and hard-won things spring from your noble head. But the rest of you isn't living at all.'

I stared at my reflection in the mirror. 'I've never been touched by a man,' I said.

'Oh, I will touch you,' he said. 'Here. And here. And here. Then stop, according to my agreement with my wife. But a painting takes time. And we shall take ours.'

We did take our time. Over days and weeks, rolling into months, Fuseli painted me with the same intensity and confidence he brought to everything. He wouldn't let me see the portrait, but I was mesmerised by the sketches and watercolour studies pinned to his walls, sometimes overlaying one another, as if he couldn't draw them fast enough – courtesans, lovers, eavesdroppers, voyeurs – women with high-dressed hair and stiff bows, or in various states of undress; women from behind, from the side, sitting, bending, touching, strolling, engrossed in a book, looking out a window, bare breasts like bright lights, at one with their bodies. He enjoyed saying that females were emotionally flagrant and feckless, but these were drawn in exquisite detail, with honesty and empathy. And now he turned his gaze to me.

We were fiercely alert to each other, and drew ever closer, meeting nearly every day, if not at his studio, he came to my new house in Store Street. We read each other's work, argued over translations, shared what we knew of the dramatic events unfolding in France. Fuseli could be irritable and itchy, but I could tell he feasted, as I did, on our rich conversation. He never kissed me, never once removed his own clothes in the time we spent together, but when I posed for him, he studied the contours of my landscape by slow touch, sometimes with a trailing finger, a soft paintbrush, a feather quill. The back of his knuckles once grazed my breast as he shifted the draping shawl.

I remember people in Lisbon who spoke of the rolling earthquake some thirty years before as if they relived it every day. The undulating ground, a wave, a swell, a peak, and seawater crashing through walls. Sensations like that, more than words, are all I have to describe my awakening to my own trembling being. I had wanted women to choose reason, not romance; friendship, not sex; companionability, not carnal abandon. But here was I, bursting into brilliant bud and new leaf. I was not a delicate flower at all, I never had been, but a tall birch that bowed with the wind, whose leaves shimmered in any light, and shuddered at a breeze as small as a whisper.

'I have to go to Paris,' I said one day, when we met at a coffeehouse to read the latest news. 'If ever there was a time, Fuseli, it's now.'

'You dangerous radical, you.'

'Because I want to turn the world upside down? Shake the rich from their gilded cages, banish despots, and lift the poor?'

'You think the world a much better place than I, Wollstonecraft.' He couldn't help a crooked smile. 'But we shall go to Paris, and see for ourselves.'

Johnson signed on as soon as he heard, and Mrs Fuseli wanted to come. How could I object? I would be with Sophia gladly to have her husband's company every day. I was surprised when she arrived for the journey looking less like Marie Antoinette, and more like me.

'I took you as my inspiration,' she said. 'As you say, "nearer to Nature."'

'Then I'll take it as flattery,' I said.

On that hopeful Tuesday in June, we set out in a carriage for Dover. If we stopped only for refreshment and fresh horses, we would be to port in a half day, waiting at most six hours for a fair breeze and a sailing tide to Calais. We could be in Paris in two days, three at the most. But at our last coaching inn, we found a crowd throbbing with news. The Tuileries Palace had been attacked, the royal family thrown into Temple prison, the Assembly dissolved, and Lafayette driven out of the country. Paris was thrown into confusion and chaos.

'It seems our travelling party is finished, then,' said Fuseli.

'All of us are unnerved, but this is our chance,' I said, trying to salvage it. 'To see it up close. In all its vibrant colours.'

'I think the principal colour is red, and it will spout from the necks of people like us,' he said. 'A French revolution will not tolerate oglers, especially the English variety.'

'Paine is there. He'll protect us.'

'Paine is hailed as a hero for now, but just wait for his fall.' I looked at Sophia, expecting she would side with her husband. She had dared to come, without her usual dripping jewels and high hair. I found her, in her more natural state, even more beautiful than I remembered, but she looked less guarded without her costume, less sure. She rubbed her gloved hands together, looked between her husband and me. We locked eyes as she drew in a breath.

'If Mary thinks it safe to go—'

'I cannot guarantee our safety, Sophia,' I said. 'But I can guarantee a moment that history will never forget. That *we* will never forget.'

She and I looked to Johnson for support, but he traded a defeated look with Fuseli, and shook his head.

'It's not worth our lives, Mary. We should turn back.'

A few days after our return to London, agitated that I hadn't seen Fuseli, I was surprised to find a great canvas wrapped in cloth and tied with twine delivered to my house, along with the folded indigo shawl, and a note: 'Here you are, as you've appeared to me, in waking life and dreams, the goddess I have seen.' My mouth fell open when I pulled away its covering to see myself, as tall as I was in real life, standing with only the long shawl loosely about my shoulders, brocade silk velvet dripping with Venetian fringe, its deep indigo against my ivory skin, the natural rose of my cheeks, autumn hair, bare breasts, round belly, a fierce, loving gaze. Fanny's carnelian ring ablaze on my hand. Close up I could see the peaks and troughs of his brushstrokes – feel the pressure of his fingers, the subtle turn of his wrist – these, his most intimate marks. What had seemed like recklessness on his palette and wildness in style had resolved to unity. Stepping back, I saw a woman on fire, pulsing with force and fury, waiting to make love to the world. She was everything we had argued over, that I had argued against. Desire inchoate, and not one ordinary thing about her. Fuseli had fixed me, incontrovertibly, as a caster of spells, the heroine of an epic tale I was writing myself.

In a fit of voracious gratitude, almost desperation, I sat down to write him, wrote again when I heard nothing back that evening, and after several more attempts through the rest of the week, felt a panic rise inside me. Even his place at Johnson's table sat empty. Not knowing what else to do, I wrote Sophia, in whom I'd sensed an unlikely ally on our aborted journey to Paris. I told her I'd formulated an idea in my head, how we might enact our own revolution, in our own lives. She invited me for tea that afternoon, greeting me in high collar and close sleeves, hardly any make-up, her hair pinned up neatly. We sat opposite each other in their dark turquoise drawing room on a pair of green velvet sofas. Fuseli's paintings governed every wall; creatures of myth and dreams, foreshortened, distorted, exaggerated, dramatic figures thrown into contortions that evoked both terror and the sublime.

'Tell me about your revolution,' she said, pouring champagne instead of tea, and getting right to the point.

'I have no right to your husband's person, I know that. But to his mind alone, I stake some claim.' I took a sip of champagne, willing myself to go on. 'I thought that we might live as the French do, right now. All strictures gone, all rules upended for the cause of liberty.'

'Liberty, you say?'

'Love's very essence is liberty, isn't it?'

'A ménage à trois, then? Is that your purpose?'

'He has abided by your agreement. I can attest. It isn't sex with him that I'm after.'

'Love and sex are little acquainted in this house.'

'My proposal arises from the sincere feeling I have for your husband, for his genius. All I ask is the satisfaction of seeing and conversing with him daily. I don't think I can live without it.'

'You want to live here, with us?'

'Live lightly, not impede or impose. To give him, frankly, the one pleasure he cannot find with you.'

'Has he told you that?'

'He finds you endlessly alluring,' I said.

'But not his equal in mind? Or is it *your* judgment that I am not his equal.'

'I'm not here to judge you.'

'Yes, you are. You find me vain, frivolous, infantile, capricious. One begins to wonder whether you aim less to free women than abolish us altogether, while you play the impoverished writer, forsaking temptations of the world for what you think are higher claims.'

'We would be complete, the three of us. Body, mind, heart. Believe me, Sophia, if I thought my passion criminal, I would conquer it or die in the attempt. Immodesty, in my eyes, is ugliness.'

'How repressively didactic.' She stood, and walked to the window. I remember the swish of her taffeta skirts, a cool pride I'd never seen.

'It was my idea to send you the painting,' she said.

'Your idea?'

'Fuseli hates to let even one go. He wants to keep everything.' She turned and swept her arm across the extravagant exhibit of paintings. 'As you can see.'

'But he could've kept it, if he'd wanted it. I don't desire to look at it myself.'

She folded her arms across her chest and looked at me. 'When Henry and I made our "agreement," as you call it, he told me I could have an affair with anyone I cared to, with one caveat: that I didn't fall in love. I was surprised, because he believes himself incapable of it. I know that he treasures me, in his way, but if he were to love me in the way I wanted, he would give up too much of his power, which is what he seeks most of all. And if I loved someone else, he would lose all of it. As him loving someone else would threaten mine.'

'You said yourself he's incapable of love.'

'*Believes* he's incapable. Resists with all his armaments: wit,

226

reason, cruelty, sex – whatever will defeat it,' she said. 'But only because it terrifies him.'

'You think I terrify him?'

'Being swallowed up by the other, lost, dominated, diminished, that's what frightens him,' she said, fingering the ruffle at her wrist. 'He thinks it the sign of a weak man.'

Sophia came to sit next to me on the sofa, our thighs touching through our dresses. I had seen her voluptuousness in his drawings, in person, but here I felt it, the heat of her.

'We've been together nearly every day. In the most intense, elevated conversation,' I said.

'That is his game, to keep you in his thrall.' She tipped her long neck back to drink the last of her champagne, then rolled the stem in her fingers. 'Henry Fuseli is a conqueror, Miss Wollstonecraft. And he has conquered you.' She set the flute down and turned her face to mine. 'The painting is done. He'll move on now to the next shiny object of his desire.'

'Then why did you send me the painting?'

'Because when I saw it, finished, I knew you were no longer merely an object, someone to be conquered, you were the subject. He has uncovered a deep, dark well of desire in you, and glimpsed your raw power, which is the one thing he respects above all else. And because he *is* a weak man, I could not take the chance . . . that he might be capable of love. I had to remove it from our life. First, the painting. And now you.'

I could feel my chest heave, breath shortening. 'Please, Sophia. I'm begging you.'

'You are banished from our home. From our life.'

I stood abruptly. 'You can't do this to me. Fuseli won't let you.'

'You have the painting to remember him by. I think that was generous of me. But my husband has agreed. He will never see you again.'

Johnson found me in a heap on his doorstep. He sat beside me, offered his kerchief, and let me weep. He seemed to know all, before I said a word.

'You can't possess a river,' he said. 'It always flows away.'

I wiped my eyes. 'You won't believe what I've done,' I said. 'In a fit of pique I ran all the way home, and cut the painting off at the neck, and threw away her body – *my* body. All I have left is my head!'

'Well, at least you're left that!' he said, trying hard not to laugh at the absurdity. We both were.

I put my face in my hand, humiliated. 'Your friend Godwin was right about him. I should have listened.'

'Godwin is right about a good many things, but he doesn't know what's right for you.'

'It's some defect in *me,* Joseph, some compound of weakness and resolution – my wayward heart invents its own misery.' I pounded my curled fist on my knee. 'Why am I made like this? I feel desperate to understand the whole of my existence, some greater purpose or meaning, but here I am wailing like a child who longs for a toy she cannot have.'

'You might grow tired of it as soon as you got it.'

'I think the toy grew tired of me.'

He took my fist gently and uncurled it, slid his slender fingers through mine, and pressed our palms together. 'So you're in a jumble now. You've lost your mind, along with your heart. It happens.'

228

'But never to you?'

'I guard myself too closely. I am a voyeur, Mary, sense desperate for sensibility, which I can only get from keen souls – the rare geniuses – who feel it, and live it, as you and Henry do.'

I had never heard him call Fuseli by his given name, nor utter any name with such tenderness. This, too, Godwin had understood. Johnson held our joined hands to his chest. 'Love was never to be mine,' he said. 'But I wish to be close to it, in all its strange and wondrous variegations, as often as I can.' There was a soft silence between us.

'I know I can be petulant and stubborn, Joseph, but I don't know where I'd be without you,' I said. 'I never had a father *or* a brother. Not really. You are both to me. I love you, as my dearest friend alive.' I wiped my dripping nose. 'But I really don't know what I shall do now.'

'Mary, you're the bravest person I know.' He clutched my hand even harder. 'And yes, they run the guillotine now, day and night. No one knows who will be next. But Paris is waiting for you.'

I closed my eyes, trying to image forth my future. It was a blank to me, but not blackness, little bird, not despair.

I squeezed his hand back, and lifted my gaze to his. 'Neck or nothing, Joseph. I will.'

Mrs B

7th September 1797

Every gleam of hope was seized upon by all. Mary began the day asking after her 'little bird.' Marguerite had gladly consented to visit her each morning at the wet nurse's home nearby. Mary told Fanny to be sure to talk to her, and wiggle her feet, the way she'd done with her own brother Charles, and that one day her little sister would surprise her with a belly laugh, and she would never forget it. Dr Fordyce was often in attendance, watching for signs in the patient, and between bouts of fever or rigours that seemed to settle into a pattern, allowed Mary visitors, a steady stream of them that didn't stop all day. A few friends sat with Mr Godwin in the parlour, pulling in chairs from other rooms, and simply refused to leave until they saw her.

Mrs B helped Mary into presentable bedclothes, brushed her hair and pinned it up loosely, sat her against some pillows, spruced up the posy of love-in-idleness she'd brought up from the garden, and opened the windows to bring more outside in.

She stayed in the room, or the adjoining study, never far, to be attentive to when Mary needed rest. On this she claimed more authority than Fordyce, who granted it to her. As for visitors, Mrs B had more experience than anyone with scenes like these, but she'd never seen a mind so tranquil under an affliction so great. Mary was all kindness and attention, dwelling with anxious fondness on her friends, asking more questions than she answered, but with a wisdom about her condition.

The midwife understood that there's a course to most illnesses, and as many variations as there are people. With childbed fever there might be nausea, vomiting, swelling, soreness in the belly, pains in the head, back, breasts, hips. The tongue, at first moist and white, might become covered in white fur. If it progressed, there would be other things, worse things, but Mrs B didn't fill her head with them – it was only inviting trouble. The patient listened steadily to her friends' advice – orange rinds and Peruvian bark for the bleeding, and a strengthening diet overall: blancmange, flummery, calf's-foot jellies, and hartshorn, as if there was no doubt of her getting well. Mrs B plied her with sips of tea and broth, a few bites of gruel, but Mary had no appetite, much as she wished to have one. The midwife made sure to give her fresh linen cloths dipped in cold vinegar and applied to the bleeding three or four times a day, which seemed to help.

Mary seemed most glad of seeing her old friend Joseph Johnson, who pulled his chair close to her, set a thin book on her table, then put his elbows right on the edge of the bed and leaned in so far that Mrs B thought he might lay his head on the pillow with her. She was accustomed to intimate moments, and didn't mind. The house was used to her now, there was no attempt at privacy. People like her, the midwives and helpers, often grew invisible in the room when big things were afoot. There was no blame in it, just so much activity, it was natural to let lesser things blend in.

She could tell Johnson held a special place for Mary.

'Translations in four languages. I've brought you the German,' he said. 'Your little book has caused quite a stir. Even Fuseli's read it!'

'Fuseli,' she said. 'I thought he wouldn't even speak my name.'

'Oh, your name is on every tongue in the literary world,' said Johnson. 'With near-universal praise.'

'Only "near"?' said Mary, with a wincing smile.

Mrs B took that as her signal that Mary needed to shift position.

'The few who don't admire it simply don't understand it. Their souls are all shrivelled up, and they don't know what to do with such fresh honesty.'

Mrs B helped Mary shift her weight and turn toward him. Johnson wanted to help but didn't know how.

'It's your opinion that matters,' said Mary, when she settled in. 'Well, you and Mrs Blenkinsop.'

Johnson took the midwife in. 'Even got you reading it, have they?'

'Best I can, sir.' She tucked Mary's covers neatly around her. 'I didn't know people could write books like that.'

'That's because they haven't. I don't quite know how she's done it, but it's a new mode altogether.'

'The way she turns feeling into thinking and thinking into feeling—' Mrs B stopped herself. She'd said more than she meant to.

'No, I agree. It captures the mobility of her soul.'

'I've never been outside England myself. But I feel like I have, when I read it.'

'Exactly. Why, I suspect she'll make a fashion of long, solitary, questing journeys. Very romantic. Probably all to the frozen North!'

'Wouldn't that be something?' said Mrs B.

'It's almost as if she travels beyond the bounds of mortality itself.'

'I'm not dead yet!' said Mary with a quiet laugh.

'Oh, I'm such a buffoon,' said Johnson. 'Of course you're still here. Look at you.'

Mary seemed tired, but Mrs B could tell they didn't want to let each other go. Her eyes closed after a while, she drifted off, but Johnson stayed by her side for the longest time, holding her hand in both of his, eyes glistening with tears. When he finally got up to go, he kissed Mary on the forehead, and thanked Mrs B for letting him sit with her.

Fordyce was there after his lunch, when Mary woke with a start, hot cheeks, and a racking cough. She looked wild-eyed and frightened, as if she'd had a terrible dream, or delirium, and couldn't quite catch her breath from it. Her pulse was racing, and she clutched her stomach in pain. He examined her joints, knees and elbows, and found them red and inflamed. Mrs B tried to cool her with a damp cloth, but the fever was coming on fierce.

She was tired of the fight, and fell into a hard sleep.

'It isn't good, Blenkinsop,' said the doctor. 'I don't like it at all.'

'Is she dying, sir?' said Mrs B in her straight-out-with-it way, though she knew the answer already.

'Well, let's not build a coffin just yet, shall we?' Fordyce slumped in a chair, splayed his legs. He worried the cloth on his thighs, that way men have, and studied the patient from six feet away. Finally he filled his big belly with air, and sighed. He wasn't obviously drunk, but contemplative, more than usual.

'I haven't lost a spouse,' he said. 'Lost two sons, though, and that was plenty. George, he was an infant, barely two months. Influenza. But William. He drowned in the Thames. Eleven, he was.'

'I'm sorry, sir.'

'I've two daughters, though, Matilda and Margaret. They look after me, get me through it. Good ones, they are.'

''S right to count blessings. To think what we have and not what we've lost.'

He looked at Mrs B, his hooded eyes filled all the way with tears.

'You never get over it, Mrs Blenkinsop. Not ever.'

He sat for a while, then tottered to his bag, pulling out a small amber bottle. 'Twenty drops of laudanum ought to get her through the night.'

Mrs B shook her head. 'None of that, sir. She won't have it.'

'Well, then. Let's hope for some rest for her. I'll be back in the morning.'

He snapped his bag shut and started to go.

'Will you tell Mr Godwin? Before you leave?'

Fordyce stood on the threshold and considered it. 'We mustn't tell Godwin, not yet. But in the morning, let's start her on a wine diet, shall we? The least we can do is ease her way.'

Mary W

I am broken, little bird, and Paris is broken with me. 'Be my eyes and ears,' said Johnson. But I'm on the outside looking in, or rather, the inside looking out, deep in the Marais, closed up on the sixth floor of 22 rue Meslée, tall shuttered doors and iron-grilled windows, with a cold that consumes me. My hosts, called away unexpectedly, have left me with a surfeit of servants who think it a favour to give me peace, quiet, and not just a room but a whole floor of my own, when what I'm desperate to have is conversation. But what would I do with it? All my fine French phrases fly away, while theirs swirl so fast around me I can't catch them. If I can barely ask for a baguette and some butter, how will I ever form sentences on this great turnabout in human affairs? I know I've sought refuge in another country to heal my wounded heart and lose myself in the grand sweep of history. I tell myself that dreary winter must give way to spring, and if men and women can reimagine the world, why not I reimagine my life?

The day after Christmas, at nine in the morning, I heard a few solemn strokes on the drum and the wheels of a cart. I climbed the stairs to the attic to watch the king pass through eerily empty streets in a hackney coach, on the way to being tried. A throng of guards in blue coats and red collars clustered around to keep would-be rescuers away. The air was so still, as if all Paris held its breath. People flocked to their windows, but all the casements were shut. I can scarcely tell you why, little bird, but tears flowed from my eyes when I saw Louis sitting with more dignity than I expected from him, on his way to a near-certain death sentence.

That night I couldn't dismiss the lively images that had filled my head all that day. And when the true dark descended, bloody hands shook at me, and death in frightful shapes took hold of my imagination. For the first time in my life I couldn't put out the candle for fear of being extinguished myself.

Three weeks later Louis was dead. Again, I dissolved to insensible tears when I heard it. I knew the world would never be the same, a king tried and executed as any ordinary citizen, as he should be. But as soon as his head dropped from the guillotine, it was said, people rushed to plunge their hands into his blood and shout 'Vive la République!' I couldn't help but feel that the turning tide had murder in it, and wondered at what cost in human dignity, this change we sought.

When I finally ventured out, I found a city scarred. Dirty streets, splashing mud, sinkholes between paving stones. Grey everything. The buildings were tall and close together, the streets so narrow I couldn't even see the sky. Taking a walk consisted of pressing my body against a building every few steps to avoid being run over or splashed by a speeding carriage. Pulled-down statues of saints and monarchs left empty pedestals and marble piles. Haunting signs, never removed, warned not to cheer for the now-dead king. The names of shops, streets, and bridges eradicated any tinge of the royal, but no maps of the new city existed.

'Don't speak English on the streets,' said Helen Maria Williams, a London writer who'd preceded me in her move to Paris and invited me for tea. 'You might be a noble in disguise.'

'Do *I* look like a noble?' I said.

'Or an English spy.'

Helen Maria, with her far better French, had quickly become a well-known salonniere in Paris. At Chez Williams, generals, diplomats, and politicians mingled with poets, philosophers, artists, and actors – old and new, French and foreign. It was a heady atmosphere, every conversation charged with a sense of personal danger, even if softened by fancy fabric and fine manners. She was fond of saying that her love for the French Revolution was born of her nature, and that her political creed was entirely an affair of the heart. To understand the general good, she said, one need not possess the wisdom of a philosopher, only the *sensibilité* of a woman.

She had wide blue eyes that took up most of her face, a long, thin nose, a petite slip of a mouth, abundant curls, and dressed like a Greek goddess. It was all the fashion now *not* to be fashionable, to eschew the elaborate silks, satins, and pinched waists of the old regime in favour of light cottons, gauze, and sheer India muslin, high waists and slitted skirts that showed a woman's true form and liberated even her stride. Helen Maria's only jewellery was a double chain of pearls wrapped about her slender neck, a delicate armour. I could have loved her myself.

It was well known that she protected Girondists on the run. We'd all seen them lose ground to the more radical Jacobins, who seemed hungry for everyone's head. Only a few months before, the people of Paris had butchered thousands of prisoners – priests, beggars, prostitutes, royalists, and ex-courtiers – anyone deemed an 'enemy of the Revolution.' Women were raped and men tortured before jeering mobs. But the most indelible image in my mind was that of the Princesse de Lamballe, Marie Antoinette's close friend, rumoured to have been stripped naked, breasts and vulva cut off, and dragged through the streets when she refused to disavow the queen. It was at least true that they cut off her head and mounted it on a pike outside the queen's prison window. The wild cruelty of it, so far beyond the meant-to-be-more-humane guillotine, haunted me. It was natural that English enthusiasts began to have doubts, some turning away from the Revolution in disgust. Eliza and Everina had begged me not to go to Paris, even Johnson had second thoughts, but I was determined to go, and stubborn, as I so often am.

But with *our* king now throwing in against France, all English were the enemy.

'I'm beginning to wonder whether we're guests or prisoners, the brave ones or the fools,' I told Helen Maria, thankful to be sitting in a drawing room where the language, even the gestures, were ones I recognised, with someone who felt like a kindred soul.

'It's hard to be certain of anything,' she said. 'You must know by now that Paris is a nest of gossiping vipers and vile rumourmongers: who's escaped, who's invading, who's planning a coup, who's under arrest? And most important, who's bedding whom.'

I smiled. In a world turned upside down, the old morality reeked of the ancien régime. No one seemed to take marriage vows seriously or thought discretion necessary. Divorce was legal. Love affairs, and the rushing in and out of them, were an apt expression of the moment's purest ideals. And why not? I'd argued for it myself. If people could overcome the tyranny of kings, why not the tyranny of unequal marriage? Sexual liberty and political liberty now went hand in hand. These were lives lived in the open. A revolution in full flower.

'I barely speak the language,' I said. 'How will I know the false reports from the true?'

'Well, don't believe it when they call me a "scribbling trollop" or a Jacobin prophetess with bloody talons.'

'You have my word,' I said.

A shadow crept across her pretty face. 'The one true thing is the hard slice of the guillotine. What's not known is whose head will be next. But not many of our countrymen and women are staying to find out. What about you, Miss Wollstonecraft?'

I clasped my hands in a tight ball. Should I go or stay? I still felt newly arrived in Paris, still believed in bearing witness, held true to the ideals of the Revolution, and hoped it might yet right itself. But I wanted to live.

'The carriages are filled with fleeing Brits,' she said. 'I can get you a place in one, but it's the only spot I know. If you can leave tomorrow.'

I twisted Fanny's ring on my finger. I felt Helen Maria's pure and sensitive heart, her patience while I thought it through. I was a free woman here, but with nothing, and no one, to protect me. But had I ever had anyone to protect me?

'Well,' I said with a false shrug. 'It's natural children do mischief when they meddle with edged tools. We shouldn't be surprised.'

She leaned even closer and put her hand on mine, as if to say, I know you're afraid. We all are.

A servant brought out a bottle of champagne and poured us two glasses. She raised hers to mine. 'If you intend to stay, I will show you a Paris you will love, that will love you back. Here you're free to follow your heart, wherever it takes you. We're all having a bit of the Revolution for ourselves. And you shall have yours.' We clinked our glasses and drank to that.

I didn't tell her that the pain of missing Fuseli was intense and real. I wanted relief but still believed joy impossible for me, in this life, anyway, even if I saw it all around me, couples throwing off social mores, and living for the sake of love alone.

Perhaps out of fear of being hurt and humiliated again, I was suspicious at first of the tall, handsome American, Gilbert Imlay, who appeared in my life like a leading man on the stage. Frontiersman, adventurer, businessman, land speculator, diplomat, writer – he was charming, direct, often light-hearted, sometimes shrewd to the edge of unscrupulousness – almost anything one wanted to see in him. Like that great shape-shifter Zeus, Imlay could be gopher, swan, cloud, or a shower of gold.

It was April, spring finally peeking through, and I felt it all the way to my toes. Tulips in Luxembourg Gardens. The fruits of my French study finally paying off, a feeling that I belonged and was right where I ought to be. We English who'd chosen to stay drew together anxiously, at salons, the theatre, parties, and private dinners, where I was celebrated as author and philosopher, where women and men flocked around, flattering me: I had a charming grace, a fascinating look. I was voluptuous; they admired the way I let my hair fall carelessly out of its pins, the softness of my voice, the sharp blade of my wit. They liked the sound of my muscular name in their mouths: Wollstonecraft.

We were at White's Hotel in the 2nd arrondissement, at a gathering of French, English, and American cosmopolites who considered themselves stalwart citizens of the world, all love of liberty and hatred of kings. Helen Maria was there, people from Paine's circle, others I'd met once or twice at Johnson's table, including the American pamphleteer and poet Joel Barlow and his wife, Ruth. After a toast to the British women authors who'd been friends to the Revolution, I could feel Imlay watch me as I threw about my new French, laughed with my head tossed back, interrupted, argued, said precisely what I thought about everything, to everyone. And when I didn't know how to say what I meant, I said simply 'Oui, oui, oui!'

'Be careful with your "Oui, oui, oui,"' said the mystery man. 'In case you chance to say "Oui" when you don't mean to, *par habitude*.'

It could have been a line straight from Fuseli's mouth, but this man wasn't like him at all. Where Henry was compact, intense, refined, and florid, Imlay was as open as a prairie field, the new country of America personified. Optimism with ambition, openness with raw desire, energy unbound. He was forthright in his flirtations, witty, but unaffected. I guessed him about forty, with thick hair swept back from his tanned forehead and wrinkles around his eyes when he smiled, which he did easily. His face was angular, his complexion ruddy. He had a natural dignity that comes from a love of forests and wide-open spaces. He looked like a man who'd slept on the ground under the stars, eaten fish from rivers, and liked it. He was brawny but graceful, in a simple white shirt, stiff collar, and brown jacket. Some said he fashioned himself after Daniel Boone, but there was a softness in him too.

At first I resisted Imlay's charms, put off by his self-possession, but soon warmed to his poetic descriptions of exotic Kentucky, its rolling fields and farms, an unimaginable expanse of wooded wilderness; an Arcadian dream where strong men and strong women were building new lives as equals in the effort. Freedom, he said, was enthroned in the heart of every citizen, and their only master. We were both friends of the Revolution in France, but feared where it was headed. We agreed the king's death had done little to improve people's lives. Bread was as dear as ever, and they were still poor.

I read Imlay's novel (surreptitiously) over two nights, and found him arguing against the slave trade, the massacre of native tribes, inherited wealth, monarchy. He called marriage 'a state of degradation and misery for women,' and apparently believed, as I did, that all impositions on freedom, including strict divorce laws, were anathema to the liberty of all. Even more, he'd written about a heroine, 'a beauty in tears' victimised by a despotic husband partial to drunken sex. I couldn't help but think of my own father, my sister Eliza, or shake the feeling that I was looking at myself in a mirror. I had never wanted to be a man, but if I ever did, I would have been Imlay down to his boots.

Soon we were tête-à-tête as soon as we came together, only stopping when we parted, and then found it hard to part at all. As spring swelled, we took long walks around Paris, which I now saw like a fairy scene that touched my heart: charming boulevards, elegant gardens, the sweet smell of clustering flowers.

'That first night when I saw you,' he said. 'I secretly made you my singular mission.'

'What, to conquer me?'

'We Americans don't conquer so much as throw off our oppressors, and then make deals in our interests.'

'What about my interests?' I asked.

He laughed and pulled a pink blossom off a tree and smelt it, almost unconsciously, before flicking it into the wind. 'It seems clear you stand for yourself, Miss Wollstonecraft, and value your freedom as much as any man values his.'

'I am not in pursuit of a marriage "deal," as you can imagine, Imlay, but I do believe that mutual affection might be the principal solace of human life. The thing that makes everything else tolerable.'

'Do you speak from experience?' he said.

'Do you?'

He stopped and looked away from me, down the arcade of leafing trees that lined our way, with his hands on his hips. I could see the answer on his face. Gilbert Imlay was blushing.

'Let me just say that I've dabbled in affection, probably exceeding what I should have, but not the mutual sort. Mostly I find there's one person more in love with the other, whose "affection" grinds down all gratification into guilt.'

'I'm guessing *that* person is not you,' I said.

'And I'm guessing it's not you, either.'

My ideas about sex, I knew, were still mostly theoretical. Here was a man who was the furthest thing from it. He was flesh and feeling, and inviting me, directly and without pretence, to share mine with him, as his equal. I was thirty-three years old, on the verge of thirty-four. I felt the pull of Imlay strongly, wanted to believe in him, yet still resisted, maybe because Helen Maria whispered in my ear, 'Be careful of that one, you know, he's got a woman in every port.' And though everyone seemed to adore him, without exception, I took gingerly steps.

Then Tom Paine invited me for dinner at a hotel in the elegant Faubourg Saint-Denis to meet a woman younger than I was – Anne-Josèphe Théroigne de Méricourt – a failed singer-turned-courtesan, turned-militant-and-legend. She had a Jeanne d'Arc sort of beauty, wild, cropped dark hair framing her heart-shaped face, a great crown of white ribbons, and a rose at her breast.

'I've heard that in the march on Versailles,' I said, 'you led the charge in a red riding coat on a black horse, sword in hand and pistols ready.'

'Oh, I'd heard a white riding habit and round-brimmed hat,' she said, with a flashing smile. 'In fact I spent most of the night in bed, depressed, though I did go to the palace next day to watch the royal family removed and marched to Paris. A sobering sight.'

'But Théroigne has a plan to form a legion of Amazons to fight for Paris and the Revolution,' said Paine. 'Don't doubt she'll do it.'

'Women must bear arms, same as men,' she said. 'That's what will make us citizens.'

'I wish men would turn their bayonets into pruning hooks, and give up war altogether,' I said.

'We must compete on their field. They won't give it to us any other way. Deep down, the spectacle of a liberated woman terrifies men. They'd rather make monsters or whores of us all.'

'We want the same thing,' I said. 'But not so we can be more like men. I'd prefer they be more like us, frankly – in our truest form.'

'Are there no "manly" virtues you would want for us?'

'Reason. Moral rightness. Strength, courage. The same as I want for all people. Based on education, not birth or status or title.'

'Don't you believe in heroism?' said Paine, enjoying our parrying with each other.

'I do, but war doesn't teach men heroic virtues. It's right to defend your own country under attack, but most wars are fought for financial gain, and valorise greed. A soldier is trained in cunning and artifice.'

'Exactly how women seduce men,' Théroigne said with a wink.

'Yes. How easily private tyrannies become public ones.' Théroigne leaned forward, her beatific face now fierce. 'But we too wish to gain a civic crown, Wollstonecraft, and the right to die for our liberty, which might be dearer to us than to men, since our sufferings under despots have been greater.'

'But who decides who will die? Those with power.'

'Then let us wrest the power away, by any means. We're in a battle for our lives.'

I was taken with her, as Paine knew I would be, and in the middle of May, insisted that Imlay come with me to see her speak about the rights of women on the Terrasse des Feuillants in the Garden of the Tuileries. I knew he would feel about her as I did.

'Let us raise ourselves to the height of our destinies; let us break our chains!' she yelled to the crowd, in her tight cropped jacket, full skirt, sash, and sword. 'But let us also stop and think how we will wield our power, or else we are lost!'

I turned my head to watch Imlay watch her. Even when he was in profile, all his feelings were on display. He turned to me with a conspiratorial smile, his eyes brimming with excitement. Here was a man not threatened but thrilled by the 'spectacle of a liberated woman.' But when he turned back to watch her, I saw his mouth gape in horror. Market women in red pantaloons and caps, who'd terrorised the streets for weeks, were pushing their way to the front, arms raised, with stones in their fists. The first stone flew over Théroigne's head, the next missed her by a sliver, but then she took a direct hit to the forehead, blood dripping down her nose and into her hair. The women breached the steps, knocking her down. I lost sight of her, but Imlay, taller than I was, could still see.

He grabbed my hand.

'We have to get out of here. Now!'

'There's no one to save her,' I said. 'Is anyone even trying?' But I knew he was right. Most of the crowd seemed to be staying, some shouting, others watching wide-eyed with their hands on their mouths. Imlay steered me through, with as much courtesy as he could, but I could feel the force of his hand, and when some of the crowd started to turn and flee, he stepped up his pace. I was panting and frightened, fearful for Théroigne, whom we were abandoning to her fate.

'Please tell me!' I yelled. 'What were they doing to her?'

'Just hurry, Wollstonecraft. Can you walk faster?'

I tried to keep up with him, holding my skirt with one hand, but I tripped over someone else's feet and nearly went down. I felt Imlay catch me under the arm; he pulled me closer and quickened to a run. When we were finally well clear of the crowd, we found a bench and he sat me down on it. My lungs were fanning, but I couldn't catch my breath. Standing in front of me, as if keeping watch, he wiped his forearm across his brow.

'You're pale as a sheet. Are you all right?'

'I feel dizzy and faint,' I said, with both hands on my hair. 'And I've lost my hat.' I didn't care about the hat, but it made me feel vulnerable.

'Better your hat than your head. Here, put it between your legs.'

He sat beside me as I began to find my breath again, patted my back with touching concern.

'It'll be better soon. Is it better?'

I nodded, but I couldn't get the image out of my mind, Théroigne, so vivid and brave a person I'd met just days ago, standing on the terrace like a wounded child trying to grasp what was happening.

'Deep breaths,' said Imlay.

'What were they doing to her?' I said. 'You have to tell me.'

'Just breathe.'

Finally I sat up. I had to know. He could see it in my eyes.

'They were tearing off her clothes,' he said. I saw his Adam's apple rise and fall in his throat. He gripped his hat in his hand. 'And smashing her skull with stones.'

My chest collapsed. I covered my eyes with my hands, but it didn't take the image away.

'I know,' he said. 'I know.'

'We are lost,' I said. 'She was right.'

I don't remember how long we sat like that, in stunned

silence, me blinking back burning tears. What I do remember, little bird, is the breeze through my hair, how soft it was on my cheeks, delicate and calm. For a moment I couldn't comprehend how those things could live side by side, the awful and the sublime. But in time Imlay peeled away my hands and took them in his. I looked into his sad eyes, and saw that he was as shaken as I was.

That was the day we couldn't be parted, not for anything.

He took me to his apartment in Saint-Germain-des-Prés, up a winding staircase, and into a series of rooms with warm parquet floors, all the walls, doors, even shutters painted a perfect robin's-egg blue. It had begun to rain. Imlay lit a candelabra, took my hand, and led me to his bed. We fell into it wordlessly, but with complete understanding. We both wanted, needed, an act of love to erase the hate we'd just witnessed, still raw in our minds. There was no desperation in it (that would come later), but an abiding kindness between us. His eyes glimmered with sympathy, his kisses were softer than soft. Imlay was at ease in his body, and he made me at ease in mine. Together we made ourselves a place of safety.

We were soon tangled in bed linens, both spent, my hair spilled across the pillow, our skin moist with sweat. I reached my hand to the dappled light from the curtained window. He pressed his palm to mine, lined our fingers edge to edge. The carnelian stone in my ring seemed lit from within. Imlay spun it round on my finger.

'From a former lover?'

'You, the jealous sort?'

'The interested sort,' he said, and asked with his eyes if he could slip the ring off my finger. I let him do it, let him try it on, but it only went as far as his first knuckle.

'You can't have it,' I said, turning toward him. 'It's all I have left.'

'Oh,' he said, with a crease in his brow. 'Dead, then?'

'Yes.'

'I'm sorry.' He laid his head on the pillow to face mine. Except for two ravines from his cheek to his jaw where he smiled, his skin was taut and burnished by sun, the most perfect golden brown. His strong chin sprouted flecks of brown and white.

I felt the indentation the ring had left at the base of my finger, studied the thin circle of white skin. 'Strange. I haven't had it off since that day.'

He replaced the ring with a light touch. 'You must have loved him very much.'

'Her,' I said. 'I loved her. Very much.' Fanny still, after all this time, made tears fall from my eyes. Imlay caught one on his finger, and put it on his tongue.

'Hmm. Salt,' he said. 'I guess you're human after all.'

'What else would I be?'

'I don't know, Mary. I've never met a human quite like you.' It undid my proud heart to hear him call me by my given name. All the shame of loving, unloved, all my agony, I forgot. Within two weeks I was Imlay's 'dear girl.' When I chanced to catch myself in a mirror, I could see a lustre in my eyes, my own cheeks the colour of rose petals, and just as smooth. I heard cheerfulness in my voice, and felt a kind of universal love of everyone. Helen Maria told me my smile was bewitching, and if I wasn't careful, I'd win every heart and soul down to the last man or woman in Paris.

A Frenchwoman who'd read my second *Vindication* and

wanted to impress me told me she thought love affairs silly and demeaning for both parties, not worth the effort, and certainly not the drama that inevitably ensued. How could I tell her that I now disavowed myself? Fuseli was right after all. Passionate sex was an elemental ingredient of being human. But it was the union of two hearts, the joining of love with lovemaking, that mattered. At last I was part of the Revolution, an adventurer with Imlay in building a relationship between a man and woman, a love affair between equals. Where Fuseli was the tinder and spark, Imlay was my raging fire.

'Tant pis pour vous,' I said to the Frenchwoman. Too bad for you.

When eighty thousand Parisians marched at the end of May to protest the price of bread, they demanded the moderates be kicked out and the Jacobins take over. Many of our friends faced arrest; it was announced that all resident aliens had to chalk their names on their doors. I knew my hosts would be accused of harbouring me, so installed myself in a small house three miles out of Paris, in Neuilly, where I might escape being spied upon.

The cottage was snug, with thick stucco walls, a stone hearth, low beamed ceilings. It was furnished, but I bought myself a simple walnut writing desk, where I read and wrote during the day. In the afternoons I took long walks in nearby forests and fields, revelling in Nature and breathing its cleansing air. My principal company was an old gardener, who wanted to do everything for me, even make my bed and bring me grapes – the best ones he saved for me. He warned me against the brigands and vagabonds who hid in the woods, but I felt untouchable.

Imlay was my night visitor. I would meet him at the gates of the city as soon as the sun started down, both of us full of hungry kisses. Every evening was a celebration of our closeness. We enacted our ritual, in all its varieties, and then with a candle, a plate of grapes, and rarely a stitch of clothes between us, quizzed each other about near everything. Sometimes all the way to morning.

'Surely, we can find something to disagree about,' he said, pulling me close.

'Well, I've had an anonymous letter warning me that you're some sort of spy or other, and that I should steer clear. Imlay's nothing but trouble, was the message. Though they didn't say exactly which side you're on.'

'There are so many to choose from.'

I laughed and pulled one of his books off the table by my bed. 'It's said that you couldn't possibly have written this, Mr Imlay, or a novel to boot, and that they are merely a cover for more nefarious activities.' I flicked the pages in his face, which made him laugh too. He took the book and read the title page, pretending it was the first time:

'*A Topographical Description of the Western Territory of North America, Containing a Succinct Account of Its Climate, Natural History, Population, Agriculture, Manners and Customs*, What a colossal achievement!'

'To my point,' I said.

'Yes. How could one man possibly have accomplished so much, and in only one book?'

'This is one of my favourite passages,' I said, taking it from his hand and turning to a page I'd marked, 'which ought to be familiar to – whoever wrote it.'

He crossed his arms under his head and lay back to listen.

'"Here an eternal verdure reigns,"' I read, '"and the brilliant sun pierces through the azure heavens—"'

'Soul of a poet,' he said. 'Couldn't possibly be me.'

'"Flowers full and perfect, with all the variegated charms which colour and nature can produce, decorate the smiling groves—"'

'He's very good,' said Imlay. 'Do go on.'

'"Soft zephyrs gently breathe and the air gives a voluptuous glow of health and vigour that ravishes the intoxicated senses— "'

I stopped, because what had begun as a joke between us, these written words, now moved me greatly. Imlay turned his head to look at me. I found it hard to go on.

'And the sweet songsters of the forests,' he recited from memory, 'warble their tender notes in unison with love and nature.'

I was speechless. Not because I doubted him, I didn't. But because he was gorgeous to me in that moment, a revelation. I had never met a human quite like *him*.

'I love you, Mary. I don't want to be without you. When all this madness is done here, I want us to be together, in America. To build a life there. Our life there.'

My happiness was beyond anything I'd dared imagine. We had long, quiet evenings, read aloud to each other, forged plans for a simple cottage with a garden on the banks of the Ohio River, where we would write and study, argue for our causes. We slept skin to skin.

Then one day he wrote me, apologising that he couldn't come that night, with business to attend to early the next day.

How quickly despair fills every cranny of doubt, little bird. They were old feelings, I knew, but so near to my surface that I couldn't keep them down. Trying to flee my fears, which I knew to be irrational, I walked eleven miles the next day to Versailles, never having seen it with my own eyes. It seemed important to the book I was writing for Johnson, important as a human being telling the tale.

The day was warm, with grey tufted clouds dulling the light. I was surprised to find myself the only person in the deserted palace, walking alone through its grand salons, one for war, one for peace, the Galerie des Glaces with its arcaded mirrors facing the windows that looked out on the gardens. The fountains were dry. Grass choked everything. Flowers spilled over their weed-ridden beds. Hedges that had been tamed and coerced into grotesque shapes to please the human eye seemed to displease Nature, which now made a mockery of them. But stranger still was to stroll the enfilade of the king's and queen's separate apartments, seven rooms each, distinguished by the colour of their flocked wallpaper and matching damask drapes, blue, then green, then gold, then salmon, and on and on, with framed portraits, and paintings on the ceilings of the Roman gods, male for him, female for her. A thick layer of dust sat on the gilded furniture, the beds closed up in their heavy curtains. The air was chill, with dampness stealing inside. Moss and mould crept over the window frames.

It was twenty times a Mitchelstown, a hundred times as sad.

'You don't know the pleasure it gives me imagining the day when we can live together,' I told Imlay the next evening when he met me at the gates, restoring my faith. 'And how many plans I have, thinking of our cosy cottage, simple garden, why, even our chickens will be convivial.'

He had a pained look on his face.

'What have I said?'

'It'll take time, Mary. And money. Lots of money. I've a scheme for it, but you must be patient.'

'Everyone always tells me to be patient. Patience be damned! My heart's found peace in you, and hope in our plan.'

He took my hand when I reached for his, but the rest of his body went rigid. 'Can't that be enough? For now? You're so quick to feel and say everything. I can hardly keep up sometimes.'

I felt a shiver in my heart, a fleeting sense that I would lose him. I knew I couldn't bear it. 'Of course. Your dear girl will wait. I promise.'

He kissed my forehead and retired to bed alone.

I vowed to myself not to press him, knowing my ardour might drive him away. I was terrified to need him as much as I did, and to think that he didn't need me. How could we be equals if our feelings were not the same, if the experience of our union did not equate one to the other? And when his visits to Neuilly lessened, he claimed to be all consumed by his new business scheme, a familiar melancholy was my companion instead. He asked me to give him time, to believe in him, to try to control my feelings, but it was a gargantuan effort.

One evening I went to our meeting place at the gate, but he didn't come, nor had he written to say he wouldn't. I fretted all night, woke early, and took my chances going inside the city gates to find him. The rain ran almost like rivers in the streets. Wet all over and frantic, I didn't realise until too late that I'd cut near the Place de la Révolution, where executions proceeded daily, in front of a wild, ogling mob. I found myself in front of the Cabaret de la Guillotine. People streamed past me, some with picnic baskets despite the squall. Hawkers sold blade-and-timber souvenirs, people passed out programs with the names of that day's victims. I'd stumbled into a ghastly carnival scene that only intensified my panic. I looked down to see my boots awash in blood, a river of its own, all the way from its macabre source.

Imlay looked confused coming out of his door at Saint-Germain to find me, sopping wet and in shock. But he pulled me inside, took me into his arms, hard.

'Paine's been arrested,' he said. 'Helen Maria's gone into hiding.'

'Oh God, Imlay.'

'We have to get you away from here, Mary. Out of France if possible.'

'I don't want to leave. My book isn't done. And I don't want to leave you.'

He rested his chin on the top of my head, his strong arms crossed on my back. I could sense him thinking it through, feel him nod, the way he did when concocting a plan. I could feel his lungs fill up against my chest.

'Here's what we'll do,' he said. 'I'll register you at the American Embassy. As my wife.'

'As Mary Imlay?'

'It won't be a real marriage. You won't give up your legal rights, nor I mine. But at least you'll be safe.'

How quick I was to give away my name, little bird, to save my neck. We would keep our dignity, not sacrifice our independence. I would live according to my philosophy, and he to his – that's what I told myself. But I can't deny the powerful temptation, then, to let Gilbert Imlay seal our bond, more sacred to me than any legal marriage could be, by putting pen to paper and making his name mine.

By the end of summer we were living together at Saint-Germain. Imlay founded a trading company with Joel Barlow to seize opportunities around the English embargo on French trade. America would be only too glad to supply soap, wheat, whatever was needed, and Imlay was uniquely positioned to make it happen. Though his days were filled with 'minding the main chance,' we passed the evenings by candlelight in our cosy blue nest of rooms. We took supper, read aloud to each other, had long conversations about the future, ours so seemingly tied to that of France. A thousand pounds, he said, was what was needed to finance our American dream. It didn't seem right to me that our simple farm should cost so much, but he felt energised and I, cherished. Our hearts, at least, were aimed in the same direction.

When he announced that he had to go to Le Havre for a while, more than a hundred miles away, I tried not to show my trepidation. His company would focus largely on Sweden and Norway, which were more than willing to take Bourbon silver off French hands in exchange for legal currency. We'd be very rich, he said when he hugged me goodbye outside his waiting carriage, and very soon. And then we would sail to America.

In September I suspected I was pregnant; by October I knew it. I relished the idea of becoming a mother, and Imlay seemed delighted by the news, vowing to return to Paris as soon as he could. He made me promise to watch over myself, and our child-to-be. I overflowed with tenderness toward him, and toward myself. Our child was the embodiment of true love and the revolutionary values we held most dear: trust, loyalty, equality. Except for Imlay's absence, my life circled round and became whole, my happiness complete.

Paris, meanwhile, was in chaos, the Revolution falling to tragic pieces. I watched secret police kick in doors, searching for the remaining Brits, arresting them in public. Imprisoned Frenchmen and women we knew, Girondists all of them, prepared to feed the guillotine with their necks. In mid-October the Jacobins executed Marie Antoinette. She'd been governed by 'uterine furies,' they claimed, and deserved what she got. It was shocking to hear them argue that the new France must be more like ancient Rome: men would make the laws, women should obey them, each sex in its rightful place. No divorce, no inheritance, no legal representation, no form of protest would be allowed for women. Even statues of Lady Liberty were felled for the more masculine Justice.

While I felt an unstoppable life force fluttering inside me, it seemed that France was dooming women, and daring its own demise.

Imlay didn't come and didn't come. His letters were sweet but impatient. Why did I press him? Why did I doubt his plan? Question his ambition? He never doubted mine. And then came word that Helen Maria had been arrested. I couldn't imagine her being carted off to a jail cell, and went to visit her as soon as they allowed it. She put on a brave face, at first, as she would.

'Women make the best prisoners, just as they will the best citizens,' she said. 'There's a true spirit of fraternity here, or sorority – acts of care and compassion among us – why, we cheer up even the gloom of a prison!'

I put my hand on hers, as she'd done for me when we first met in her drawing room. Tears pooled in her eyes.

'But I'm terrified, Mary,' she said, cupping her other hand around her slender neck. 'At night I feel the blade quivering over my head and can't sleep a wink.'

I rubbed my thumb across her knuckles.

'I was cocky,' she said. 'I thought by the sheer exuberance of our humanity, there'd be no stopping the world we could make together. But brute force has defeated sentiment, and the lust for power triumphed over reason.' She bowed her head and shook it. 'I meant to be the spectatrice, not the spectacle itself. Now I lie awake wondering if I can be one of the bold ones who dance my way up the steps to the guillotine, sing a song, recite my principles, or just tell them to go to hell. Mostly I think I'll simply weep for my life.'

'Imlay will think of some way to save you, Helen Maria, I know he will. He always has a scheme. And knows people on all sides.'

'That he does,' she said, slipping her hand from mine. 'But I learnt some time ago never to wait for Imlay.'

'I don't know what you mean,' I said. 'He's on the same side we are. For the cause of good.'

'I think the one thing clear to most everyone but you is that Gilbert Imlay is for the cause of Gilbert Imlay.' I didn't know what to say.

'Do not wait for him,' she repeated with greater force, and a sympathetic glance at my protruding belly, which I made no effort to hide. 'I know you're in love with him. But don't make the mistake, as many have, of imagining your passion singular. I've been violently in love with him myself.'

When I walked out into the open air, I threw up into an overgrown bush. How could she not have told me, or he? I knew there'd been other women in his past, but I believed his past well behind him, and far away. Here it was in my face; an omission that felt like a lie, that began to feel like a trail of them.

My letters to him got longer, his terse and less frequent. I started mine trying to be light, and ended weeping on the page. I asked why he hadn't told me about his affair with Helen Maria. He reassured me that it was long over, that he'd never lied about his past, and he loved *me* now, like a goddess. But my mind made monsters to taunt me. 'My head aches, my heart is heavy; my happiness depends wholly on you,' I wrote to him. I thought we'd made a paradise together, but now our world seemed like that unweeded garden at Versailles, choked by everything.

My spirits rose again when Imlay invited me to Le Havre. I packed my things quickly before he could change his mind. Helen Maria, who'd just been freed from prison and was plotting her own escape from the city, begged me to burn my half-written book on the Revolution – sure that if discovered, the pages would land me in prison, pregnant or not. I couldn't bring myself to do it; the work mattered too much. Not just to Johnson and me, but to all the curious world that was watching the contortions of the Revolution and holding its breath. I felt renewed by Imlay's wanting me again, but I wouldn't give up my work to be with him, or him for my work, and so, willing to risk my life for all of it, swept past the guards at the gates with my manuscript hidden under my skirts, pretending not to be terrified.

I hated Le Havre, but was glad to be with Imlay again. It seemed everyone there had come to make their fortune, crooked or not, and he was no different with deals instead of ideals the currency of the town, densely packed against a high seawall. I felt confined and claustrophobic. I couldn't get a Parisian newspaper, and had left most of my books behind, so determined to finish my own book before the baby came. Imlay had rented us a large house with a view of the sea. He liked to watch the ships go out, rising and falling on the waves. I envied the seagulls the smooth glide of their open wings. I decided to embrace his trading venture, do what I could to support him, and try not to ruffle his moods. Imlay seemed content to have me in his bed again, which I took as happiness enough.

I took a walk every day, and worked more intently than I had for a long time. Shopped for groceries, made meals, ordered fabric from Paris to make baby clothes, altered my own clothes to fit me. When Imlay was away, I might leave him a leg of lamb smoking on the board to lard his ribs when he returned home. I found linens for his shirts in Le Havre, and heard myself using 'us' more than 'I,' a matrimonial parlance that surprised me. I told myself that I'd succeeded in negotiating a domestic partnership without clogging my soul by promising obedience. The book began to take shape. Imlay read what I was writing over my shoulder and heartily approved.

In May I gave birth to your sister, an experience so exhilarating, I told Imlay I felt like I'd scaled the highest peak in the Swiss Alps, and breathless with the beauty of it, wanted to go again as soon as possible. I had only the help of a nurse who was convinced mother and baby would die without a doctor in attendance, and was mortified I wouldn't stay in bed for more than a day after, insisting on going down for dinner the next night. But, trusting my own body, I found labour the most natural thing in the world – not smooth work but a triumph, without any terror in it. Imlay and I marvelled at our newborn daughter, sometimes gazing at her for hours, only surrendering her to the other's arms. Those first weeks he doted on me with constant and gentle attention. Baby Fanny, named for my dearest friend, went everywhere with us, out to dinner, down to watch the ships come in, to the market. She took only my milk, and Imlay loved to watch her nurse at my breast, 'so manfully,' he said, 'I reckon she'll write the second *Rights of Woman*.'

But we soon lost him to the waterfront for long hours, negotiating with sailors and captains helping him skirt the English embargo and escape the notice of French authorities. I knew he and Barlow were desperate to capitalise on the steep rise in prices in France, and the brisk market for illegal goods. When Robespierre prohibited the French from owning luxury items, I came home one day to find a trove of Bourbon-crested silver platters, candelabras, and tea sets splayed and stacked across our dining table. They held no allure for me as objects, but it was impossible not to think of the real people they'd been taken from, not only aristocrats but émigrés, even victims of the guillotine. It could have been people we knew. Imlay bristled when I brought it up. Why did I see the wrong in things instead of what could be right?

He brought a young Norwegian captain from a prominent shipping family, Peder Ellefsen, to stay with us, while he and Barlow bought a French three-master for their scheme. Ellefsen was small built but strong. Despite his leathering face – too old for such a young man – he had a dimpled smile, a mop of yellow hair, and clear blue eyes. He loved to listen to Imlay's tales of Kentucky, enthralled as he was with the American wilderness and the legendary Daniel Boone, whose autobiography he'd read. He told Imlay, in such a soft voice for a sea captain, 'You remind me of Boone. I imagine him just like you.' Imlay said that he'd met him, just once, but that Boone was his hero too.

I knew that our future in America, maybe even bringing Eliza and Everina with us, depended on the ship setting sail with the silver on it, landing safely in Norway, and fetching a fair price. Still, I wanted no part in their plot. It was a dangerous business. I couldn't condone it, except as a way to feed the starving people of France. But when an anxious Imlay was called away to Paris the day before the ship was to sail – some knavery by his underlings, he said – he asked me to see the ship off, and I agreed.

From our house we had often marvelled at ships sailing in and out of harbour, but close up to the *Maria and Margarethe*, hearing the wind snap her great sails, and the groaning creak of that whalelike hull, was another species of experience. A ship was a leap of imagination, an expansion of human possibility. This one bore our shared hopes in her pregnant belly. I was to give Ellefsen his last orders, and I did.

Soon after Imlay left, Robespierre fell victim to his own blade and timber, and at last the Terror was done. France breathed a heavy sigh of relief; we all did. I wanted to be in Paris with Imlay, not alone in a place I didn't like, with the sole care of our child. Le Havre only made sense if he was with us. I felt abandoned one day, talked myself out of it the next, and was back to it that night, as soon as the sky pitched to dark. I wrote long, loving letters telling him that all I wanted was for the three of us to be together, and to be revived and cherished by his honest love, but they soon devolved to recriminations.

He responded with silence, all my insecurities reinvigorated. And then one day, without warning, he came home. He greeted us warmly, held his 'Fannikin' close, apologised for being away, and made love to me as he always had. But by next morning he was tepid to both of us. He seemed agitated, and bridled when I asked him if he'd come to take us back to Paris with him.

'I have to go to London,' he said, setting his teacup on his saucer with a spilling clang.

'London? We'll go there with you, then.'

'There's been some bad business, Mary. The knavery I suspected. I've lost money.'

'I know it's demanding, a new baby, but she's the best baby, and will travel well—'

'I'll take care of you and Fanny while I'm gone. Just tell me what you need.'

I sat across from him, stirred a splash of milk into my tea, something to occupy my own shaky hands. 'It wounds me when you conceal yourself,' I said. 'I ought to be the one person you can say anything to, without disguise.'

'I need to be in London when the English lift the embargo, make contacts with the right merchants. It's an opportunity I cannot miss.'

'We don't need all the money you think we do.'

'I can't have a wife and child in tow.'

'I'm not your wife,' I said, but the words were bitter on my tongue.

'No,' he said, icy, draining his cup. 'But I intend to honour my commitments.'

I reached for his hand across the table. He took mine, but his fingers were limp. 'I don't want you to be with us out of a sense of duty. If you don't love me as passionately as I do you, you shouldn't be with me at all.'

He loosed his hand from mine. 'Don't talk like that. You sound desperate.'

'Should I be?'

He looked out the window toward the churning sea. 'I have serious business to conduct. Why do you take that as an insult to our love?'

'If you could let go of your obsession with making a fortune, we could be happy. I thought you were a man of ideas and imagination—'

'I'm a man of commerce as well, Mary. Why can't you love me as I am?'

When Imlay sailed for London, I took Fanny back to Paris, hoping it would feel like home. The city was reopening, to itself and the world, but my own life grew small. Some friends were dead, others had escaped the country, Helen Maria in Switzerland, the Barlows in Hamburg, Paine still languishing in jail. Fanny was a wonder, and I adored motherhood, but I couldn't take her everywhere. With no help, and hardly any means, I had to refuse invitations, stopped reading and writing, did everything myself. The apartment in Saint-Germain felt empty without Imlay, and since I'd refused his offer of money, out of pride and principle, I couldn't stay there on my own, and didn't want to.

I took new lodgings with a sweet German family. The father was always sunny, helped with the children, doted on his hardworking wife. They seemed to rest in each other's company, laugh and tell stories, finish each other's sentences, as if they spoke a language invented just for them. It was the life I wanted with Imlay. If he could only see them as I did; the perfect happiness they'd made without any fortune to speak of, except the love they had for each other – I knew he would return to us.

I had argued, in the book I'd just finished, that if men could learn to value familial love more than power, money, and land, despotism would die a natural death. Imlay had agreed with all of it. I wondered if it was only theoretical to him, while for me there was now no difference between the public and private, home and history. Back and forth in letters, we each argued our case.

When I finally relented and accepted his offer of support, I found Marguerite first thing. She was young and willing, with black hair, a fair heart-shaped face, and dark, shining eyes. She became devoted to Fanny, and vice versa, and eager to help with anything. I could write again, study my French, take walks, shop alone, and go to soirées and salons, where I was greeted as 'Mrs Imlay,' which made me feel that it was true enough, in the way I needed it then. I didn't want to be legally bound, but the solace of his company, the thrill of his physical being, I couldn't live without. I would rather die than have him fall in love with someone else, as I often convinced myself he had, and I thought sometimes he hinted at. I made it a point to meet new people, and felt my old charms returning. Men were drawn to me, but I only taunted Imlay with them, and was faithful.

That winter was the coldest anyone could remember. Bread was dearer than ever, meat scarce, hardly a vegetable to be found. People burned their furniture for warmth. My spirits sank, and not even Fanny's sweet temper could revive them. A virulent cold took hold of my lungs, and I worried I might die and leave her alone in the world without any parent at all. In one of my darkest nights, I wrote Imlay that if anything happened to me, he must promise that Fanny would stay in France, with the German family, because she would be freer there, and feel loved.

I had a letter from him right away: 'Business alone has kept me from you. Come to any port, and I will fly down to my two dear girls with a heart all their own!' What had my imagination done to me? How sick was my mind that I let myself doubt him so thoroughly? I felt confused and hopeful all at once. England held no appeal for me, not any more. But Imlay was there, and he was calling us to him.

We sailed for England in April, with Marguerite so violently seasick, and Fanny restless and mad, that I felt I had to hold them both together for the long passage. Here I was again on choppy seas, heading for an uncertain future, to a country I no longer loved. The only thing that got me through was a vision of Imlay spotting me in the crowd coming off the ship, pushing his way through, and pulling me into his arms.

But he wasn't there to meet us. The disappointment was crushing, but I didn't show it. I was the one leading the charge for our small brigade, and couldn't give up, not yet. We'd left everything behind; all our hopes resided in him. I dashed off a note and booked a coach to London the next day. The man who did greet us, though he looked like Imlay in every respect, seemed more like a polite stranger. There were no kisses, no long embrace. I wanted to grab his lapels and shake him but instead held my tongue.

266

We shared a house in Charlotte Street, but it was cold. Shared meals, but they were distant. Shared a bed, but Imlay slept on the far shore, and never pressed me to his heart the way I'd hoped, the way he had before Fanny was born.

I had no energy for anything. Not for a walk, for reading or writing, not even the simplest household chore. I felt the way I had when my mother turned away from me, when Father hanged darling Betsy from my favourite tree – some mix of anger, desperation, grief – even worse when Fanny took her carnelian ring from her own finger and closed it in my palm, then took her last breath and left me for ever. The way I felt when Fuseli rejected me, refused to see or talk to me, despite how I'd opened myself to him. And now this.

I refused all company, even Johnson, who came nearly every day only to be turned away. He wrote me letters, but I didn't answer. Marguerite tried to force me to eat, but it was a struggle to lift my head. She laid clothes out for me; some days I dressed in them, but sloppily. Mostly I wept, and wept some more. Sweet Fannikin, not yet one, had just learnt to walk. She would come to me with her doll to coax me to play, but my limbs were heavy and my spirit weak. She put the doll in the crook of my arm, stood very close, and kissed my cheek. My sorrow had made a child of *me,* and it was my young daughter, your sister, who tried to comfort me. I was conscious of feeling nothing but the merest sense of being alive. If the house had been burning, I would have thought it too much effort to rise. I was not well enough to mother anyone, little bird, not strong enough to leave Imlay and start again. The world, and Fanny most of all, would be better off without me.

Mrs B

8th September 1797

As Mrs B fussed about, fulfilling her morning duties – check the bedpan, replace the water in the basin, dip clean linens in cold vinegar – she turned to find Mary awake, staring out the wide-open window, very still, the way she'd been that first day, with a faraway look. The midwife turned to close up the panes.

'Must've left it open all night. Didn't even notice.'

'Leave it. Please. It's like sleeping outdoors.'

Mary'd had a fever in the wee hours, Mrs B remembered. The rounds of hot and cold hardly seemed separate anymore. It wasn't easy to recall which was which, and when. She was happy to leave the window open now. The room smelt of sickness; it was hard to be rid of it. And the autumn morning was apple ripe, mists clinging to the ground, slowly warmed away by the soft September sun. Mrs B felt Mary's forehead, her cheeks. They were damp but cool.

Mary put her slender hand on top of the midwife's, and

searched her tired green eyes. 'Am I dying, Mrs B?'

Mrs B took Mary's thin wrist in her fingers, and found her pulse, slow and faint. 'It's not for me to say,' she said.

She didn't believe in hiding things from patients or their families, but she believed in not giving up hope where there was any at all to be had.

'What about Fordyce?' said Mary. 'What does he say?'

The midwife sat Mary up slowly so she could pat the pillows behind her, give them more air. 'Dr. Fordyce recommends a wine diet. He believes it might be of some benefit.'

'Of course he does,' said Mary with a half smile. 'But I'm not much of a drinker.'

Mrs B laid her gently back against the pillows and returned the smile, unguarded. 'Shall we brush those teeth, then?'

Mary nodded. Mrs B didn't have her usual salt and charcoal, but it would've been too much anyway. She used water and a rough cloth instead, taking her time. Mary's tongue was hard and thick; the white coating had turned to brown fur that stuck to the edges of her teeth. The midwife cleaned each one as best she could.

There was no order to dying, but there were signs.

'What an irony it would be, wouldn't it?' said Mary. 'Me, finally content.'

Mrs B didn't answer. Didn't think it needed answering. But she felt relieved when Marguerite knocked on the door, bringing little Fanny in with her. No matter how sallow Mary's cheeks, her eyes sparkled at the sight of her girl. 'Bonjour, Maman!'

'Bonjour, ma chérie!' said Mary, patting the bed.

Marguerite lifted her onto it. Fanny sat cross-legged beside her mother.

'Have you seen your little sister today?'

'Yes. And we took flowers from the garden. For the nice woman who looks after her.'

'I'm so glad you think she's nice, Fannikin.'

'She gives me sweets.'

Mary shot a look at Marguerite.

'I took them to her as a gift. Some caramels, hopjes, from my Dutch cousin. I just wanted to thank her for looking after little Mary.'

'How thoughtful, Marguerite. Thank you.'

'You'd like her. She's good-hearted and gentle, sings songs while she suckles. A Scottish girl.' She turned to the midwife. 'And a redhead! You'd like her too, Mrs B.'

'What about my little bird?' said Mary, her voice catching in her throat. 'How is she today?'

'Très, très bien,' said Marguerite.

'She's getting fat, Mama! Even her tiny feet.'

'Isn't that lovely,' said Mary, stroking Fanny's hair.

Desperate for her mother's touch, Fanny leaned into the crook of Mary's arm, resting her small head on her shoulder. She made spiders with her fingers, crawling them in the air.

'Today, Mama, we found a spider in the kitchen, but we didn't kill it. We put it outside, because I told Marguerite that you like spiders, and wouldn't want it to die.'

'I admire them more than I like them. But I'm glad you saved its life.'

After a moment, and without any warning, Fanny looked up into her mother's face and said, matter-of-factly, 'Are you going to die, Mama?'

Mary looked down at Fanny, still nestled against her. How

keen children were. Fanny, with her natural curiosity, always wanted to know everything, and Mary encouraged it. Why should now be any different? But the whole room held its breath.

'I am, sweet Fanny. I am.'

Marguerite all but gasped, and had to turn away. Mrs B kept her gaze steady on mother and child. Just like that, it was said out loud, and done with.

'But does that mean we can't play any more?' said Fanny.

'There will be so much playing, Fannikin. You have Papa, and Marguerite, and your sister will want to play hoops with you sooner than you think, and you'll have to teach her, of course, and then you'll make friends at school, and hardly notice after a while.'

Marguerite turned to the window, her ribs heaving.

'May I play school in your study, Mama?' said Fanny, already on to the next thing.

'If it's all right with Mrs B,' said Mary, glancing at the midwife. 'She's our guest.'

The midwife held her arms out for Fanny, who climbed into them without a second thought. 'I'll take you there myself.'

In the study Fanny climbed right onto the chair, stood up, and reached for the cracked quizzing glass hanging around the gold frame over her mother's desk. She put the velvet ribbon around her neck. 'I'm allowed,' she said.

Mrs B had no doubt of it. The door was open, and she could see Marguerite turn to look at Mary, who reached out her hand.

'Don't be afraid of me. I'm still who I am.'

Marguerite went to her bedside. 'I wish I were half as brave as you.'

'It's not bravery if you're not afraid, dear Marguerite. I've seen you, seen you be fearful, but it never stopped you, not once. You've followed me to the ends of the earth.'

'I would do it again, from the very first day. All of it.'

'So would I.'

Mrs B could see Marguerite pinching the elbows of her sleeves. 'I don't know what will become of me, without you.'

'You'll stay here. For my girls. Who need you. It would be a great comfort to me—'

'Of course I will, if that's what you want. They're my family too.'

'I know maybe one day you'll want to have your own family—'

'I don't wish to marry. I'm not only your servant; I'm your pupil. And I've seen what it's put you through.'

'I know you have. But not all men are hopeless. You don't have to marry them, you know.'

'You've given me a taste of my own liberty. Married or not, why would I ever give that up?'

Mr Godwin knocked lightly on the bedroom door, and peeked his head in. 'Morning, ladies. All safe for me?' he said, with his usual worried smile.

At the sound of his voice Fanny rushed to the door to greet him. 'Papa!' she called.

Mary watched as Godwin lifted the little girl into his arms and brushed the hair out of her eyes, asking her where she'd been all morning, and how she got the fresh scrape on her knee. Fanny put her arm around his neck and toyed with his ear while she answered, and he listened, his face darkening or brightening according to the vicissitudes of her story.

Mrs B stood in the threshold. The morning breeze coming

in from the window kissed the scene.

'I think I ought to have some of that wine, Mrs B,' said Mary, with a smile that was equal parts love and sorrow.

Mary W

When you read this, I'll be gone. My soul was calm, the tempest subsided. Nothing was left but an eager longing to forget myself, escape all anguish, all thought – fly away from this hell of disappointment. Some vision, like a liquid dream, appeared, but I couldn't catch it. I was aware of my head turning, but it was no longer my head, the sinews in my neck, not my neck. My hands, not my hands. 'A little patience, and all will be over,' I said to myself, dissolving into blankness, at last, oblivion.

I woke to Imlay's face in mine. One vein at the side of his head bulged purple. He shook my shoulders in his hands, trying to rouse me. 'What have you done, Mary? Wake up!' He slapped my face lightly, but my eyelids were too heavy to open; my head bobbed and fell onto his chest. He hoisted me up from the bed, but I was a rag doll in his arms. 'Think of Fanny!' he said, gathering the back of my hair to hold my head up. 'Your little girl!' I mumbled her name, or his name, but the sounds that came out of me weren't sounds I knew, or a voice that was mine.

Imlay walked me around the room, strong hand at my waist, asking me questions, sometimes soft, sometimes shouting, making me answer. He must have found the empty bottle of laudanum by my bedside.

'How much did you take, Mary? What time did you take it?'

'Why are you here?' I kept asking him, even as my knees buckled under me. 'Why did you come?'

'Your letter,' he said. 'I read your letter.'

A doctor came, who gave me purges until I vomited everything in my body – what felt like everything I'd ever ingested, violently so. I was turned inside out, outside in, weak and listless. I was an empty vessel, without a will of my own, neither to live nor die. Either seemed too much effort.

It was then I caught sight of Marguerite at the door, wiping tears away, and Imlay, through the crack, trying to reassure her. She always spoke rapid French when she was upset or afraid. Imlay's French was halting, but his voice calm. Then I saw Fanny, burying her face in her nursemaid's skirts. Even then, too sweet for the world.

'Ça va aller,' Imlay said to Marguerite. 'Tout ira bien.'

'Ça va aller,' she repeated, stroking Fanny's hair. 'Ça va aller.'

This was my coming back to consciousness.

The next few days I rested, woke, wept, refused to eat, stared out at the barren sky, and slept some more. Imlay often sat in a chair by my bedside, reading, sometimes aloud. But he felt more a guard than a guardian, I understood, lest I try again to end my life. Once a day Marguerite would bring Fanny in, little legs wrapped around her hip, but Fanny reached for me as soon as she saw me.

'Mama's tired,' Marguerite told her. I caressed my little girl's honey-gold hair.

'Forgive me, darling Fannikin. We'll play soon. Very soon.'
Which was the most I could muster. When I began to sit up in
bed, then moved to the parlour, then took tea and toast, Imlay
didn't speak to me of love, but commerce.

'You can't live on the sofa, Mary. There's no future in it.'

'Is this a sofa?' I said. 'I thought it was an abyss.'

'A sense of purpose. That would help.'

'Thank you for knowing so cleverly what I need.'

He managed a rueful smile. 'You move onward. Outward.
It's what you do.'

'Perhaps "flee" would be a better word.'

'A trip would do you good.'

I looked at him, some ember of hope in my hollow heart.
'Together?'

He started to pace. 'I know I've neglected you,' he said, 'but
only because of the worries pressing on me. If we could find out
what happened to the silver, the lost ship—'

'Ellefsen's ship?' His tight turns around the room made me
dizzy. We knew the *Maria and Margarethe* had never arrived
in Norway. There were reports that Ellefsen had unloaded the
silver in the dead of night and then sunk the ship, or planned
to; indeed, there were rumours of such a wreck near Arendal, all
the treasure lost. But the ship had lately reappeared, battered,
with no silver on it. Ellefsen had been arrested and released,
awaiting a formal inquiry. By now I hated the whole crooked
business.

'Our future depends on it,' he said, scraping a chair across
the floor to sit across from me, our knees touching. He clasped
his strong hands together. 'A thousand pounds. That's all. We'll
go to America. Be farmers – read, study, write – the way we

planned. If you can just find where the silver's gone.'

'You want *me* to find the silver?'

'I have to go back to France to track the other end of this business. And you hate it here. Think of it, the sea, the air, something to do—'

'And you, successfully dispensing with me—'

He pulled a folded page from his coat pocket. 'I've already written the commission. It authorises you, Mary Imlay, my best friend and wife, to undertake the sole management and direction of all my affairs and business in Scandinavia. You are my helpmate, my equal. The only person in the world I trust entirely.' He unfolded it and handed it to me. 'If anyone can find what was lost, or make the case for restoration, it's you.'

My eyes scanned the words, but my head was swimming. I didn't understand why Imlay clung to the ship as our salvation, but certain words teased me: 'trust,' 'best friend,' 'equal.' There sounded a future for us in it, the utopia I'd imagined for so long. Still, I didn't know if I had the strength to take it on, to pack my things yet again and go.

'*Then* we'll have a glorious holiday,' he said in response to my hesitation. 'You, me, Fannikin.' He knew this would lift my chin.

'To celebrate.'

'And you'll give up your commercial venturing, your speculations? We'll go to America?'

He looked down at his hands, ground his palms, the way he did when he was thinking. Then looked at me squarely with soft brown eyes. 'I believe in you, Mary,' he said. 'I need you to believe in me.'

I sighed and looked out the window, trying to decide

whether I could, after all, still believe.

'I won't be separated from Fanny,' I said, as if negotiating terms.

'I've spoken to Marguerite. She'll go with you both. She wants to go.'

I didn't have the wherewithal to resent him presuming to speak to Marguerite without consulting me first, but marvelled at her willingness to go.

'How can someone so afraid be so intrepid at the same time?' I said.

'Elias Backman expects you in Gothenburg. He's our partner there. Knows all the details and has begun a lawsuit on our behalf.'

'To think that a month ago she'd never even left Paris.'

'He'll make any necessary introductions.'

'And suffers such awful seasickness. But still she longs to go with me?'

Imlay sat back in the chair and studied me. 'You make everyone's world bigger, Mary. You can't help yourself.'

Within a week we were in Hull, where Fanny, Marguerite and I stayed in a house as cold as a tomb, with fewer comforts, waiting for a vessel to take us to Sweden. I wrote the first of my letters to Imlay an hour after we arrived: 'Imlay, dear Imlay, am I always to be tossed about thus? Shall I never find a haven to rest contented in? How can you love to fly about – dropping down in a new world, cold and strange, every other day? Why do you not attach to those tender emotions round the idea of home, which even now dim my eyes?'

But I might as well have been talking about myself. Imlay

was right about me, I'd been on the move since before memory began. Onward, outward. From Spitalfields to Barking, to Yorkshire, back to London, each time holding out a singular hope that I could reinvent myself, as my wayward father had, half believing that the next place would be different. But Bath, Lisbon, County Cork, Paris, Le Havre – they were all mine. No matter what setbacks, I did push forward, went somewhere else, tried again. Imlay was right, too, that I didn't want to be in London, his being there aside. If not for our endless separations, I would never have returned to a place that had lost all charm for me, for which I now felt a repugnance that amounted almost to horror. I had no doubt most of London would turn against me if they knew I had a child out of wedlock. My own country no longer made sense to me. Moving did, as it always had. Locomotion was the only thing that had ever given me new life.

On a morning in mid-June the captain sent word that we were to be on board in a few hours. My spirits were agitated. All week in Hull I'd woken in fits of trembling. Now that departure was imminent, I knew I'd been wishing that Imlay would save me from it. But he never came. When we set out, on a vessel hardly designed for passengers, the winds changed again, leaving us afloat at anchor for another week in a misty fog that might as well have been purgatory. Marguerite was seasick from the first moment on board, and needed my constant care. A fidgety Fanny, gay as a lark, wanted to run about on her newfound legs, fall, get up again, and play. Imagine my guilt at stealing a glance out to the cold, grey sea, flashing on my secret wish that it might become our tomb.

You needn't know all the details, little bird, of the lost

treasure ship that was the aim of my journey; Imlay knew most of them already. I went because I needed to believe that if I succeeded in some way, at least secured restitution for our loss, Imlay would see that I was indispensable to him, that he couldn't be parted from me. I could turn him around and back to us. But I see now that the mystery of the ship was not my true purpose, nor even whether Imlay and I would be together. Rather, I sought the answer to the deepest mystery of my own life in that moment – whether I should live or die.

The captain agreed to put us on shore at Gothenburg, where Elias Backman awaited me, but rough conditions forbade it. I caught sight of a lighthouse not far away and asked to go there. The captain, surprised by my determination, put out a signal for a boat to emancipate us (after eleven wearying days at sea), but for two hours no one came. Finally I used all my rhetoric to persuade the good-natured captain to let me have the ship's boat, which argued against all his instincts and, he hastened to tell me, broke general rules. 'But I see you like to break rules,' he said when he relented, and three sailors hoisted the boat in minutes, promising to row us to the lighthouse where we might recruit a pilot for Gothenburg.

'I don't see a single soul,' said Marguerite as we neared the little island. Her fear always acted as a feeler before her adventuring spirit, but I didn't listen until we landed, alarmed to find only two hermits who emerged out of their wretched hut. We made out that they had no boat, but some miles over there was a dwelling, they pointed past an outcropping of giant rocks, and we could try there. Our sailors didn't want to risk their captain's wrath, but for two guineas took the chance.

For two hours they rowed. I should have enjoyed the fine weather and good till, but fatigue showed on their young faces. We saw no dwelling of any sort, and they kept glancing at their own ship in the distance, making jokes with each other I couldn't understand. Only one of them spoke any English.

'Why do you keep looking at your ship?' asked shy Marguerite.

'That good breeze?' said the sailor. 'Maybe the captain sail without us.' The other sailors laughed, but only to cover their anxiety.

Marguerite looked concerned for them, for us, but she held Fanny tight and sang to her, which for a while calmed us all. Sunbeams played on the ocean, ruffled by the lightest breeze, but the wild, majestic coastline was littered with dark rocks jutting over the sea like the brute materials of Creation. I was more like the sailors, putting up a good front, but even I felt uneasy when the shore seemed to recede the harder they rowed, the tide pushing against us, wanting to carry us farther away. There seemed no end to it, no arrival possible. With dusk soon to be closing in.

When at last we turned into the most picturesque little bay, we saw a small boat coming toward us, rowed by a lone man with a scruffy beard. Marguerite, who'd come to trust our rowers, looked alarmed when I said I'd soon release them back to their ship, but when the man introduced himself, with good English, as the lieutenant who commanded all the pilots on that coast, she climbed gladly on board. Soon a cottage came into view, overlooking the whole bay, and his plump wife appeared at the door, waving us a welcome.

The house was clean, with a sort of rural elegance, its simple muslin beds, curtains, table linens all dazzling white, the floor

281

strewn with juniper sprigs. Fish, milk, butter, cheese, dense dark bread, and brandy were instantly spread on the board. The lieutenant and his wife doted on Fanny, who ate ravenously, tasting things she'd never had, and ending with rose-hip jelly smeared on both her cheeks.

I needn't have worried about darkness closing in, as night never moved beyond a bluish-purple twilight that gave everything an ethereal glow. I was eager to see whether our honest tars had regained their ship, so the lieutenant gave me his telescope. I climbed some rocks and spotted the vessel underway with a fair gale on a calm sea, watching until it dwindled to a mere dot and disappeared from view. I was glad for them, followed by a sudden panic. They were the last link to our old life, now gone. We were entirely cut off, alone in a new world. There was no turning back now.

Feeling a fit of trembling coming on, I sat on the ground and pulled my knees to my chest, resting my cheek there, bone to bone, the way I had when I was young, and closed my eyes to still my breath. When I opened them, the most remarkable thing happened, little bird. I saw, in the azure eve, brilliant patches of earth popping all around me, the most exquisite verdure. And then a clutch of wild pansy caught my eye, peeking over a dark stone. I took one of its perfect blossoms in my fingers, love-in-idleness, sprays of sunny yellow radiating from its centre and deep violet petals, velvet against my cheek.

I felt a sudden peacefulness wash over me. I knew it was Fanny Blood, not inside me but all around, in the glow, the never-night, holding out a lamp for me, a talisman against the darkness. I'd been without her for so long now, she'd soon be ten years dead, but here she was, Fanny, who had taught me to believe in the possibility of spontaneous pleasure and argued always that we were right to expect happiness. She was whispering a way forward, as she always did, one footfall at a time.

I didn't want to go to bed, my senses awake and imagination busy. And nothing could equal the beauty of that northern summer night. All Nature seemed at rest, even the rocks, in deep repose. I kissed little Fanny's cheek as she slept, my emotions vibrating on the brink between ecstasy and agony that gave a poignancy to all my sensations. I felt alive again.

Writing at midnight without a candle, I penned a letter to Johnson telling him I thought I would turn my travels into a book of some sort, and hoped that he would publish it. Then I tucked the violet blossom in a letter to Imlay, feeling strangely hopeful.

And so began our midsummer journey in the great wild North. By horseback, carriage rides, boat trips, ferry passages, long walks, ocean swims, and flights of fancy did I travel, and by travel I mean think, and by think I mean try to relocate myself in the world, and the world in me. Only a few weeks before, I'd wanted to die, aiming at tranquillity, but instead almost destroyed the energy of my soul – almost pulled out by the roots what makes it mine. I had come here, I knew, to find it again.

I confess that I wrote often to Imlay, usually at night when I was most fragile, to report the progress of my journey, but instead poured out my fears. I pleaded with him not to taunt me with promises he couldn't keep, implored him to decide once and for all whether we would live as one or part for ever.

But between those lines I lived another life.

In Gothenburg – a clean, airy, wealthy town with canals running through the streets and endless rows of trees – Elias Backman welcomed us into his lively home, with a French wife and four little sons. Marguerite was back to her convivial self, surrounded by familiar things. Each night before supper we'd repair to a side table to eat bread and butter, cheese, cured salmon or pickled herring, and a glass of brandy, always in the same order, same dishes, same *Skål!* to our good health, as the Old Norse had done. I smiled and did my part, and at supper quizzed Backman about everything – the ship, the lawsuit, the Ellefsen family – but learnt nothing new. He told me bluntly that I was a woman of observation because I asked men's questions.

What I remember best is falling in love anew with my little girl. What an interesting creature she was, noticing everything, tirelessly curious. (How I envied her the magic of existence, seeing things for the first time.) Even when I fell into darkness, her smiles twined round my heart and stopped my self-pity. Seeing her frolic with the Backman children – how free she was, naturally kind, generous with hugs, happy to be tickled and tossed about, same as the boys – reinvigorated my belief that all children are the same if only they be treated so. But worry over her future slipped in, the oppressed state of her sex. Would she be forced to sacrifice her heart to her principles, or principles to her heart? I was determined to cultivate her finer feelings, but in lending blushes to the rose would I sharpen the thorns that would wound her – by unfolding her mind make her unfit for the world she'd have to live in?

I wondered if that was what I'd done to myself. It all swirled inside me, the rosy tint of morning, the flush on Fanny's cheeks as she played, the remembrance of colour rushing to my lover's skin, and mine. My eyes glossed with tears. Why must all roads lead to Imlay?

When I told Backman I wanted to go to Strömstad to see the damaged ship for myself, he offered to accompany me but said that I should then go on by myself to Tønsberg to meet the judge in our case, and it would be best to leave Fanny behind. I hadn't been away from her since her birth. The thought of it nearly gutted me. But worse, how could I ever have thought of parting from her for ever? When I'd wanted to die, the cleaving felt necessary to save her. An unhappy mother was a cruelty she didn't deserve. Now that I began to want to live again, I couldn't bear being torn away. 'Please don't leave us,' said Marguerite, the night before we left.

'But you're content here. You can speak French all you like. And Fanny, she has so much to distract her. I don't think she'll even miss me.'

Marguerite pinched the muslin elbows of her nightdress.

'I'm not worried about Fanny,' she said. 'It's you.'

'But I've often travelled alone.'

'That you'll leave us here and never come back.'

'Of course I'll come back.'

She hugged herself closer and pursed her quivering lips. Marguerite's face always gave her away. I put my hand on her cheek and tilted her head to meet mine.

'I won't hurt myself, Marguerite. I promise you. I'll come back.' She nodded, but the worry on her face remained.

'Ça va aller,' I said to her. 'Tout ira bien.'

To see the careening of a three-masted sailing ship, a heaving down at high tide, as Backman and I did at Strömstad, is to watch mere men and their ropes topple a wounded giant against her will and nature. How strange it was to see the dignified *Maria and Margarethe* felled and lying on one side, sails torn, masts snapped in two, her hull exposed with its rotting craters and holes – barnacles, shipworms, and seaweed clinging to it, feeding away. I felt a keen sympathy for her plight. It was so like my own.

'Is she beyond repair?' I asked Backman.

'No, but she'll be here a good two months, I guess. And cost a good deal.'

'Will Imlay have to pay?'

'I'm supposing that's why *you're* here.'

'But the silver's disappeared. It seems unlikely we'll recover it.'

'Then it's on you to persuade someone to pay for what was lost, isn't it?'

'Wouldn't the judge do that, if he finds for us?'

'It's a complicated business,' said Backman. 'I'm supposing Imlay would rather rely on the pressure you might bring to bear, to settle with someone. No one wants the stain of a matter like this.'

'Well, why not Ellefsen?' I said. 'His family's got money enough.'

'If he's the one who lost it,' he said with a shrug.

Seeing the ship hove down like that was as if I'd seen a vision of our future (or my own) having been dashed on the rocks and adrift at sea, now run aground. It made me redouble my commitment to her restoration, if not Imlay's and mine. But when we settled at our inn, I was disappointed to find no letter from him. My being there was a chance, but a year before he would have taken it. Each time the post arrived and there was nothing from him was a fresh abandonment. Where was the man who'd been alive to our shared feelings, to imagination, our deepest principles – alive to touch, to kisses, beating hearts, and bodies in flight? If only he were here with me, this romantic country, these fine summer evenings, wouldn't it turn his heart away from the coarseness that hardened it? I felt his absence as wrenching physical pain, and wondered what my existence was without him, without my daughter, without anyone.

My letters were alternately plaintive, pleading, or proud. I was the abandoned woman, an exile pleading for return. I wanted to awaken his feeling, if not his guilt at having treated me unjustly. I berated him and enumerated his faults. But each time I posted a letter, I berated myself. How far had I fallen from the 'Wollstonecraft' who'd argued against the victimisation of women, the sort glorified in the novels I hated, capable of nothing but raw emotion; objects of male desire but never the subject of their own lives. All sensibility, no sense. Had I become the very woman I'd railed against?

Then something else began to stir inside me. On the morning I was to leave for Norway alone, a dish of coffee and crisp linen revived my spirits. Backman warned me that the roads were notoriously rocky and slow, so I determined to go by sea. The coast was known to be dangerous too, with rocks lurking just below the surface of the water, but it seemed the better means. The air was pure and balmy, producing the most voluptuous sensations. I wrapped my greatcoat around me and lay down on some sails at the bottom of the small boat I'd hired, its motion rocking me as we went. I crossed my arms under my head to watch the grey morning bloom with purple clouds, then gold, then pass to silvery white. How often had I felt myself a particle

287

broken off from the grand mass of mankind, all alone, and then something sublime and beautiful dilated my emotions to make me feel that I was still part of a mighty whole.

The clouds came into my vision, drifted across and away. But I didn't want to keep them. Why would I?

I was the sky.

At Tønsberg, Norway's oldest settlement, I met first thing with the thoughtful, good-natured Judge Wulfsberg, who had charge of our case. He said a fair inquiry would require him to interview everyone involved and that I should expect to stay three weeks at least, or I might as well not have come. When he saw the look on my face, I told him about Fanny, and lamented that I hadn't brought my daughter with me. What I left out is that I no longer knew who I was without her. She had come to seem, even more than Imlay, my true anchor in the world.

The judge had found me a charming room in a quiet inn with a commanding view of the sea, ringed by an amphitheatre of woods.

It was almost evening, and I wanted to feel it on my skin. Standing under a towering grove of aspen and beeches, I turned my face to feel the whispering softness of those western gales. They almost died away that time of night, the leaves trembling into stillness. A light shower had fallen; the juniper, the underwood of the forest, exhaled a lush perfume that enveloped me. Even the moon seemed to say hello.

No one at the inn could speak English or French, which was a good pretext to dine alone – and they let me at a late hour, which became my habit. Sitting by myself in the little dining room, with its tall white-trimmed windows, I was surprised to find that I relished my aloneness. Each singing scrape of knife and fork, delicate clink of glass was mine, every taste and thought my own.

With three weeks to fill and so much time by myself, I began to occupy the space it afforded, as it occupied me. I took long, blissful walks in pine and fir groves, struck with a mystic reverence, a sense that they were conscious of their own existence and the pleasure they gave. Fanny Blood walked beside me; I could hear her voice warbling over the heath. I found a swimming rivulet just out of town, but soon wanted to bathe in the sea. A young woman, with ice-blue eyes, proposed rowing me across the water among the rocks to a place she knew, but since she was pregnant, I took the oars and learnt to row, soon becoming expert, even going by myself, my thoughts keeping time with the oars.

Nature was my first and, most days, my only companion. Its beauties seemed even more alluring than when I was young and sought refuge in it. Living for so long in cities, I'd come to think that mixing with the human race, in all its varieties, forced us to examine and lose our prejudices – that it was a culture of science, history, philosophy, and art that led to judgment and taste. But I remembered now that it was the countryside that gave birth to my imagination, to sentiments that were the true source of taste, and inquiries that expanded my soul. The horrors I'd witnessed in France had cast a gloom over everything, but they began to dissipate, and in their stead came the healing embrace of the natural world.

One day I climbed to the vestiges of a fort battered by the Swedes long ago. The only human about, I reclined on the mossy down, lulled to sleep by the prattling sea. A balmy gale woke me; I turned my head to follow white sails as they turned the cliffs. Fishermen cast their nets, seagulls hovered over the deep. Everything harmonised into tranquillity, even the bitterns called in cadence with the cows', tinkling bells. It was the finest summer I'd ever known, with magic everywhere.

I began to write again, with a freedom I'd never felt. It was the book I'd told Johnson I wanted to write, though not the one I imagined. It seemed at first like a nosegay of unconnected remarks, observations, and musings – my own travelogue – lightly bound by letters to an unnamed lover. But as I abstracted Imlay, the outlines of my own self became sharper. How often had I written under a man's name, or as a high-minded philosopher who spoke of things that 'one' believed. This was different on the page, surging up from uncharted depths. The 'I' who wrote was not a passive woman in pain, but the thinking, feeling hero of each little tale.

While Nature was recalibrating my senses to the sublime, I found I was finely tuned to my emotions, the whole awful, wonderful gamut of them, and that they in turn interacted with place, culture, history. The Norwegians seemed the most naturally free people I'd seen, no feudalism, no firstborn sons inheriting everything, instead, farmers tilling their own small plots of land, a free press, religious tolerance. Perhaps knowledge hadn't yet enlarged the grand virtues, extended their humanity to the whole human race, but among the peasants I saw such simplicity, so much overflowing of heart and fellow feeling. I could see that all their exertions were for the good of their families. It was hard not to be touched by it, hard not to feel my embitterment diminishing, and my own battered ideals revived. If only power-seeking, money-grubbing men tended to the hearth at home, the world would be a gentler place for all.

I wanted to live again, write again. I recovered myself in the purity of the air, the trailing summer light, the ink on the page. I could feel the taut sinews of my thighs, my ribs braced, lungs like bellows. It was as if I'd faded away before the withering touch of disappointment, but in the mirabilia of this place become visible again, my mind and body reanimated. My desire for Imlay, for the peace we once shared, had made me forget the respect due my own emotions; sacred emotions that are harbingers of the delights I was formed to enjoy. Nothing could extinguish that heavenly spark.

I missed little Fanny, but I was happy alone for those three weeks. I could no longer even bear to think of being no more – it seemed impossible that I should cease to exist, this active, restless spirit, equally alive to joy and sorrow. In moments I thought of that ship hove down in Strömstad. Were her leaking holes resealed by now, sails mended, hull scrubbed clean and laid with copper? Surely she was ready to be righted, as I was, and take to the open sea.

What a long time it takes to know ourselves, little bird, and yet all of us know more than we're willing to own, even to ourselves. But I rejoiced at having turned, in that strange solitude, a new page in the history of my own heart.

Don't think that my entreaties to Imlay stopped. They didn't. His letters to me, scant, were sometimes gloomy, other times buoyant. Some filled me with dread that his fickle attentions had already moved elsewhere – he hinted at it – which sickened my heart anew. Yet he spurred me in my quest, our shared purpose, and threw me a crumb now and then. Yes, he would meet us in Hamburg when it was all done, and we would go to Switzerland.

291

He still believed in our future life. But another aspect took shape in my letters back to him, a feeling less of desperation than hope that as I was restored to myself, he would see what he was losing if he lost me. The sublime was on offer to him too.

'I don't think the case will proceed,' Judge Wulfsberg told me when I met him in his office to hear his determination.

'But Ellefsen was arrested,' I said.

'And released on a bail of ten thousand riksdaler, thanks to his wealthy mother,' he said, rubbing his forehead. 'I'm afraid there's not enough evidence to convict him. And given the family's position, not much likelihood of it.'

'But what about the silver he took, and his plan to sink the ship?'

'I believe that was the plan, but I'm not sure it was Ellefsen's.'

'I don't know what you mean,' I said.

The judge scratched under his wig and sighed. 'The thing that continues to nag at me, Mrs Imlay, is Ellefsen's claim that it was you who gave him his final instructions.'

'I did.'

'Why wouldn't Mr Imlay do it himself? Something so important.'

'Imlay trusted me to do it.'

'I can see that. But I wonder whether there was another plan, from the start, and Ellefsen was told to disregard yours.' I felt my stomach churn.

'Think of it,' the judge said. 'Most of the silver's removed before Arendal, perhaps before it even sets sail, Ellefsen takes his agreed-upon share, but the plan to sink the ship goes awry, so now there's a battered ship to contend with, cost of repair far exceeding what the ship is worth, and the silver unaccounted for. But if such a plan had gone right, one might recover the costs of the ship *and* the silver from insurance, and never have to produce either.'

My heart was pounding. 'Imlay wouldn't do that.'

'Perhaps not.' The good judge took off his spectacles, eyes full of sincere feeling. 'But you might consider, if his only chance to recover anything from this debacle is an out-of-court settlement from the Ellefsens – the only characters in this drama with the means to pay – it is a stroke of genius to send Mary Wollstonecraft to lend her eloquence and reputation to the cause.'

Hearing him call me by my own name startled me. Not because it felt false, but because it felt true, and the central contradiction of the life I was living. Not wanting to be anyone's legal wife or property, insisting on my independence, living by my principles, yet wanting the rights of a 'Mrs Imlay' to the point of desperation – the right to his strong hands, his first smile of the morning, last kiss. The right to need him, and be needed in return. But the thought that I had offered up my name, surrendered my own cause to nefarious dealings, rocked me.

'You're wrong, Judge,' I said, my throat clutching. 'It simply cannot be.'

'Certainly Imlay has more supporters than detractors. Quite an intriguing man, I take it. A sort of Daniel Boone type?'

'Did Ellefsen tell you that?'

'Perhaps you ought to go see Ellefsen for yourself.'

'I'd planned to. And I will.'

He took my hand warmly when I stood to go. 'I hope I am wrong, Miss Wollstonecraft.'

Sailing through the islands that led to Risør, where Ellefsen lived, I saw two hundred houses packed together under a high rock just beyond a horseshoe bay, with only planks to walk between them. It looked like a place 'bastilled' by nature, shut out from all that opens the understanding and expands the heart. I found there a hotbed of secrets and shady business among its inhabitants that almost frightened me, a sordid love of money. Men smoked pipes and made deals. Their breath, hair, clothes, and couches reeked of it. If this was the place that birthed Ellefsen and his family, I held out little hope for a resolution, and an answer to the mystery of the silver ship.

'I wish none of this had ever happened,' he said, when he sat across from me in the drawing room of the inn where I was staying. Peder Ellefsen wasn't threatening at all, but diminutive and humble, the way I remembered him, same dimpled smile and soft voice. He looked uncomfortable dressed as a gentleman instead of a sea captain, with the same tossed mop of hair. His whole look begged my sympathy, but I didn't intend to soften.

'We aren't here about wishes, are we, Mr Ellefsen?'

'I know what you think I did, Mrs Imlay,' he said, almost rushing to get it out. 'But you've got no proof.'

'I know that now. We seek restitution, that's all. If your mother was willing to bail you out for half what the silver was worth, why not settle with us?'

'My mother will refuse, as a matter of principle. She's a very strong woman.'

'I'm a strong woman too. I believe in what's right, and fair.'

He clapped his hand on his knee, surprising us both. 'What's right and fair about it?' he said. 'The plan failed, but I'm the one left holding the bag.'

My jaw clenched. 'Was there another plan?' I asked. 'Different from the instructions I gave you?'

He looked out the window toward the bay, kneading his cap in his hand. I could feel his wanting the whole business done with.

'No one believes me anyway,' he said.

'Then why did you agree to meet with me?'

He locked his blue eyes on mine. 'I thought you might ... understand.'

'What is it you'd have me understand, Ellefsen?'

He ran his fingers through his hair. It seemed he was thinking how best to say it. Both of us steering around rocks lurking beneath the surface.

'I liked Imlay right off. His big view of things, grand schemes. No limits, not like here. Every man making his own way in the world. I believed in him.' A reluctant smile formed on his lips. 'It impressed me that he knew Daniel Boone.'

I could feel my shoulder blades pinch together, and remembered Judge Wulfsberg's words. 'I think Imlay only met Boone once,' I said. 'He never told me otherwise.'

'Why would he? That he swindled an American legend out of thousands of acres of land in Kentucky, and had to flee the country to escape the debts, writs, suits, and claims against him? That's why he went to France in the first place.'

I could barely speak. 'I'm quite sure Imlay didn't tell you *that*.'

'Wasn't Imlay. I only found out after. I was bragging to my first mate, he's an American too, about Imlay knowing Daniel Boone.

It was him told me.'

'He had first-hand knowledge?'

Ellefsen shrugged. 'Said that was the story going around.'

'People make up stories all the time.'

'When he said it, something inside me, I don't know, it seemed true,' said Ellefsen. 'Maybe I imagined Imlay as something he wasn't. Something better than he is. Maybe I overlooked some things because of it. Me wanting him to be what I wanted him to be.'

Oh, little bird! Ellefsen's words slapped my face like a bracing cold. Some veil was torn away and I saw that I was the same as he was, wanting Imlay to be what I wanted him to be. But I knew that my want preceded even Imlay, when revolution was in the air we breathed. We all wished to push it as far as we could, pledged not to miss its shimmering possibilities. Our utopian ideals were tested by the truth – blood in the streets, lost friends, exile, treachery, the sadness – but I didn't dare give up on them now that I felt myself and the world conjoined. In the midst of all that, I met Imlay, wide open, free, and loving. He was a believer too. All my lost optimism I invested in him, in the dream of our 'partnership of equals' in the pristine wilderness of a brave new country. New world, new life, new love, new me.

Imlay invested in other things.

Now I wonder how I could have thought he would change, when my own father had not. Even when I demanded that he stop violating my mother, laid my body across the threshold of their bedroom door, he had simply stepped over me. Why wasn't that proof enough? The good men I'd known – John Arden, Richard Price, Joseph Johnson – couldn't help but be who they were. I denied Imlay's nature because I disliked it. But he was true to himself. It was I, little bird, who hadn't been.

Love was a want of my heart, and what I deserved. What every human being deserves. Then, I asked myself, what was the defect in me that I could not accept that the Imlay I believed in was as slippery as the silver ship, and never to arrive?

Mrs B

9th September 1797

Mrs B slept on the settee that night, fitful, wakeful. She felt herself overflowing more than usual, a roll of her fleshy belly, a swollen foot dangling off the edge. She was used to waking up in strange places, beds, chairs, now and then floors. She wasn't home, that was always the first thought in her head, but now a second thought wedged itself in: she had no home, not any more. Not like it was. At least she'd spent enough nights in the Godwin house to know its sounds and smells, its rhythms and rounds. Judging by most things, she'd slept till late morning. But she didn't expect laughter.

Mrs B rubbed her face and set aside the book, which she'd fallen asleep reading. The laughter was wafting in from the bedroom, she realised, right through the open door. It was Mary's laugh, and a man's laugh, one she didn't recognise. She gathered up her loose corset and tiptoed toward the sound, near enough to see them – Mary and Godwin sitting against the pillows, side by side atop the covers, him with all his clothes on, save shoes, and her in her chemise and blue shawl, trading a near-empty wine bottle between them, another dead one on the bedside table, a corkscrew, and two unsullied glass goblets. It was Mr Godwin's laughter; she'd never heard it before.

'Pot-shotten, jug-bitten, drink-drowned, high-flown!' he was saying. 'Wait, and drunk as a wheelbarrow. That's a good one!'

'But why would a wheelbarrow be drunk?' said Mary.

'Why would a lion? Or a fox? Fox-drunk, lion-drunk? Never made any sense to me.'

In between they chortled, and took turns tipping the bottle back.

It was more exertion than she'd seen from Mary in the last day, and she had to give Fordyce credit for it. Many things might mark the nearness of the end – a wild countenance, delirium, sighs, low spirits, lassitude, weakness. The face might flush or pale; weak pulse, hard pulse. Usually, there'd be rattling lungs, that slow, awful death by drowning. The lucky ones were fey, she'd seen it before, with unnaturally high spirits, but this was another thing altogether.

Mary pointed to a hole in Godwin's sock, his big toe sticking out. 'You've got a hole in your sock!' She giggled.

'I've got no time to darn my socks,' he said, wiggling his toe. 'I'm a very busy man.'

'I would darn your socks,' she said.

'Have *you* darn my socks, *the* Mary Wollstonecraft?'

'Not Godwin?' she said, her laughter subsiding.

He looked at her, and, though her eyes were sunken, cheeks hollowed, and all the light fading from her face, seemed to see

299

only beauty. '"Godwin" is not good enough for you. Better that I should be William Wollstonecraft.'

Mary put her hand on his arm, concentrating all her energy on a smile. 'We're equals then, aren't we? Just as we promised we'd be.'

'No, Mary.' He placed his hand on hers. 'There does not exist your equal in the world.'

They sat like that, shoulder to shoulder, thinking their own thoughts. She rested her head against his, entwined their fingers.

Mr Godwin sighed and turned his face to the ceiling. 'If only I'd met you in Hoxton, and stolen you away somehow, we'd have twenty-two years together by now. I can hardly forgive myself for missing you.'

She put her chin lightly on his shoulder. 'Oh, we wouldn't have liked each other at all then,' she said playfully, but there was pain beneath it. 'We have to believe that every step we've taken, even the ones when we were lost, led us to each other, right here, right now.'

Godwin traced the carnelian round of her ring. 'And I guess you wouldn't have met your Fanny Blood.'

Mary closed her eyes and nodded. 'I could almost believe in Heaven if I thought Fanny'd be there to greet me.'

He squeezed her hand. 'I know you loved her best.'

She looked into his eyes. 'But love doesn't always accord with happiness, much as we want it to,' she said, holding tightly to him. 'I have both with you.'

Mrs B had to look away. She left the door as it was, so as not to disturb them, but sat on the settee in stockinged feet, let her corset go.

'I know, with all my being,' she heard Godwin say, 'that we

300

were formed – whoever or whatever formed us – to make each other happy.'

'You are the kindest, best man in the world,' she said. 'You'll be happy again. You will.'

'I have not the least expectation I will ever know happiness again.'

'Please, for the girls. For our little bird. They must believe in it.'

'What would you have them believe?'

There was a long pause. She thought of the way Mary looked up and to the right when she was thinking, the line of her jaw, the fullness of her cheeks. Mrs B saw her in her mind's eye, restored.

'In love, that melts into friendship,' she said, 'and friendship that melts into love.'

After that, there fell a quiet that only a kiss can bring. Mrs B rested her elbows on her knees, hung her head, and wept.

After Fordyce came in the early afternoon, mostly to declare the wine diet a success, Mary slept for a good few hours. There was nothing, any more, to do. Visitors still sat in the parlour downstairs, wringing their hands, keeping Godwin company, hoping for one last word with Mary, but she'd said all the goodbyes she had in her. How different it was, Mrs B thought, waiting on death instead of birth. And still, perhaps the same. Both were a coming and going, a hello, a farewell. She hoped wherever it was Mary was going, it would be like another womb: no want, no thought, no pain, only sustenance, Heaven, and God's love.

Reading, she fell asleep herself, hard and dreaming, and when her eyes opened, the first thing she saw in the shaft of gold light pouring in through the window was a spider finishing her web, knitting its gossamer filaments into a perfect whole. She heard Mary stir in the next room, a light moan, complaining of thirst.

'How strange to be as happy as I've ever been, and now to leave,' she said, after Mrs B dripped water into her mouth from a soaked cloth, then dabbed her parched lips with it.

'Water,' said Mary. 'How lovely.'

'All the water you want,' said Mrs B. 'What else can I do to ease your way?'

'What can I do to thank *you,* for having eased it already?'

Mrs B looked down at Mary, surprised to feel no pity in her heart but a caring beyond what she'd ever known, in all the births, the stillbirths, the miscarries and unwanteds, the children birthing children, the wee worn-out dead babes whose mothers refused to surrender their bodies even after the stiffness set in. And now this, a woman whose caring she felt in return.

'There is one thing,' she said, a tremolo in her voice. 'It's about my James.'

'Your husband, James. I remember. Of forty years—'

'Died twelve days ago. In our bed. Right next to me, while I slept.'

'I'm so sorry,' said Mary, reaching for her hand. 'If only you'd told us, Mrs . . . Will you tell me your name?'

'Parthenia,' said the midwife.

'Parthenia Blenkinsop,' said Mary, her voice thin and breath shallow. 'What a wonderful name.' Her heavy lids flickered; she tried to fix her gaze as best she could. 'It's so hard talking up at you.' She patted the pillow beside her with a thin hand, the one with the pretty orange ring. 'Lie on the bed with me?'

Mrs B looked down at her old black mules. Without a word, she slipped them off and stretched herself long on the bed to face Mary, feeling all her own weight, and gravity. She put her tired head on the pillow.

'Now, about your James.'

'It's just, there are things I wish I'd said. And I thought, maybe, if you see him . . .'

'Tell me.'

'Last night I tried to think of the words. I guess I thought maybe you could mix them with yours, and make mine prettier.'

'Tell me your words, then.'

'The thing is, it wasn't any great passion that drew me to other women's bedsides, but a sort of penance.'

'Penance for what?'

'When I was young, I believed it my duty to God, and the purpose of marriage, to make children, and I let my heart hope for it too, which I thought was sinful, wanting what I couldn't have. I thought God meant to punish me, but that I could be redeemed in His eyes helping other women have their children. But my husband, my James, he never did blame me. I knew he wanted a child, or maybe just wanted me to have what I wanted. He was kind to me, always, even though I turned away all those nights, year after year. I made my heart cold to him, cold to myself. Sometimes he'd reach for my hand, and I'd pull mine away. And then we just stopped. But the day he died, it was the saddest day of my life. And there's no reward at all, I see now, when I've lost the one man, right here on this earth, whoever loved me.'

Mary nodded, her flat grey eyes now gleaming with tears.

'And I am filled with regret that I didn't tell him: I wish

I'd loved you better.'

A single tear creeked down Mary's cheek. Mrs B dabbed it away with a corner of her apron.

'I hope I will see him, Parthenia. Because I'll tell him for you, exactly that.'

'I know you don't believe, like I do,' said Mrs B. 'And after these last days, well, there've been times I wasn't sure if *I* could believe still. If I could forgive Him taking my James – and then you.'

Mary pinched her dry lips together. Mrs B heaved herself from the bed, wrung out the cloth in cool water, and pressed it to Mary's lips.

'But what I've seen and heard here, in these days with you,' said Mrs B, 'well, none could do all this but God with all his might.'

'Do all this what?' said Mary.

'All this – sad and glorious beautiful.'

Mary W

Before I left the wild North, I had a letter from Imlay, fresh proof of his indifference. He said our fortunes were inseparable, that he cherished tender feelings for me, and would do what was right, but it sounded like a burden. I was weary of travelling but sensed there was no home for me in him, no place to rest. I might as well have tried to lean on a spear.

My amiable innkeeper insisted that I couldn't leave Norway until I saw the cascade outside of Fredrikstad, and said he'd take me himself. On horseback we took a road that wound along a gurgling river through woods of white-barked aspen and birch, deep oak. It had rained hard. Shimmering drops of water clung to the blazing leaves. A few of them fluttered down, they had lost their colour and curled inward at the edges; a harbinger of autumn. We tied up the horses and set off down a narrow footpath through an ancient forest that nearly crowded out all light, full of aged pines with fine silvery cobwebs strung across their rusting needles, spiders making new life from old.

Before we could see it, we could hear it, the ferocious roar shattering the woodland quiet. When we reached the waterfall, I wasn't prepared for the overwhelming power of it, a crashing torrent exploding out of the cliff above us. My gentle guide saw how I marvelled at it, and, by the elbow, led me to a small plateau where, if I didn't mind the spray on my face and clothes, I could reach my hand out and feel it. There was only room for one of us. He stepped back onto the path and let me alone. I reached for it slowly with a shaky hand. The icy cascade pounded my fingers, numbed them almost instantly. I closed my eyes and turned my face to the spray. My own feelings merged with the tumbling water itself, pouring out of me, unstoppable. I felt my own infinity, and insignificance. How easily it could – if only it would – toss me to the river below, and wash me full away.

Nature was my cathedral now, and this, a baptism by deluge, or as good as last rites. The sublime seemed to thrive at the knife's edge between life and death, earth and Heaven, unchained by misery and grasping at immortality. But this hurtling tempest seemed like something getting free.

How I envied the water.

'You say my letters torture you; I won't say what yours do to me.'

Imlay didn't meet us in Hamburg. We sailed alone to Dover, but he wasn't there either. He met our coach in London, had found a place for us, a maid, a cook. But not with him.

'You say my letters torture you,' I wrote to Imlay. 'I am not, and never will be, a mere object of compassion. I can take care of my child. I want no protection without love.'

When I pressed the cook, poor woman, she admitted that

306

Imlay had taken a lover, an actress with a strolling troupe, and that they shared a house, and had all the time I was away.

'I am agitated. My whole frame convulsed, my lips tremble as if shook by cold, though fire circulates in my veins.'

Why was I made this way, wandering to and fro in a vale of darkness as well as tears? The deep hole at the centre of my being gaped open, a ravenous maw. I couldn't go back there, not again.

The old voice – where did it come from? – whispered in my ear to put an end to all these struggles.

'Forget that I exist. Be free, Imlay. Let us both be free.'

All emotion beaten out of me, and nearly too numb to cry, I kissed each of Fanny's fingertips and held her close. She'd thrived for those weeks without me in the North, and I knew she loved Marguerite almost as much as she did me. I was grateful she was too young to understand, or to ask why tears come as close to pleasure as to pain.

I do not know how to describe the certainty that everyone you love, in the order that you love them, will be better off without you.

What happens next, little bird, is not the end of my story but the start of yours.

On a cusp-of-winter afternoon, I rowed alone to Putney Bridge, and paid the halfpenny toll for foot passengers, thinking, as I turned the coin in my hand, that another day I might have laughed at having to pay for the privilege of killing myself. There was scarce anyone about, which was best for my purposes. Can you see me, walking back and forth on the bridge long enough to soak my wool skirts with rain, to make myself heavy, as if my depression were not weight enough? I wanted to sink fast, drown my endless suffering, arrive at some eternal place of rest. No more thinking or feeling, no railing against the unjust world or the injustices done to my own heart.

Without a prayer or even a goodbye to the awful world, I climbed the low wall and plunged into the waters under the timbers of Putney Bridge, eyes closed, mouth open, intending to swallow the roiling river to help it swallow me. I have never told another soul what followed, not even the boatman who saw me jump, and dragged me, barely conscious, out of the murky tide.

I woke to him pressing on my belly and slapping my face and, though weak, tried to bat his hand away, despite my violent choking on river water. I was gasping for air, my ribs heaving. He sat me up on a slatted seat and made me hang my head to let the river run out of me, then clapped my back with both hands and didn't stop until my lungs were clear. I scarcely knew who I was or where, but the old man, with a degree of tenderness I still recall, circled a heavy blanket about my shoulders and, after a few minutes, without a word, placed a cup of gin between my shaking hands.

His face, all that tethered me to this life, was a weathered map, with deep grooves going every which way, pointing in no direction at all. I couldn't contain its goodness, or what I'd just done, which crept back into my awareness in small sips, and had to look away. The rain had stopped and the air was soft. I watched the water curling against the side of the boat, rocking us like a cradle. I don't know how long we sat like that, we two, but he asked nothing of me.

Finally, I took a ragged gulp from the cup and felt the burn of gin down my throat, pure sensation, perhaps too numb to feel the pain of being alive. Too numb to locate any emotion at all. That's when I remembered that watermen get paid to dredge for suicides.

'How much will you get for me?' I asked him, still reaching for every breath.

'A penny, if I'm lucky. But a pint on top if you've a tale to tell.'

'You'd trade my story?'

'If it's a good one, I'll have a four-pint sleep tonight.'

I pulled the blanket closer. 'I meant to die,' I said. 'That's all.'

'They all says they meant to. But I've never seen a one off Putney twice.'

'There are other bridges.'

He drew his chin back and grunted as if he knew better. ''S not the way thinkin' goes, when yer not straight-thinkin'.'

I let the blanket fall away from my shoulder, with not even the strength to keep it up. He leaned over and pulled it back into place.

Such a small gesture, but it was everything.

'Let's let the grim stream wait another day,' he said to me.

I drank the rest of the gin and handed him the empty cup with a small nod of thanks, surprised by a shiver of gladness that he'd saved me. He took up his oars, a slow pulling start for shore. I looked at my hands, coming back to feeling, the skin on my fingers puckered and white. That's when I realised Fanny's ring wasn't there.

In that instant, I blinked and saw everything with shocking clarity, as if I were still in it: the frothing water closes above me. I sink in the slow darkness, my torso thrust upward, arms floating backward; my skirts and hair billow around me, pushed and pulled by the current; eyes open, gazing upward as if to catch some last shard of light, mouth sealed by instinct, and then, when I can hold it no longer, an involuntary spasm of breath that drags rancid water into my nose and mouth, filling my lungs. My eyes widen with panic, my limbs flail in slow motion, and I'm alone – the cold, hard nothing of being nothing – and then at last surrender, my body flaccid, all exertion ceased. I am free of all pain, all feeling, all past, present. All resistance gone. The only sound is my own heavy heartbeat inside me, sluggish and faint. I am overcome with the most perfect floating stillness and tranquillity – my body itself becoming water.

Just then, some small thing brushes my cheek like a kiss. My eyes open but can barely make out what shines in the dark near my face, all alone in the watery world. As it rolls, end over end, away from me, I see it, the gleaming silver band of Fanny's ring, its carnelian round flashing as it floats away, having slipped from my finger.

A hand that seems to be my own, disembodied, reaches for it, dragging the water's weight, fingers outstretched, but I cannot grasp it. I can only watch its faint glint, receding in the darkness.

Stay with me, please.

I want to live.

Instead, blackness wraps around me like a cocoon. I have no sense that it's an ending, because I have no sense, no thoughts, at all.

But then, little bird, but then!

Time circles back for me, bends, and breaks.

Something, somewhere, pulls me from the dark and explodes inside me, a rush of vivid scenes that fly at me like memories with wings, shimmering and breathing, moments from my life, most keenly felt, an infinite gallery of my own experiences coming at random, one on top of another, side by side, singular, then merging into one, a sweeping view of my entire existence, but every detail and colour exact, all light and movement just as it had been. I relive every emotion precisely as it had felt, every wound and disappointment, but enchantment too; and not only my own feelings – I can go inside someone else and know what they'd seen and felt, know all the sadness and joy they carried from their own lives. Not only people, but animals and things – the whole universe alive to sensation and feeling – now alive to me! There is no progression, not even time at all, a second and a thousand years, both and neither. Everything at once and separate, present, and then gone, but indelible. Everything I have told you, little bird. All this reached for me and gathered me in its arms. Carried me across the gateway, and back to life.

I lifted my head to see the boatman looking at me, as I looked at him, a boundless sympathy between us. My mouth hung open, my jaw quivered, but no words came out. What words could there be? I wanted to grab his sleeves with both hands: did you see what I've seen? That my heartbeat, like yours, is the heart of the world inside us? That everything touches every other thing, and love, even the darkest corners where no light lives? That we float, all of us, in the same water, on the threshold of eternity? And you and I, alive in it now. Right *now*.

Of course, with his kind grey eyes, he saw only a woman who'd jumped into the Thames off Putney Bridge, and escaped with her life.

311

When we reached the river stairs, he climbed from the boat and held out his hand to steady me. I offered him back his blanket, but he refused it.

'Almost forgot,' he said, pressing something into my palm. 'When I pulled you up, you was holdin' on to it for dear life.'

I looked down to see the carnelian ring, its perfect circle, returned.

When I opened my mouth to say something, he shook his head, no need. But I knew, looking in that good boatman's face, that he was right. I would not jump off Putney Bridge again, or any bridge, not drink laudanum, not cut my wrists, but live to claim what joy was mine – the fierce, unruly, grim, defiant, soaring joy of being human.

And now, little bird, you too will do the same.

Sorrow, my sweet girl, will bring you to your knees, time and again, but so will beauty, so too love, enough to rise again, to try again, to live as all beings wish to live: free.

ACKNOWLEDGEMENTS

First thanks for this novel goes to Emma Parry, my wonderfully intuitive agent, who knew I was struggling to let go of Dickens, who'd captured my imagination for so long. It was the two hundredth anniversary of Frankenstein; Mary Shelley was everywhere. 'What about Wollstonecraft?' she said. Who did, capture my imagination entirely, especially those eleven days between giving birth to her daughter and her own death from puerperal fever. How could one possibly say goodbye? What would she have her daughter know? But until Emma reminded me recently, I'd forgotten that when we had that first conversation, I'd just lost my own beloved mother, quite suddenly (though to a long illness), and that my seventeen-year-old daughter, the youngest of my children, was getting ready to leave home. I see my mother in both my daughters (and my son), her natural belief in equality that lived in every fibre of her being, as it did in Wollstonecraft's. Of course it would be a mother-daughter story; I just didn't know that when I started. But I think Emma did.

Still, taking on the iconic Mary Wollstonecraft – 'the mother of feminism' – felt like an enormous responsibility. I wanted to shape her unruly life into a good story with just enough mess left in it. (We are nothing without our messiness.) Caroline Bleeke, my gifted editor, helped me do that with her gentle but exacting sense and sensibility, making the book better at every turn. I'm also grateful to Amelia Possanza and the whole Flatiron team for the great work they do for writers and their books, especially Sydney Jeon, Jordan Forney, Nancy Trypuc, Marlena Bittner, Keith Hayes, Kerry Nordling, Donna Noetzel, John Morrone, Emily Walters, Malati Chavali, Megan Lynch, and Bob Miller.

I also stand on the shoulders of giants, the great Wollstonecraft biographers: Janet Todd (*Mary Wollstonecraft: A Revolutionary Life*), Claire Tomalin (*The Life and Death of Mary Wollstonecraft*), Lyndall Gordon (*Vindication*), and Charlotte Gordon's dual biography of mother and daughter, *Romantic Outlaws*. Each of them made Wollstonecraft come alive for me, in broad strokes and exquisite detail, leaving just enough cracks and clues in her story, and their unique versions of her, to find my own footing. But there's no giant like Wollstonecraft herself to humble a writer. Her letters, novels, and other prose gave me an intimate glimpse of her intellect, but also her humanity – her humanness – so full of contradiction and complexity, like all of us. To be sure, the best lines in the book are straight from her mouth and pen. I hope the ones that are mine do her justice.

Thanks to my once writing group, who read first chapters forever and seemed never to tire of it (at least they didn't tell me so): Lynn Hofflund, Kim Philley, Erin McClure, but especially to Tish Thornton, my remarkable friend and editor-on-call, who'll pick up the phone at the drop of a hat to debate the uses of the semicolon, or just as easily pivot to the meaning of everything. Tish was part of a reading group five of us started to stay grounded through the strangeness of the pandemic year. While I was finishing the novel, fretting, doing the usual weird writer stuff, we read *War and Peace* and then *Middlemarch* to each other over Zoom, every single word. Which certainly puts being a writer in perspective. And makes you reconsider the semicolon, not to mention dependent clauses and lots of other points of grammar, not to mention what shapes people, and history. The experience would not have been the same without the deep understanding and friendship of Elizabeth Tullis and Lori Benton.

I'm grateful to the Alexa Rose Foundation and the Idaho Commission on the Arts for making my work possible, and the work of so many artists.

I'm always grateful to my father, who is the reason I'm a writer. But any book I write is for my children – Atticus, Phoebe, and Olive – a record of things I've meant to tell them, or that bear repeating, but also everything that they've taught me. This one is also for my best friend and touchstone, Josie Fretwell, who can run a pandemic reading group like nobody's business, but who has also, for so many years, held my hand on this thorny, astonishing trip of being human, and a woman, in a world such as this. We've navigated so much of what's in this book, as all women do: desire, dependence, despair, love, freedom, power, purpose. We grew up together, sometimes flailing, as we figured out how to argue for our subjectivity, our experience, our needs, as equal to any man's – and not back down. I can never remember if she's sun and I'm moon, or the other way around. We take turns, like light and shadow. I cannot imagine what my life would be without her.

Finally, David Nevin is my rock, the man who reads to me every night in his rich, honeyed voice that tells me everything will be all right, and if not, that love, and books, are the beauty we have right now.

SAMANTHA SILVA is an author and screenwriter based in Idaho. Over her career, she has sold film projects to Paramount, Universal, and New Line Cinema. Silva graduated from Johns Hopkins University's School of Advanced International Studies. She has lived in London, briefly in Rome, is an avid Italophile, and a forever Dickens devotee. Silva is currently adapting her debut novel, *Mr Dickens and His Carol*, for the stage.

www.samanthasilvawriter.com
@samantharella